SANCTUARY'S WARLORD

BOOK 1 OF THE SANCTUARY SERIES

NIKITA SLATER

To my mom.
Thank you for your love, support and advice.
You gave me my first novel and I've had my head in the clouds ever since.

PROLOGUE

In 2020 humans were warned, melting ice and rising sea levels were going to release disease into the world. We were warned that the effects of this disease would ravage the world unlike anything humanity had ever experienced. More than half the world's population would fall. Still, countries warred. Still, they ignored the warnings.

In 2022, in a South Pacific country, formerly known as the Solomon Islands, a new, never before discovered illness arose. Some described it as the plague, others described it as a twisted version of Ebola. The world ignored this terrifying news. Countries were at war, nuclear threats were common, dangerous synthetic drugs were being sold illegally, food shortages and unpredictable weather patterns created an untenable financial burden for governments. Citizen unrest led to riots, police actions, the rise of gangs and out-of-control crime rates. Politicians, military, media and law enforcement were too focused on their domestic struggles to turn to the medical crisis in a little-known island country. By the time they took notice, some of the world's biggest cities were on the verge of being consumed by an angry planet.

In 2025, after the disease wiped out half the South Pacific and spread to each continent, it became known as Necrotitis Primeval, or Death Kiss. It was a hybrid of a new type of flesh-eating bacteria. The people who contracted the disease became known as the Primitives. There was no known cure. The incubation rate was minutes, no one was immune, and the results were irreversible. Once a person became infected, they would rapidly return to a primitive state, focusing only on their base needs. Food, water, reproduction. They attacked without conscious thought, devouring everything organic in their path. Humans, animals and plants became food. They would mutilate their prey, mutilate themselves in their driving need to scratch and bite.

By 2030, Death Kiss had ravaged the world, collapsing all systems of government, destroying communications, electrical grids, everything essential to society. Pockets of humans banded together, creating towns and cities, protecting their new homes by whatever means necessary. Anarchy became a way of life as humans fought to survive. Fought each other, fought the Primitives.

By 2050, Sanctuaries had risen from the ashes of great cities, taking in the terrified refugees that clawed for survival. But many of these Sanctuaries fell under the pressure of high populations, lack of resources and bad leadership. Birth rates increased as birth control became less and less available. But death rates climbed even higher. Medication was no longer widely available, infrastructure was falling down all around us, bands of people fought not only the Primitives, but each other in a bid for territory and resources. It quickly became apparent that only the strongest could survive this hostile world.

My name is Taran and I was born on April 27th, 2047. I watched as my parents and five-year-old brother were taken by illness. Not the Death Kiss, but a common flu. The virus and harsher winters took out more than half of the remaining Northern population, forcing the rest of us to relocate. With a band of survivors, including my grandparents and sister, Skye, I walked South for weeks and months, in search of Sanctuary. Finally, after a gruelling journey, including the loss of my sister in the Nevada riots and the subsequent fall of the Las Vegas Sanctuary, we arrived at the Tucson Sanctuary. I was taken in, but my grandparents were refused entry. They were left to survive outside the city walls. An impossible feat, especially at their age. Primitives rove the land looking for new victims. No one can survive the Death Kiss without turning. From birth, I've been taught that a bitten human is a dead human.

ONE

YEAR 2073

TARAN

4:00am is my favourite time of day. Everything is hushed, the sky is still dark. Soon, first light will attempt to break through on the horizon. Things smell a little fresher, as though kissed by mother nature while we were all sleeping. I'm reminded that our planet still lives, still breathes, though we've done our level best to bring the fucker down with us.

I crouch next to the shell of a burned-out vehicle, my back pressed against the cool metal door panel. It's part of the barrier wall around our Sanctuary city, built on the ashes of Tucson. What a joke. There's nothing welcoming about this Sanctuary. Except that it's relatively safe from the Primitives. But it's no kind of real sanctuary. If it was, then the self-elected leader and his rabid crew of enforcers would open the city to anyone and everyone in need. Instead, they've locked it down tight, only accepting select individuals; men who can work and women who can bear children.

I found this out the hard way when I was taken in as a teenager while my grandparents were left outside the barrier to fend for themselves. I hadn't wanted to leave them behind. I'd kicked and screamed as I was dragged into the city. I don't know what happened to my grandparents. Probably dead. Not many survive the outside world without sanctuary. I'd been taken because I was old enough to get pregnant and young enough to have many babies for a civilization that relies on population renewal. As soon as I entered the city I was given citizenship and a husband.

A train whistles loud and clear, piercing the morning stillness.

"That's the signal," Emery whispers from beside me.

I nod and indicate that she should stay and keep watch as we'd discussed, while I cross the barrier wall. Her worried eyes are on me and I can see the argument threatening to leap to her lips once more. She'd older, more experienced, can handle weapons better. I shake my head and double-check the rifle slung across my back. She may be the better choice in some ways, but I'm not risking the woman who has become everything to me in this terrible post-apocalyptic world. We both know she can't scale the wall in the time I can. I'm smaller, faster and tougher.

She sighs her resignation and presses her fingers into my shoulders, giving me her sternest, most motherly look. I offer her a half smile and nod, promising silently that I'll be as safe as I can. She drops her hands from my shoulders and picks up a charcoal pen, running it under my eyes and over my cheeks, chin and forehead. She uses her thumbs to rub it in, blending it over my face but leaving the heaviest marks under my eyes. She does this for two reasons. One is to protect my skin from the sun. Sunscreen is a commodity that only the rich have access to and my skin is fairer than most as I'm from the far North and Sanctuary is located in the Sonoran Desert, in what used to be Arizona.

The second reason is more important. Darkening my face gives me more of a chance to blend in if I run into Primitives on the other side of the barrier. For some reason, the first thing to decay on the bodies of the infected is their skin. It darkens, becomes splotchy and eventually rots, peeling away from the skeleton until they become little more than walking death. Of course, I should also smell like them if I truly want to get away from them unscathed, so the face trick only works at a distance.

"Be careful, Taran," she whispers, worry clear in her tone.

"Always." I shoot her a cheeky grin and pat her leg before standing. I reach over my head for the metal frame of another car and pull myself up, the sound of her husky chuckle behind me. I grin. We both know I'm not exactly known for being careful. I'm part of the Sanctuary rebellion, we both are. The rebels are a group people who stand up to the harsh authoritarian regimes popping up in most Sanctuary cities, including ours. They're a scourge I fully intend to help bring down by doing my part.

I'm opinionated when I feel passionate about something and I can be reckless in pursuit of my goals. I've terrorized poor Emery with my disdain toward the Authority. She thinks I'll eventually be caught doing something illegal and executed or turned out of the city; both the most common sentences for treason against a Sanctuary.

I quickly lose sight of her as I'm forced to crawl through a section of beams that juts out, pointing toward the city like giant skeletal fingers. The climb is taxing, a brutal test of endurance. I'm lean, leaner than I should be. Too often I give my food rations to the hungry illegals that crowd our city slums. I know this isn't a smart choice. That I'm depleting the strength that I desperately need to survive in this tough, uncompromising world. But it's all I have to give back to the underground community that has sheltered me for more than a decade.

The climb becomes steeper as heaps of twisted metal and concrete, leftovers from old vehicles and collapsed infrastructure, thin out toward the top. I've been climbing for almost an hour now, never stopping. There isn't time to stop. I must complete my task as quickly and quietly as possible. My breath comes out in short, sharp puffs and my muscles are screaming at me. I know I can do this though. I've done it dozens of times. It's one of my most important tasks among the rebel faction; lead the refugees rejected by city officials into our Sanctuary. A dangerous, but necessary job.

I've reached the pinnacle of my climb, about twenty feet from the very top of the wall. A wall built to keep out the Primitives. Or so we're told. In reality, the wall, built all the way around the city, also serves to keep the citizens trapped within and make sure the refugees are kept out. We haven't had a Primitive attack in almost a year. And though they are easily distracted and driven by instinct, they're fast and they can still climb, if they believe the object of their fixation, fresh meat, is on the other side.

I crawl headfirst into a section of metal piping, squeezing myself through the narrow space. The top sections of the wall are impossible to get through, topped by massive sections of metal plating and barbed wire. The tunnel is a tight fit, but I've been this way before. My shoulders and hips are just barely small enough to get me through. I climb out the other side and breathe for just a moment, sitting on top of the barrier, looking out across the vast landscape. Shadows are giving way to morning sun, blazing its way strong and sure over the top of the Rincon mountain range, to the East of the city. There are five mountain ranges surrounding our Sanctuary, but I'm headed Southeast this morning.

I breathe deep, taking in the early morning scents. Metal, dust, desert. The beauty laid out before me, stretched out for miles below my dangling feet, is an homage to the resiliency of our planet. Our home. Mother Nature struggles to shake off the aftereffects of humanity, while still providing sanctuary for those of us that survived the culling of our species.

I shake off the grim nostalgia and begin my descent. I'm wary now, careful to move fast, while twisting my head this way and that, searching out the city police. Or worse, the military, a squadron of savage men entrusted with our safety, guarding us from the dangers of the outside world, while holding us hostage from within. The men who helped create a city of hundreds of thousands, forcing us to follow laws that are created by the strongest because we have no choice. They are cold, cruel, angry. Hand-picked by the city's authoritarian leader and Warlord, Diogo Fuentes, for their aggressive, dominant tendencies. The few run-ins I've had with them have been far from pleasant.

Luckily, I'm small, plain, unassuming. Meek to those that don't know how to look for a strong personality filled with belief and conviction behind the exterior of a simple girl. The last person they would suspect of being a leader of the rebellion. The woman who has caused constant upheaval throughout Sanctuary. One of the people they've been trying to ferret out for the past several years with no success.

Our Sanctuary was built from the ruins of Tucson, one of the few habitable areas left on the planet. Not usually plagued by intense storms and tornadoes, the area is protected by an expanse of desert and the mountain ranges. The northern countries have been rendered mostly uninhabitable to humans through increasingly long cold winters and severe storms. Without easy access to electricity and gas, the conditions are too harsh to survive. Flash freezing, illness and, finally, mass migration took out half of the Northern populations while the Primitives took out the rest.

Beyond that, I figure the founders of New Tucson Sanctuary thought the Primitives would be less likely to cross an expanse of desert and mountains to get to a few surviving uninfected humans.

They were wrong. Nothing can stop a Primitive. They will cross oceans, mountains and deserts in search of new victims. Though they don't come often to our home, they do show up once in a while, forcing us to defend our city, defend the survivors of a dying race.

"Fuck!" I automatically yank my hand into my chest. I'd grabbed hold of a piece of twisted metal that cut into my palm, slashing it. Blood runs through my clenched fingers and over my leather vest.

I glance down and then squeeze my eyes shut as the ground far below glares up at me, mocking me with its distance. There's a short platform of sorts several feet below me. I climb as best I can using only one hand, and then drop down the last few feet. My legs buckle as I hit the hood of an old Plymouth Chrysler. I'm forced to throw my weight backward, so I don't slide off the slanted hood and hurtle toward the ground below. It's dangerous enough, climbing around up here on old cars that can shift at any moment. I land on my ass against the windshield. Pain shoots through my tailbone and I grit my teeth.

I need a moment to recover, to regain my purpose, but I don't have time. Instead I check my hand quickly, assuring myself the damage doesn't look as bad as it feels. I drag the scarf from my face where it's wound around my head, protecting my lungs from the endless dust kicked up by constant winds sweeping across the desert. Today the wind is calmer, so protecting my face isn't as big a concern as it is on other days when the relentless sand fills mouth and nostrils, burying itself in the skin of anyone foolish enough to wander outside the wall.

I wrap my hand, using my teeth to tighten the makeshift bandage and then curl my fingers and flex them out. Though pain shoots up my wrist and arm I can still move everything that should move. No nerve damage. The cut isn't as deep as it looks then. I stand, sweep my gaze across the distance, squinting toward the meeting area. A rock formation off in the distance, close enough to the tracks that refugees can jump off the train and run to the relative safety of the rocks while waiting for their rebel contact. Me.

The train passed hours ago. They'll be crouched in the shadows of the rocks as the warming sun reaches out to scorch everything in its path. This is part of the reason I need to reach them quickly, get them into the city. The heat becomes rapidly unbearable to anyone outside and exposed. But they won't be able to get into the city without the papers tucked safely into my vest. Papers that will give them the legitimacy they need to enter the city legally. Give them access to housing, food rations, doctors. When the forgeries fail, I take them over the wall as illegals and they're forced to live looking over their shoulders for the rest of their time in Sanctuary.

Today I'll be escorting a family of four, including two children, and a couple. Six people total. I've done it before. A dangerous and illegal task. If I'm caught I will be branded a traitor. The punishment for treason is being stripped of citizenship and turned out into the desert. Sometimes death, depending on the severity of the crime, although, being expelled from Sanctuary is as much a death sentence as outright execution.

Ignoring the pain in my hand I make my way to the bottom of the wall, climbing as fast as I safely can. I groan my relief as my boots hit the dirt sending up a cloud of dust. Stretching my back, I scan the horizon, shading my eyes against the blazing sun peeking over the mountains. It'll be around 6:30 am. Not my best time. I'm going to have to hustle.

I pull the hood of my vest up to protect my head and set off at a light jog, zigzagging across the landscape, heading for the rock formation. The day is completely clear, so anyone scanning the ground from above will likely see me. It's not illegal to leave Sanctuary, though we do need passes to come and go. Fortunately, I know a damn good forger so I have a pass. Still, it's best to avoid the guards and patrols until I'm ready to re-enter the city.

It takes me a further half hour to reach the rocks, my steady run slowing to a lope as I get closer. I squint at the shadows, seeing nothing at first. Then a man steps out, waving me down. I approach cautiously, staring at him. I'm instantly on alert. Though he's giving the impression of easy comradery as he waves, he doesn't look like either of the men's pictures on the papers. In fact, this guy is much bigger, well fed, muscular. He looks nothing like any of the refugees I'd helped over the years.

I have no choice though. Even though I'm suspicious, I can't ignore the plight of these people. They're coming up from Puerto Rico, a place that's now completely uninhabitable due to high sea levels, storms and Primitive infestation.

I slow down to a walk, eyeing the guy as I approach.

The closer I get, the bigger, more intimidating he seems. He's much taller than me and he has a commanding presence that screams Authority. Wide shoulders, head up, back straight, legs spread apart. His arms are crossed so he obviously doesn't see me as any kind of a threat. His biceps bulge with muscles and my heart sinks as I realize he must be part of the city military. They're all built like this.

His face is covered by a bandana and he's wearing sunglasses to shade his eyes from the intense glare of the sun. Sunglasses are a rare item, which means he's well compensated too. High up in the Authority.

"Hello," I greet him as I approach, aiming for a disarming, light tone. Hoping my light, friendly attitude will give the lie I'm about to make some added authenticity. "Nice morning for a hunt, eh?"

Hunting fresh meat is one of the most common reasons to leave the city. Hunting is tough though. There isn't much to hunt in the desert unless a person makes their way to the mountains and I'm not equipped for that lie. No bag, no back-up and only one weapon.

He doesn't acknowledge my greeting. Says nothing until I've halted a few feet away from him. I stand with my arms loose at my side, my right hand near the base of my rifle, ready to fight if I have to. I've made it this long without capture, I've no intention of being taken now.

Finally, he speaks. "Give me the documents."

Fuck.

Somehow he knows.

I widen my eyes innocently and reach into my vest, pulling out my city residency and re-entry papers. He takes them from me, glances over them and then drops them in the dirt. My mouth falls open. Those papers are worth more than clean water. They're my passport to safety. Though fake, they're still worth a lot.

I bend to pick up the papers before they can drift away in the hot breeze, but he steps forward and grabs my arm, stopping me. I gasp and become rigid in his hold. No one has taken hold of me without my permission in years. He's close enough that I can feel the heat from his big body, smell the masculine sweat. His grip doesn't hurt, but it's solid. Probably unbreakable.

"The other documents." His voice is menacing and rings with authority.

My mouth goes dry. Out here in the desert, away from the city, though we aren't far, there is no law and order. And while the justice system in Sanctuary is fractured and vastly unfair, it's something. This man could too easily snap my neck and walk away from my dying body. No one would know what happened or where to find me. The only people who would care about my disappearance are rebel friends.

"I don't know what you're talking about," I whisper.

At first I don't think he hears me, my voice carried away in the wind. But then he leans closer, until our faces are only inches apart. He lifts a hand, tugs his scarf down and removes his sunglasses revealing his entire face.

Diogo Fuentes.

I've only ever seen him at a distance, but recognition is as swift as a punch to the stomach. His strong, rugged features with grim lips and flat eyes are recognizable to every person held hostage within his city. This man has stolen the freedom of nearly 200,000 people, dictating their lives. He is the enemy in a world filled with despair and fear. He's everything I despise.

He could be a handsome man if it weren't for the hard lines around his mouth and eyes. The dead look to his eyes.

The pure evil he's perpetuated throughout one of the last remaining Sanctuaries in North America. His hair is cut severely short, a scar running from his ear into his hairline.

"Obey me, girl." His deep, cruel voice is laced in ice. "Or I will search you, strip you bare and walk you naked through the gates of the city before handing you over to my men."

TWO

DIOGO

I stare down at the woman, finally within my reach. The Desert Wren.

Named after the elusive prey animal because this mysterious woman is able to flit through my security with the speed and ease of a small bird and lead her flock to safety. She is also rumoured to be small and plain, like the wren. I believe the woman in front of me to be one and the same, though none of my people have managed to set eyes on her. A thorn in the side of both military and police for years, she's managed to avoid capture, her identity a complete mystery. Though we suspected she was rebel allied, she could've been an elite. Hell, she could've been an officer.

Not at all as I'd imagined her, this woman seems a pathetic creature. Shaking, barely lifting her eyes off the ground when I speak. Her face is purposely covered in dirt, her clothes are those of the poorer factions of the city, worn and frayed. She is small, not a characteristic that is highly regarded in a society that needs big, strong people to survive.

Yet when I hold her arm I sense a stiffening, a reserve, not the subservience she's trying to sell me.

My blood rushes in anticipation. After years of searching for this woman, this legendary enigma, I finally have her in my hands. I can detect her delicate scent, made more noticeable by the heat of the sun and the heavy clothes she's chosen to wear for protection.

"Give me the papers now."

She tilts her chin fractionally, her eyes lifting to mine for a second before dropping. That second was long enough for me to see fire, rage and defiance in those intriguing grey depths. I want to eat her alive, throw her in the dirt and show her how well-earned my brutal reputation is. I want to accept her as the prey animal I've caught in my trap and allow the savage hunter inside me free reign with this sweet little morsel.

"Do you know who I am?" Though I soften my voice slightly the menace is still there.

She doesn't speak.

I glance down her body. Though rough, her clothes are not ill-fitting. Thick, hardy and snug to her form, they are built to protect her from the wall and the blazing sun as she walks a distance into the desert.

Without warning, I drag the rifle from her and toss it away. Then I spin her around so she's facing away from me. She squeaks in protest and struggles, wriggling in my hold as I run my hands over her body. First her pants, looking for pockets. There are none. I run my fingers across her middle, running them inside her waistband to see if there's anything tucked away. She grips my wrist and tries to yank as I slide my hand down the front of her pants. Her strength against mine is negligible, like a child's.

"Stop it!" she hisses, her fingernails scrabbling at my skin.

I ignore her fight, turn her back around and reach for her vest, gripping the fabric at the neck. I tear down the front until the entire thing is shredded and laying open. As I bare her, papers tumble out, falling to the dirt at our feet.

I reach for them as she dives for her rifle. I catch her by the back of her hood, no doubt catching hair too, and drag her with me as I grab a fistful of papers. Some are caught by the wind and carried away. It doesn't matter. I have more than enough evidence right here to arrest and prosecute the little rebel. I keep a tight hold on her, ignoring her flailing arms while I flip quickly through the papers. Yes, these are exactly what I need.

I wave them in front of her face. "Explain," I demand, using my grip on her hood and hair to tip her face up.

The dirt smeared all over her creamy face bothers me. I can't tell what she truly looks like. Just the general features. Sharp chin and wide grey eyes that dominate a petite face. I shove her hood back and pull a handful of hair from where it's been tucked into the back of her vest dragging it foreword. It straggles down around her shoulders, a dull brown colour, but I can tell that it's dirty, filled with desert dust. It'll probably shine much brighter when it's clean. The curves of her small breasts are just visible from beneath the two halves of her torn vest. Her breastbone and ribcage are clearly visible. I have an urge to see her cleaned up. See what she really looks like.

"I was meeting some friends before my hunt. They asked me to hold onto their papers until we meet up, so they wouldn't be lost or destroyed." She's speaking fast, her voice is strong, though there is a quaver to her tone.

"You lie." The untruth makes me angry. I despise liars. I shake her by the hair. Her hands fly up to grip my wrist, but she can't loosen the hold.

"I'm not," she insists.

"These," I shove the papers in her face, "are a forgery. I know this because I set up the entire scenario. I made up the Puerto Ricans. Gave them names, lives, a past. Whatever you needed to play your little game."

Her mouth opens but she doesn't speak. She has nothing left to say. She's been caught red-handed. The look of horror that flashes across her face before she can smother it is sweet to behold. I have finally captured the illusive Desert Wren, the woman I've been seeking for so long I was starting to doubt she actually existed. Now she belongs to me.

Somehow this idea has taken on new meaning. I've wanted to get my hands on her for so long that my motivation to do so has grown unclear, fuzzy. Through the years, her daring and intelligence had morphed from annoying to intriguing. With each new report that she'd somehow managed to smuggle more people into the city, my anger had gradually turned to curiosity and finally pride. The police mandate has always been to capture and prosecute rebels involved in illegal activities. My plan should be to extract information on the growing rebel faction in the city. My methods are not nice and I don't soften for women, particularly criminals. If I deal with her as a traitor of the city, she will be tortured and then expelled or killed.

But even before I came here today, took on the task of capturing this rebel leader, I knew this wasn't going to be the plan. I've admired her from afar for years. Such a creature can't simply be torn apart by our city justice. It would be blasphemy to dispose of her once she's deemed no longer useful. Her bright spark, the daring and defiance, the steel core of morality that I've seen in her actions shouldn't be snuffed out by the heavy hand of the Authority. I won't allow it.

She still has vital information that I need. And though the idea doesn't sit well I know I'll have to hand her over for processing. She'll need to be charged and prosecuted. I am the highest representative of the very Authority I want to save her from.

"What is your name?"

She remains stubbornly silent, her eyes now fixed on the distant horizon, no doubt planning her next move.

I grip her neck and tip her head forward, looking for her marker. She gasps and stiffens under my harsh grip. No tattoo mars the flesh of her shoulder, only a small, pale scar. Not surprising as she's a suspected rebel and the first thing they do is find a way to get rid of their identification tattoo.

I'm deeply curious about her. I want to know everything. Her name, her place of origin, her placement in the rebellion. I will get these things out of her. But it appears I may have to be more patient than usual if I don't wish to damage her. Looking down at the delicate creature, I realize that harming her is the opposite of what I want from her.

"You will regret not giving me what I want now, Wren." She frowns, her lips parting as though she wants to say something, but then her face smooths out and she continues to stare away from me. Though she's no longer fighting me, I feel that this small act is a defiance. That she's placing herself above me by refusing to speak. She will regret this as well. I drag her face up to mine, forcing her onto her toes and growl, "By the time I'm done with you, I'll make you beg to give me the information I seek."

Her eyes finally move to mine. Instead of fear I see only fire. "And I will make you wish you'd never met me, Diogo Fuentes."

THREE

TARAN

Perhaps it was a stupid thing to say. Certainly the Warlord thinks so. His hand loosens in my hair and he laughs out loud. I can see why. He probably outweighs me by more than double and is clearly well-fed and strong. His bicep is the same size as my entire head. He can snap me in half without breaking a sweat. But I need this arrogant authoritarian Warlord to understand that he doesn't intimidate me. I've come to terms with this desperately broken world and the idea of death doesn't terrify me. The idea of life without values, the life that Diogo forces upon his citizens, fills me with disgust and loathing.

He sobers and takes me by the arm, leading me toward the rock formation and around.

"Desert Wren," he says. "You are under arrest for willfully disobeying the laws of the New Tucson Sanctuary. Once we reach the city you will be processed and prosecuted. Your sentence will be forthcoming."

I want to shout at him, want to yell every indignity he's forced on my beloved Sanctuary. Want to say, *yes, you've caught me, but the rebellion is stronger than one person, it will continue to grow in strength without me.* Instead, I say, "What are the charges?"

He gives me a look that clearly says he doesn't want to play games and that I know exactly what I'm being charged with. Which, of course, I do. Still, I want to hear them from him before I say anything else.

"Please," I say softly. "If I'm to be executed or turned from the city I would like to know what I'm being accused of."

I realize that he's taking me to a vehicle. An all-terrain jeep. These vehicles are extremely rare with only the military and the elite given access to them. I've only seen them at a distance, but I'm not surprised Diogo has one.

Just when I decide he's going to ignore me, he says, "I'm charging you with intent to break the law by giving illegals access to a Sanctuary city, possession of forged documents and withholding information from an Authority. Other charges will be applied once I confirm your identity."

He means, confirm that I am the Desert Wren. Obviously, he believes so. I'm filled with pride at the thought that I've caused enough mischief to this regime to get myself noticed by the Warlord himself. Though the moniker, Desert Wren, started among the frustrated police force who were unable to capture me, I've accepted and embraced the name. A plain little bird. Solitary but hardy. It's suitable for me.

"Any one of those charges will mean death," I point out to him.

I'm not sure why I say this to the man who has the most authority in our city. The man who might ultimately decide my fate. Except there's something in the way he's looking at me, touching me. A curiosity. While he must be triumphant over my capture, as he obviously stepped in to do the deed himself, he doesn't seem overly angry at my transgressions. His manner is milder than I would've expected from a man with his terrible reputation. And I know he's capable of some truly terrible things, I've seen his public executions. It's almost as though something is muting his anger.

"Your fate has not been decided." There's an edge of annoyance to his voice as he turns me around and handcuffs my hands behind my back. I grunt when he tightens them until they're flush against the skin of my wrists. Though my hands are as small as the rest of me I won't be able to slip them through the metal cuffs.

His finger brushes the bandage on my palm. At first I think it's an accident, but then I feel his touch again, probing the bandage, moving it to look at the flesh.

"You've been hurt." He sounds almost accusing, as though I did it on purpose or something. I twist around to look at him. His head is bent and he's still looking at the small wound.

"I'll live," I say drily. What's up with the Warlord? One minute he's threatening me with torture and prosecution, and the next he seems almost concerned over a small cut. I wonder if he's this attentive with the rest of his prisoners.

He escorts me to his vehicle, and opens the door, lifting me easily into the passenger seat. He slams the door shut behind me.

I should be thinking about escape, but I can't help myself, I stare around the jeep in awe. I've never been inside one that actually works. Some parts are shiny, some are dull and the seat beneath me is comfortable, not ripped. It seems to be well taken care of, not smashed and rotting like the abandoned ones I've sometimes had to use for shelter.

When he climbs in the other side I say, "I've never

known you or your officers to go easy on a rebel. According to your laws I'm a traitor. My sentence will almost certainly be death."

Why am I pushing this issue? Why is it so important to get the Warlord to acknowledge my fate? We just met, yet there's something between us. Something that transcends our respective realities. Perhaps meeting in the desert as we did, his arresting me away from the city, giving me a nickname and elevating me above the common mischief-maker, has made me brave. Put me on equal footing with this man, even if we are on opposite sides. Something in me wants him to acknowledge that he won't kill me.

He seems to wonder the same thing. He turns to me and pinches my chin between hard fingers. I flinch but hold my position. I lift my eyes to his, staring into the depths. They're dark, like a rare bitter chocolate. His gaze is serious and watchful but not wrathful. He's not the brainless, angry Warlord I always thought him to be. I think maybe the intelligence I perceive in him is almost worse than the other. I can despise an evil leader, thirsty for blood and mayhem. I fear a man that purposely cultivates a city divided by class and power and led without democracy.

"Do you wish to die, Wren?" he asks, sliding an arm behind me and fingering the hair next to my face. I'm helpless. With my hands cuffed behind my back I can't do much other than flinch. But I hold myself rigid, don't react. I honestly don't think he'll hurt me. "I've told you that your fate hasn't been decided and yet still you push. Why?"

I lie to him, wanting to avoid a discussion. I'm not even sure what my reasons are for baiting the man. "You implied torture. I would prefer a quick death."

He snorts and drops his hand. He doesn't speak as he turns the engine on and gives the vehicle gas. I take a sharp breath as I'm jolted, unable to catch myself with my hands behind my back. He reaches out and steadies me with a hand across my middle. I suck my breath in, sending him a quick look. Then he puts both hands back on the wheel and we're zooming across the landscape, racing back toward the city at a much faster pace than I left it. I'm shocked by the speed. If the rebels had access to even one of these we would be in a much better position to collect food and medicine. Another thing that the Authority withholds and doles out at their leisure. Another reason for me to hate the man beside me.

We remain silent as we enter the city gates, which are opened on his approach. They must know his vehicle well since he doesn't have to stop and produce papers. He drives through the gates and proceeds toward one of my least favourite buildings in Sanctuary, police headquarters.

It's an intimidating concrete building with rusting bars at all the windows and guards with guns at each entrance. The police station is always one of the first buildings hit during food riots, so they don't take chances with security. I've been inside three times. Once for identity confirmation and processing when I first arrived as a refugee and twice for public mischief when I was caught up in the riots. I've learned to keep my head down though and escape attention so I haven't come to police attention for almost three years.

Every head lifts, and stares follow us as we walk through the entrance of the station. It's probably not often that the Warlord bothers with petty criminals. Unfortunately, we're intercepted by a man that I know. Not surprising since Sanctuary isn't a massive city. Officer Gillert, one of the processing agents looks me over with a smug glint in his eye. His gaze lingers on my chest reminding me that my vest has been torn and left to hang open. I believe that he recognizes me too, despite the dirt. I stand stiff, my chin tilted up and my eyes fixed on the wall behind the perverted officer. He's made disgusting advances toward me in the past. Probably does it to all of his female detainees.

"Street Urchin," he announces loudly. I roll my eyes. Yes, he definitely recognizes me.

I refused to give the officer my name when I'd been arrested and I hadn't produced any papers so Gillert had named me Street Urchin as a joke because he'd found me on the street and decided I was pathetic. At the time he'd been forced to release me due to overcrowding after the riot, but he hadn't been happy. He'd wanted my name and where to find me. "You remember the last thing I said to you?"

I sigh my annoyance and pin him with a disgusted look. "You told me I'd be back in custody and you'd see me again."

"You know each other?" Diogo asks icily, taking my arm in a tight grip and pulling me back away from his officer.

"Was her arresting officer during the 2070 riots," Gillert answers, almost proudly.

I roll my eyes again and sigh my annoyance. I'd practically tripped over him trying to get out of the way of a stampede. He had no real proof that I was even involved, but he'd taken one look at my prone form sprawled on the ground and arrested me. At a guess I'd say he hadn't wanted to put in the effort to arrest any of the bigger, stronger men that were smashing the city to pieces in an effort to get the authority to give out better food rations.

I'd used the riot as a distraction to sneak refugees to the safety of the slums. I'd been heading back home when he picked me up.

"What were the charges?" Diogo demands.

Gillert shrugs. "Nothing big. Mischief-making. She was released before I could get so much as a name out of her."

Diogo grunts and says, "Her crimes are more serious this time. Take her into processing, call the Judge. I want her charged and sentenced immediately."

Gillert looks surprised, his eyes covering me with more speculation now, but still perverted intent. He steps forward, taking my arm from Diogo. "I'll take care of her, Commander Fuentes."

A dark look passes over Diogo's face. He's not happy, but he has no choice. He needs to leave his officer to do his job. Diogo is the city's leader, he shouldn't be on the ground level worrying about the intricacies of a single arrest. Still he hesitates to step away and leave.

"I want to be informed when the Judge arrives. I will attend the hearing."

"Hearing," I sneer.

His eyes are drawn to me and he raises an eyebrow. "You have something to say, Wren?"

I'm a dead woman anyway. Since I have the ear of our Warlord, I may as well make each second count. "There is no such thing as a fair trial in this city. The Judge shouldn't have complete authority to prosecute, pass judgment and sentence. The whole system is utterly flawed. Guilty until proved innocent... oh wait, no, not even that since you guys don't bother with the burden of truth, just guilty as charged."

Diogo steps so close to me that I can feel Gillert flinch away, his hold on my arm loosening. No one wants to be in the Commander's personal space. Mostly because, rumour has it, people who get this close to him die. I can feel the heat of his big body as he towers over me, stooping a little so he can look me in the face. I tilt my head back and glare up at him, searing him with my loathing. There's no point in denying my feelings, he knows where I stand. Knows I'm a rebel leader and people smuggler. He caught me outside of the city with the intention of escorting refugees inside. I'm fucked anyway. I won't bow down to the man who has caused so much suffering.

Instead of anger, I sense only curiosity as his hard eyes pierce mine. "The Judge isn't the only Authority."

"Who then? You?" I demand. I shrug my arm the rest of the way out of Gillert's slackening hold and step so close to Diogo that my chest nearly brushes his. He inhales sharply, his body curving toward mine, almost straining. "I don't recognize your authority or your laws," I say scathingly. "Your authority should've died a long time ago. We live in a dictatorship, run by a Warlord who serves the few at the expense of the many."

Anger flashes across his face, quick and brutal before he brings it under control and says icily, "You don't know me and you don't understand what you speak of, little girl. You need to stop before you say something you will regret."

I open my mouth to reply, to give him testimony of his misdeeds, when he takes my arm and shakes me. Bending even further, he hisses into my face, his breath hitting my lips and nose, "Do you wish to die? Question my authority again and I will be forced to act. We have an audience."

I'm stunned by his warning. Shocked that I'm getting this much out of him. Shocked he hasn't fallen back on his famously brutal methods when it comes to dealing with lawbreakers.

He doesn't seem to want me harmed. At least not here. I turn and look around the room. Every eye is on us, from the nearby officers to the people going through to processing.

Everyone knows who Diogo Fuentes is. No one knows who this small, dirty urchin is that's yelling at him. He's right. I should be smarter. Should hold my tongue, at least until I decide whether I truly do want to die. I should wait for processing and sentencing. If it is to be death, *then* I will speak all the words that have bottled up inside me for years. Diogo said he would be there for my judgment.

Not waiting for my response, he thrusts me toward Gillert and says coldly, "Take her through to processing."

Gillert barely touches me as he urges me to turn, like he thinks my mouthiness with the boss is going to wear off on him. He walks me swiftly away from Diogo, but before we can go through the door, Diogo's voice follows us. "She is to be treated with respect. Touch her and die."

FOUR

DIOGO

I watch them disappear from sight with a vague sense of loss. I want to be near the girl, learn her secrets. See what she looks like without the dirt. This last thought lingers. I don't particularly care if she is beautiful or as plain as the Desert Wren that she was named after. But I feel the need to see clearly the lips, cheeks and chin that go with those strange grey eyes. The more she speaks to me, the more I'm touched by her. It's not a comfortable sensation.

Nor is leaving her behind as I stride from the station. The city police are a brutal group of men. Not as bad as my elite military, but not nice either. They must be harsh in order to protect our Sanctuary from threats both within and without. But the Wren is different, they won't be allowed to touch her soft skin, to speak to her. And my concern is that they may try anyway. They may take offence at her words and do something irreparable.

Ordinarily I wouldn't care. I allow my people to do their job, for the most part uninterrupted. But this isn't an ordinary woman. She's agile, swift, intelligent and she has convictions. She has the one thing our dying world sorely needs if human civilization is to continue into the future. She has values.

She believes I lack them. And perhaps I do. I reign over the New Tucson Sanctuary with brutal efficiency. I have killed, often. Not just Primitives, but criminals. Sometimes without trial. I've had to make stomach turning decisions when they aren't necessarily the decisions I would prefer to choose. I allow only certain people into the city. People who can contribute. When the city is reaching its limits, when resources are spread too thin, I turn away all who show up at the gates. We tell them to seek refuge in the mountains, knowing full well that they won't survive.

In my time as leader, I have grown Sanctuary, have stabilized it in ways that will make it strong well into the future. I've brought my city through every imaginable trial, but in the process I've sold my soul. I am the Warlord. A reviled leader.

Even the elite despise me. They take what I can give them, they smile, they make obsequious gestures, but they don't like me. I'm under no illusion that they suffer my leadership out of love. They fear me. And that fear stays their hands when it comes to overthrowing my regime. They need me, need what I can give them. And they know I can and will crush all resistance.

Except for the resistance of a little bird. The Desert Wren. Because when I look at her, I see my soul again and I know that I must keep her alive at all costs. I will take her, keep her near me. She will belong to me, and in the process, she will become my conscience.

I get back in my jeep and make my way swiftly to the military guard station, located at the base of the wall near the city gates. These men are more than police officers. They deal in more than petty city matters. They're the military elite of Sanctuary. They are where the real power lies. They are my men and my brothers. If I had any friends, it would be among these men.

I nod toward three of them as I enter the building. They're sitting at the table playing cards. When not on duty, they're on call, and I'm usually here with them, waiting for those calls. I detest sitting in my isolated tower, a home that is nothing more than a show of power. I prefer to be on the ground, my hands in the dirt, working alongside these men.

"Where's Jorje?" I ask, stopping at the table.

"In back," says Karl. He tosses his cards in front of him and crosses powerful arms over his chest. "Heard you finally caught that little birdie bringing in all the illegals. 'bout fucking time."

I grunt and walk past them, toward the office in the back. Jorje is sitting at his desk, writing in the log book. When he sees me, he sets the pencil down and gives me his full attention. I like Jorje. He's one mean motherfucker, but he respects authority. While he makes the day-to-day decisions he never makes an important move unless it's with my full knowledge and approval. He runs the city like clockwork, executing my every command with military precision.

"Your trap work, you got the Wren?" he asks, getting straight to the point.

I nod and settle in the chair opposite him. I don't mind that he holds the power position here. This is his office, his men, his building. But he never forgets who gave him all this, who gives him free rein to do what's needed to keep control inside the city and in the surrounding countryside.

"She fell for the bait, walked right up to me before she realized something was wrong. She had the papers, caught her red-handed." I contemplate Jorje, wonder what he'll think of my plans for her. "I intend to keep her once she's been processed."

"Keep her?" he asks, frowning for a moment, mulling the words. "As in keep her with you? In your custody? You won't have her publicly executed? Make an example of her to the other rebels? We know that she's well loved. They've been hiding her for years. No amount of torture or bribery could get information on her out of the rebels we've managed to detain. A public execution will send shockwaves through the community, show the rebellion that we don't tolerate active resistance."

I consider his questions. He's right. The smart choice would be to make a spectacle of her execution. She is well-loved and she's as innocent looking as they come. Executing her would show what we're willing to do to maintain order. The complete and ruthless power of the Authority trumps any rebellion.

Yet, I can't bring myself to think about what her execution might look like. I've never had this problem before. I'm a military man. Always have been. I'm used to making the brutal choices. But this feels different. "No, I'm not willing to let her go yet. She holds vital information on the rebellion and can be of use. Right now she fully expects to die and won't be persuaded to talk. If I keep her near me I may be able to lull her into a sense of safety, get her to give up what she knows. She may be the key that leads us to Gunther and brings a decisive end to the rebellion." It would be a major victory to capture both the Desert Wren and the leader of the rebellion.

Jorje waves his hand in the air negligently. "Torture," he says.

I smile grimly. Jorje has his preferred methods of dealing with lawbreakers. He and his men are well versed in extracting information. I'm not innocent of using these methods myself.

"I prefer she remain unharmed for now."

"I see," he says, eyeing me speculatively. He doesn't like my proposal. It doesn't matter, I'll keep the girl regardless of his feelings, and he will obey my orders.

"She's wily though. She'll try to fly the nest as soon as she can. I want a full-time guard on her when I'm not with her myself. I'll update you with the details once I get her settled into the Tower."

A flash of disapproval crosses his face. He does nothing to hide it. Resources, including military resources, have always been strained. Providing a guard detail seems frivolous and unnecessary. He believes that she should be kept at the prison, tortured and executed, thus negating the need to have her watched. I remain silent though, awaiting his response.

"As you wish, Commander."

"She is to be detained if she tries to leave my protection, but she is never to be harmed. Understood?" The orders are crisp commands. I leave no room for argument.

He pauses a fraction before agreeing. "Understood. My men will do as you say."

I drop the matter. Jorge will give me what I want. He always does. We discuss the logistics of an upcoming hunt outside the city walls. A rumour has reached us of a particularly large band of Primitives that has made it into our region. Smaller groups are normal and often found in the area, but larger hordes don't tend to make it through the mountains to our Sanctuary. Our best recourse is to eliminate them before they can make it into the city.

I stand and we say our goodbyes before I make my way outside. No one says a word to me as I stride back through the building and leave. They know when it's not a good time to test my patience. And I find I don't have a lot of patience when it comes to the Wren. I don't want my men thinking or talking about her. She's about to become off limits. This idea solidifies the longer I'm away from her. I didn't like leaving her in Gillert's care. He's not a careful man and she doesn't seem to hold back with her words. She can easily get herself into trouble. And a woman that small, it would take one hard punch to the head to kill her.

I don't know why I care what happens to her. Yes, she is intriguing. Yes, I can get information from her about the rebels. But there's something more. Over the years, the Desert Wren has become an obsession for me; elusive, mysterious, daring. Qualities I admire, but that also infuriate me. I imagined this day as one of victory, capturing the Wren, making her an example. But now that I have her, I find the victory hollow, because the little bird is more than I imagined. She's passionate, intelligent, courageous. I want to know her better, understand her. Maybe I want her to understand me. I recognize it isn't logic that's driving my decisions, but an obsession I've cultivated over years. I should ignore it but there's something about this girl that I can't seem to let go of.

Finally, I give up the pretense of being impartial, get back in my vehicle and drive to the police station.

FIVE

TARAN

"Name."

I ignore the question, staring past Gillert's shoulder as he speaks. My wrists are now cuffed in front of me to a metal table. I've been through this before. I'm not intimidated and I'm not impressed.

"Identification number." He stares at me malevolently.

Again, I ignore him.

He stands and walks behind me. I tense, but I don't move visibly. I hate having a man like Gillert at my back when I'm helpless to turn and face him. He grabs my hair and shoves my head forward until my forehead nearly hits the table, lifting the hair off my neck. He yanks on the hood of my vest, dragging it down, to have a look at the skin on my neck and the back of my shoulder.

"No identity mark." He drops my hair and goes back around the table. I'm relieved when he puts distance between us again. Despite Diogo's words that I shouldn't be touched, I suspect Gillert would love to get his hands on me. He seems the type to kick elderly ladies for fun and torture small animals. I hunch my shoulders in an effort to keep the skin under my torn vest as hidden as possible.

"It's illegal to be in the city without an identity mark."

No shit genius.

I'd had it removed shortly after the rebels took me in and claimed me as one of their own. This is for our safety and the safety of the families that shelter and protect us. If the Authority knew what house I belonged to they could arrest and interrogate anyone associated. And they aren't known for their kind-hearted methods. They will turn an entire family out of the city for the infractions of one. According to the Warlord's philosophy, if one is bad then anyone associated with the rebel is a risk as well. Plus, he enjoys setting an example. There are now few within the city that would risk both themselves and their families, proving the Commander's theory that it's better to rule by fear and obedience than kindness.

"Do you admit to the charges laid against you?"

I stare back at Gillert refusing to give him anything. No fear, no information. No reaction.

"This is your only chance to speak. If you don't give a statement now, then you'll be prosecuted without a defence."

I sneer at him, finally speaking. "Your kind doesn't believe in a defence. You force confessions, lock us up and kill us. Why should I give you anything, you stupid fuck?"

Predictably, fury flashes across his face. He moves forward until he's leaning on the table, the buttons of his uniform jacket straining against his chest and stomach. He's inches away from me. He takes my hands in his and closes his fists threateningly. I hold myself still despite the near overwhelming urge to jerk back. "If you want to live to see the sunrise then you'll give me something that I can give to

Fuentes. Make me look good and I'll do what I can to help you. Maybe get you remanded into my custody." He leans back in his chair. "Now tell me your name and the house you belong to."

I laugh. Does this idiot really think I'm going to give him anything? "In what way do you think your custody is preferable to death, Gillert? I'm not giving you a damn thing. You can burn in hell right beside me for all I care."

His fists hit the table causing it to jump. He stands, his face turning red with anger. I lean back in my chair as far out of reach as I can get while still chained down. "You'll regret that you little urchin. Give me a name right fucking now!"

I can't help it, I start laughing again. The man is so fucking predictable! He calls me Street Urchin in one breath, like that's my real name, before switching gears and demanding my given name. "Fine, you've convinced me. Can I get a glass of water first? Watching you bust a neck vein is thirsty business."

His face is starting to turn purple and I think about saying something to the effect that he should be watching his blood pressure, when he comes storming around the table. He's about to reach for me when the door opens and the Warlord strides in. He takes in the scene at a glance and then turns his glacial expression on Gillert.

"You were about to lay hands on the woman?" It's clear from his voice that he's not asking a question and doesn't expect an answer.

Gillert backs away from me. I still can't really see him from my foreword cuffed position, but I can tell by the atmosphere in the room and the sweat-fear stench that Gillert's about to wet himself. "She... she... was threatening to hurt herself. I was just gonna make sure she wasn't hurt."

I twist my head around as much as I can to look at him. Is that the best he can come up with? "What exactly was I supposed to be doing over here with my hands chained to a table? Swallowing my own tongue in protest?"

"Shut up," Diogo says walking around the table. He places his hand on the chair opposite me and stares down at me coldly. Without turning to look at Gillert, he says, "You can leave, I'll talk with you later about following my instructions. Don't go far. I want the Judge sent in as soon as he gets here."

I tip my head toward Gillert as he walks by. Stupid fuck. Bet he won't even get that order right.

Diogo drops into the chair, leaning back, his legs spread and his arms held loose in front of him. I think it's a deliberately relaxed-looking pose. I can feel the tension flowing between us, like a live electrical charge. I've seen how fast he can move. If he wants, he can drop the pretense and be across the table in an instant.

I stare back wordlessly.

"I think I can safely assume that you gave officer Gillert nothing." I don't answer, but he seems almost pleased that I didn't give up my identity or anything important. This worries me. If Diogo Fuentes is pleased, then there's something terribly wrong happening in my world. We're on opposing sides of a philosophy, each practicing different moral goals. If he's happy then I can't be.

"Let's start over with the processing then," he says smoothly, pinning me with those chilling dark eyes. "Name."

I don't speak.

He nods his head a little and relaxes further into the chair, steepling his fingers in front of him. He looks different. It takes me a moment before my brain kicks in and I realize that he's no longer wearing desert gear, he's in a crisp clean uniform. It's militaristic in style, severe and fitted to his tall, muscular frame. A collared jacket over a dress shirt with creased pants. The jacket is emblazoned with the symbol of the desert hawk. Underneath are the three bars that indicate the highest authority in the city.

"Give me a name, little Wren." His voice is soft. Deadly. I feel that I'm not going to like the next words out of his mouth. And when, again, I don't speak, he says, "There are three refugees in processing at this very moment. They walked up to the gates yesterday. Two are healthy and strong, one is not. He's young and frail. Give me a name and I won't have him turned out."

I stare at him, trying to decide if this is a bluff. His story is more than plausible. It's similar to my origins, similar to many stories of refugees being taken from their families and kept within the city walls while the too old or too sick are turned away. Still, I shake my head, "I don't believe you. Your story is too convenient."

For the first time he shows real anger. Not in his facial expression, not in any real way. But I know he's angry. It's in the tightening of his body, the flare of his nostrils, the quick, obsidian flash of his eyes. He shutters it quickly, but his words are deadly as he says, "I do not lie, Wren. Ever. Learn this and remember. I won't repeat myself."

I shiver but hold my ground. "I want to see them. If what you say is true, then show me and I'll give you a name."

He leans forward in his seat, lifting his arms to rest them on the table. He almost copies Gillert's action by placing his hands over mine, but he doesn't tighten them painfully. Instead he lets me feel the tensile strength of his fingers, the encompassing grip of his large hands over mine.

"I don't compromise, little girl. Last chance, do you accept my proposal? A name for a life? Once the offer is off the table it won't come back."

Fuck. When he puts it that way, what choice do I have? "My name is Taran." I don't give up my last name.

He leans back, his expression thoughtful. I'm relieved. His touch is disturbing. It threatens without actually threatening. The authority running through his veins isn't in name only. He's been given, or taken, the position of our Sanctuary's Warlord for a reason.

"Taran. That is a powerful name," he muses, his voice caressing the syllables, sending a shiver of apprehension down my spine. "It encompasses Earth, thunder and heaven if I'm not mistaken."

I stare openly at him. He can't know this unless he has a basic understanding of either Hindi or Hinduism. Definitely not something I would've expected of a warlord or a man from this part of the world. If I'm not mistaken he's of Mexican descent with a slight Spanish accent. This intellectual side of him is far more frightening than the brash, angry heathen I always assumed him to be.

"I have no idea what you're talking about," I say coolly, staring back at him, trying to maintain eye contact.

He chuckles, but the sound isn't at all pleasant. "Don't play games with me, little Wren. You know exactly what I mean. Is your family of Indian descent? I can't tell what you look like under all that grime."

"You don't get anything else out of me, Warlord. You told me if I gave you a name that you would give me a life. Is the boy safe or are you going back on your word, demanding something else?" I shouldn't speak to him this way. I'm sure no one in their right mind would speak to him this way, not if they wanted to preserve their life. But I feel safe somehow. I don't believe he'll hurt me. Not yet anyway. He seems to want something from me.

"Be careful, Taran," his voice is calm, but there's an underlying steel to it. "You do not want to question my word."

"Then if the boy is safe I have nothing else to say." I eye him, considering for a moment. "Unless you wish to keep playing this game, a life for a question. Depending on the questions, it may be worth my time."

He shakes his head and then speaks, confirming my earlier thoughts. "People don't speak to me this way, girl. You need to watch your tongue."

"Maybe they should speak to you this way," I say sharply. "If more people tell you what a shit leader you are, then maybe you'll actually listen."

"You are stupid to bait me. If you had spoken to any of my men the way you do to me, then you'd be beaten bloody, broken and left to die," he snaps. He seems more annoyed that my mouthiness would place me in danger than he is at the way I'm speaking to him.

"Maybe I am stupid, Diogo." I use his given name for the first time. I may as well. He knows mine, so why shouldn't I speak his? The word has a visible effect on him though. A flash of surprise crosses his features, followed by a slight softening of his rugged features before he once more smooths his expression. "Maybe I do have a death wish. I've known for years that I would be caught one day. That if that day ever came I would be executed. But the one thing I swore I would do if I ever got the chance, was tell our intrepid Warlord exactly what I think of him."

"And what do you think of me?" His question isn't a dare. It holds real curiosity.

I stare at him, considering my words before replying. I

should back down. Shouldn't speak my mind. I'm beginning to see that I might actually get out of this arrest alive.

But this may be my one and only chance to get him to listen. To truly listen. We've been rioting and yelling our opinions for years. Nothing has worked and his punishment has been to lay harsher sanctions on certain areas of the city, on certain citizens, and the implementation of a city-wide curfew, brutally enforced. I pause before I speak, and when I do, my words are thoughtful. "You're a brutal man, with cold and unforgiving values. You're a tyrannical leader that doesn't know how to listen to his people. You rule with a twisted authority and you've created an unnecessary hierarchy among the people. You don't deserve to lead."

He watches me as I speak, listens to the words. Absorbs them. When I finish, he says, "Anything else you wish to add?"

I hesitate, and then I say, "You're different from who I thought you'd be, Commander Diogo Fuentes. You aren't rash, despotic, or unnecessarily evil. At least I don't think so, from what I've seen on our short acquaintance. This confuses me even more though. If you're as well educated as I suspect, as thoughtful, then it makes no sense that you would cultivate such a terrible authoritarian style of leadership."

His dark eyes consider me. I've insulted him over and over, but I've also spoken the truth as I see it. He's been the leader since well before my arrival in the city twelve years ago. In all this time I've never seen him show a kind act. Never once seen him bend to the will of the people or the majority of public opinion. He simply crushes all opposition and continues to rule through fear. Yet, I don't sense that he's at all fazed by my words.

"And you, my Desert Wren." He uses the nickname I've

been given, despite now knowing my actual name. I sense he does it for a reason. Uses the title of Desert Wren to make a statement. "You are exactly as I'd imagined."

"I don't understand," I say, frowning at him. How long have I been on his radar that he's formed an opinion of my character? And how can he do that without ever having met me? All he had to go on was my actions.

He stands and reaches across the table. I flinch back, but he only releases the cuffs. He motions for me to stand. I do, rubbing my wrists.

"I don't suppose you do understand," he says, waving me toward him. He bends to speak close to my ear as we leave the interrogation room. "But you will. In time."

SIX

TARAN

He stops me before we make it ten steps from the room and frowns down at me, his dark gaze considering. Then he rapidly unbuttons his jacket and removes it from his broad shoulders. He drapes it around me, lifting my arms as though I'm a child to tuck them into the overly long sleeves. Next, he buttons the front until my swath of exposed chest and stomach is covered.

I'm stunned. This can't be for my comfort or he would've done it in the interrogation room. Is it possible that he doesn't want others to see my exposed skin? We haven't known each other a day, yet Diogo is acting strangely possessive. Telling Gillert not to touch me, insisting that he be called when the Judge arrives. And now this.

It all seems oddly out of character of the man I imagined him to be. He places a hand at my back and guides me down the hall. I bite my lip, thinking, and then I say, "Won't it make a statement to your people that I'm wearing part of your uniform?"

He glances down at me but doesn't break stride. "It

doesn't matter what they think as long as they keep their thoughts to themselves."

"That's exactly what I mean when I call you a dictator, Diogo," I grumble.

"I take your words as a compliment, girl," he says unfazed.

Of course he would.

He leads me to the front of the station again and over to Gillert's desk. The officer stands up, staring at me nervously. He must be worried that I told Diogo he touched me. Twice. I didn't, but that doesn't stop me from flashing him a satisfied grin. The colour seeps from his skin, leaving him pale. He really is afraid of the Warlord.

"Has the Judge arrived?" Diogo asks, his voice becoming cold and distant once more.

"No, Commander," Gillert chokes out.

"Have him sent to my residence then." Diogo turns to leave, turning me with him.

"A-are you taking the prisoner with you?" Gillert spits out, curiosity winning out over good sense. It seems obvious to me that Gillert is disappointed that the woman he considers his personal prize is walking out of the station with his boss.

Diogo stiffens but doesn't address the question. He continues to walk away, as though Gillert is so far beneath him that as soon as he's out of sight he no longer exists. It hits home once again how different Diogo is treating me than he treats others. I glance over my shoulder. Gillert is burning a hole in my back with his twisted gaze. I hope I never again find myself in a room alone with that one.

Diogo escorts me to his vehicle. Once we're both inside I ask, "Why are you taking me to your home?"

"To get you cleaned up," he grunts, keeping his eyes on

the road. Vehicles are so rare that the streets are crowded with people, vendors and debris, making it difficult for drivers to navigate. I've become so efficient at transporting myself by other methods that I'd never imagined what it must be like to drive through the city.

Then his words penetrate the fog of my musings. He wants to get me cleaned up? If Diogo thinks I'm going to get naked anywhere near him, he's entirely mistaken. But I don't say that. Instead I say, "Do you often take prisoners back to your home?" He ignores me, so I push. "You don't, do you? You seem like the solitary type to me."

He doesn't look at me, but he growls, "Don't pretend you know me, little girl."

No, I think to myself, but with every passing minute I'm getting to know you better.

When a group of people are too slow to get out of his way, he drives so close to them that I'm sure he'll clip them. "Be careful, there are children out there!"

"Stop speaking, Taran," he says coldly. "I'm weary of your constant challenges."

"Then why are taking me home with you?" I snap, crossing my arms over my chest and glaring at him.

He doesn't speak again and neither do I. There's no point. He's a strange and unpredictable man that seems determined to take the course he's set out. Or maybe he is predictable and he's right, I don't know him at all. But I do know that going to his home makes me very nervous. It somehow feels significant. Like a step forward that I can't take back once I'm in. I should probably try to escape. Jump out of the vehicle and run. But I don't. I won't make it far. Diogo is in top athletic shape and I'm utterly exhausted. I'll go to his home, find out what 'cleaning up' means and then

I'll find a way out. Maybe I'll get a meal out of him before I go.

I lean back in my seat and close my eyes. It's been a long day. I climbed over the wall, I've been searched and arrested. I've been through Gillert's half-assed processing, then Diogo's strange interrogation. Now I'm headed to his house to await prosecution and judgement. I have no idea what that'll look like, but I know I'm probably not going to like it.

"We're here." Diogo's deep voice rouses me and when I open my eyes he's looking at me intently.

I turn to hide my yawn. Did I actually fall asleep?

"Come," he says, his voice gruff. He wraps one of his huge hands around my arm and pulls me through his side of the jeep. I step outside and blink up into the hot sunny afternoon.

I realize that I'm in the elite sector of the city. Not a surprise, but I've never been here before, never had a reason to access this sector. It's surrounded by fencing to help control crime against the wealthy inhabitants. It's stunning. The lush greenery surrounding us has been neatly trimmed and the buildings left standing seem to be in good order. Without people to maintain buildings and cut away the nature, the city was overtaken by greenery after the Great Fall. It's left to grow wild in most sectors, but apparently it gets trimmed back in Sector One. I've never actually witnessed something as frivolous as lawn maintenance in my lifetime.

I stare in awe as Diogo pulls me foreword towards a huge building. I barely have enough time to shade my eyes and look up, and up, at the spectacular high rise before he pulls me inside. It's one of the few tall buildings left standing from old Tucson. Some were burned down during the first and fiercest riots of 38, before martial law was instated. And others were brought down to use for as material for Sanctuary's wall.

"You live in The Tower?" I whisper shakily. The tallest building left standing in Sanctuary, it can be seen from all corners of the city.

"Yes," Diogo says, glancing down at me. He places his hand at my back once more. It's big and broad, takes up nearly half of my back. I don't mind. I almost feel as though I need the comfort. I've just entered a new world.

He pulls me into a staircase and starts climbing. My legs are shaking with fatigue and I groan out loud when we reach the fifth floor. Without pausing, he pulls me to him and lifts me right up into his arms. I gasp and cling to him for a second before I realize that he's carrying me, now running up the stairs at a dizzying speed. He's got incredible stamina. He's not even winded!

"Diogo, I can walk!" I protest, giving his arm a test shove.

He just tightens his grip and keeps climbing. I lose count of all the floors we pass. The stairwell is meticulously maintained with none of the usual shrubbery and debris that can be found in most other buildings as the neglected infrastructure crumbles and collapses all around us.

Diogo stops in front of the door with a giant 20 painted on it, sets me on my feet and unlocks it. He pushes it open and ushers me inside. I take a few quick steps away from him and then glance around. My eye immediately catches on the window. I gasp and approach it, awed by the view. New Tucson Sanctuary lays spread out at my feet, the sun shining brightly across the buildings. I love heights and have always enjoyed the sensation of being high up. Now, as I

look out at my city, I feel warmth and belonging to Sanctuary. It's a bittersweet feeling. I had to leave my grandparents
behind and forge a relationship with the city and its inhabitants. Had to find my way through loneliness.

"Home," Diogo says gruffly from behind me.

The building has rattled her, but she's quick to shutter her expression as I guide her through my home on the top floor of what used to be One South Church, now known as the Tower, the tallest building in Sanctuary. I made it my home when I became leader. A symbol of strength and power. I prefer to live up high, away from the daily stresses of my people. I don't share the Tower with many except for a few of my security men who reside on lower floors. The rest of the building is left empty. I enjoy the solitude.

Except now I've brought home an urchin. She walks toward the window and gazes out at the dazzling view of the city. She's quiet as she studies the panorama. I doubt she's ever seen anything this spectacular. But she gives me nothing in either expression or words. I feel... disappointed. I expected more from her. Perhaps the grime on her face is covering the emotion I wish to see.

"Home," I say. I want her to feel the moment. Feel our shared Sanctuary and the building.

"No," she replies quietly, without turning. "This is not my home. Home was with the people I loved."

I feel a rush of anger at her words. She doesn't belong to anyone but me. I don't want her pining for lost love. I want her to settle into her new home. Perhaps it's an unreasonable expectation considering how quickly I've come into her life and forced change. But in an uncertain world, with death lingering around every corner, we must seize opportunities when they arise.

"Come," I say sharply. "I'll show you where you can wash."

She drags her feet as I pull her through the apartment. It's large, but not built like a regular home. It was originally an office building, but I had this floor gutted until it was just concrete and my meagre belongings. I added in the essentials for living. A washroom and a kitchen. But left the rest bare.

"I don't want to shower," she grumbles.

"Nonetheless, you will." My voice is uncompromising. It's best for her to learn obedience quickly and easily so she doesn't have to learn my methods of obtaining obedience.

"I won't," she insists stubbornly.

I stop in front of a chest of drawers, open one and thrust a towel at her. I wave her toward the washroom, and when she refuses to go, I give her a small push. When still she resists, I say calmly, "If you don't do as I say then I will strip you and wash you myself. The process will not be dignified and I will not be kind or gentle. Your choice, Taran."

A shiver runs through her body, she stares a second longer defiance warring with fear, then quickly turns away to comply. Perhaps she is learning that I'm a man of my word. I would've done exactly as I described if she'd hesitated any longer. A part of me almost wishes she hadn't disappeared so quickly into the washroom. Those quick flashes of chest I'd glimpsed throughout the day were intriguing.

I stifle the feeling. She may be too young for that wayward thought. She's so small, her body doesn't seem fully formed. Perhaps mid-to-late teens. But her intellect, her reasoning, though flawed, is complete and well thought out. Not the musings of a child. And Gillert had suggested she was the same last time they met, three years ago. Though, it wouldn't matter if she was young, women are wed early in Sanctuary to give them a better chance of producing healthy, strong children.

It occurs to me that Taran could be married. Probably is married. This makes me unaccountably angry. I want to murder her husband, if she has one. I hadn't originally thought to bring her here to install her as my mistress, or my wife. My intention was just to have her near for a while. But now, the more I think about her, the more the idea feels right.

I can hear the shower running now and I wonder what she's thinking. Is she afraid? Does she think I'll rape her? I admit, respect for women is not a priority in most Sanctuary cities, mine included. They're weaker than men and thus their rights have been set aside in the face of survival. I can essentially do whatever I want with my little captive and no one would step in.

I pace as she showers. I want to go in, but I don't want to frighten her. I'm not sure why this is important. I've never cared about a woman's feelings before. I don't have time for that. The few times a year I feel the need for female companionship I fuck them and I push them out the door. No mess, nothing that gets in the way of my single-minded focus. Then, none of those women have ever been as interesting as Taran. I choose my women from among the elite, sometimes they're single, more often they're married. Sharing women is common – a practice that has grown as the numbers of women fall, especially fertile women. For me, they are just willing vessels to sate my lust. They leave and I forget about them. I've yet to find one that I want to spawn children with.

An image of Taran's slight figure bothers me. What would she look like pregnant? She's too small to produce strong children. At least not until they're born and start growing larger. Perhaps she already has children with someone else. Again, this thought disturbs me. I need to find out more about her, get her to talk. If I don't like the answers then I'll make changes to her life. I'm used to playing God in the lives of others. Why not this one insignificant girl?

I realize that she has nothing to wear other than the grimy clothes I found her in. I want those clothes thrown away, but she'll need something else to wear. Especially once the Judge arrives. I dig through my drawers and come up with a loose shirt that buttons up the front. It'll be huge on her, but it's better than what she has.

I open the door to the washroom and thrust the shirt inside. "Taran, you'll wear this when you finish." I stare hard at the frosted glass doors, but I can't see anything in the steam of the room. She'd definitely taking advantage of the hot water. This thought pleases me. She wouldn't have access to hot water wherever she lives. There's a water reservoir in this building that pumps to the various living quarters. It's been outfitted with heating coils. Such a rare commodity can only be found in Sector One, leaving the rest of the city without any means of artificial heating. Most families make do with small gas stoves and firepits. This reminds me that I have no idea what district she's from, what house she calls home.

"You have five minutes and to finish and dress." She doesn't speak. I leave the door open and sit on the bed, listening for her movements. The shower turns off and I can hear dripping as she steps out and towels off. My eagerness to see her grows with each moment until I'm up and pacing again. I resist the urge to watch her as she pulls the shirt on.

Finally, she steps out of the washroom and I stop to look my fill. The Desert Wren. Wet strands of hair trail over the shirt, wetting it until it clings to her shoulders. The collar is open at her throat showing narrow collar bones against delicate flesh. Her skin tone, without the dirt, is slightly paler than mine. Not white, but not very tanned either. Her hair is a rich, dark brownish red that will probably lighten as it dries. Slim legs poke out from the hem of the shirt, which stops nearly at her knees. My hunger grows at the sight of her.

Her face is round, her chin and nose softer, more feminine than I'd thought when she was covered in dirt. A slight flush pinkens her cheeks. Her eyes, tilted in at the corners, look large in her face. She is not beautiful, but she's not plain either. She would be easily overlooked on the street if a person wasn't interested at first sight. But the more I look, the more I feel the rightness of her appearance, of my attraction to her. She's perfect.

"How old are you?" I demand hoarsely.

She glares at me, determined to give nothing. I'm finished with her stubborn attitude. She needs to learn who she's dealing with and I need to know how old she is. I need to know that I can make her mine, take her carnally, without worry that I'm fucking someone too young. And if she is too young, then I'll wait until she's old enough. I walk toward her so rapidly that she only has time to retreat a single step before I'm wrapping my fingers around her throat and lifting her. She chokes and clutches at my wrist as I slam her into the wall at her back. I crowd her with my body, both to intimidate her and to hold her up. I've no wish to strangle her, only frighten the truth out of her. I hold her at least a foot off the floor. Her feet are scrambling against my legs as she tries to gain purchase.

I pin her with my gaze and say calmly, "Your age?"

I lower her slowly, allowing her to feel the strength in me should she refuse to answer the question again. Once her toes are back on the floor, I loosen my grip only enough for her to suck in a desperate breath of air. When she's had enough I flex my fingers threateningly.

"Twenty-six!" she gasps.

I raise an eyebrow. If she's telling the truth, then she's definitely older than she looks. She's likely been a runt all her life then. Not much of a prize for men in a world that actively seeks larger, healthier looking women. Yet, this one isn't unappealing. She has a healthy glow about her. Likely that spitfire attitude makes her eyes snap with enough fury to give her the glow.

I grunt in acknowledgment. She's fifteen years my junior. Young, but not out of reach. My gaze drops once more, lingering on the small breasts poking against my white shirt. The nipples are peaked, probably from reaction to my rough handling. She's slim all over. No good for birthing children. Especially with a warlord. A man in my position is expected to mate with a strong woman.

"Are you married?"

She frowns and avoids my eye. I sense that she's about to refuse to answer the question. I don't want to hurt or frighten her again, but these questions must be answered. "Taran," I growl down at her. She lifts defiant eyes up to mine. "Answer the question. This is nothing compared to a real interrogation. I prefer you remain intact but will choose the alternate path if you don't give me what I ask."

"And where does it end, Diogo?" She digs her fingers into mine, tugging to get my hand off her neck. Her struggles are pointless. She's like a bird fluttering angrily against its cage. "How much will you demand? Names, places, my soul? I've determined that death is preferable to betraying my friends."

"This is not a negotiation." I tighten my grip once more. I'm losing patience with her stubborn resistance. "You don't seem to understand that it isn't one or the other. Information or death. There is so much in between that your imagination can't even begin to comprehend. All I ask for now is your marital status."

Her eyes are sparkling with tears, likely from the pain of my attack and heightened emotions. She's feeling trapped.

"Answer," I growl, giving her no choice.

"Yes!" she hisses breathlessly. "I have a husband."

I shouldn't be, and yet, I'm shocked by her answer. I wasn't expecting it. Perhaps I hoped her husband dead. The urge to shake his name out of her is so strong that I have to step back so I won't harm her. It wouldn't take much. She's too delicate for such treatment and I'm not used to leashing my strength. Still, anger is rushing through me. An unfamiliar emotion. I rule with cold, calm logic so I don't take any missteps with my leadership. This woman is fucking with my equilibrium.

I briefly consider sending her back to processing. But I've known for a while now, well before I met the woman, that I was intrigued. That her ideals and conviction had captured and held my interest. She first landed on my radar when she used the hunger riots to smuggle people into the city. It took months for us to realize what she'd done. My people estimate that she was able to hide nearly 100 illegals during that time. We began searching further back and discovered that she'd been working the underground rebel circuit for nearly a decade. She would've been sixteen when she first started people smuggling.

Yet despite her work producing legitimate looking forgeries, guiding illegals into the city and generally stirring rebellion among the non-elites, we hadn't been able to discover a single clue to her identity. She is well-loved among the people. They would plead ignorance at every turn, protecting their rebel leader, even under threat.

I stare at her, taking in her defiant pose and snapping eyes. I want to demand her husband's name. I want to ensure his death with my own hands. I want her free from him so she can be with me. But I don't touch her. Now isn't the time. Instead, I jerk my head toward the door. "Come."

She follows behind me. Not too close. Despite her attitude, she's wary now that I've threatened her physically. I seat her at the table and am about to gather something for us to eat when my radio squawks. The Judge has arrived.

I allow him entry and wave him toward my prisoner. Huffing and puffing from the climb up 20 floors, he takes his time sitting down and catching his breath. He opens his diary and glances at me. "Processing didn't give me much information. Just the name, Desert Wren, and the charges."

I cross my arms and stare back at him. I don't like the officious man, yet he is our judge and has been for many years. He has several lesser prosecutors that work under him, dispensing justice on petty crimes. But the Judge is responsible for greater crimes. Crimes such as the ones that Taran is facing. Treason within a Sanctuary city is one of the worst crimes a person can commit. It weakens social order and leaves the city vulnerable.

"You may add the name 'Taran' with the Desert Wren," I tell him gruffly.

He makes a note and then looks up at me with brow lifted. "Surname?"

"None. Move on, Judge." I don't attempt civility. There's no point to such niceties. Civilization has collapsed and only the strongest survive. Those who attempt polite societal niceties are either lying or heading ignorantly toward their own deaths.

The Judge moves his gaze to Taran, taking her in with interest. I'm not pleased with his speculative look, but I hold my peace for now. Most in our circles have heard of the Wren. It would seem stranger if he simply ignored her.

"Taran – Desert Wren," he begins. "You are charged with treason against your Sanctuary city. You are charged with providing forged documents to illegals and bringing them into the city. You are charged with hiding illegals from the Authority. You are charged with inciting unrest among the citizens."

She sits unmoving, absorbing each charge. We both know what's coming, yet my heart pounds for her as we reach the conclusion. For her part, she's gripping the seat on either side of her thighs, as though to stop herself from launching at the Judge.

"Taran – Desert Wren, how do you plead?"

She lifts her lip in a sneer. "I refuse to plead anything in this mockery of a trial. Fuck you and your judgments."

The Judge stiffens slightly, his face hardening, but he doesn't otherwise react to her profane comments.

"Taran – Desert Wren, you have been judged. You will be executed for these crimes. Your sentence is effective immediately. You will be escorted to the execution hall where the sentence will be carried out. Please stand."

EIGHT

TARAN

The only thing this mockery of justice deserves is my disdain. Execution is nothing less than I expected. From the first illegal I brought into the city until this day I've known I was living on borrowed time. I say nothing, give no reaction as the Judge finishes his speech. At least he's quick and to the point. If I'm to be sent to my death, then the last thing I want is to listen to this man all day.

When the Judge rises, so do I.

"Sit down." Diogo's voice cuts through the room like the edge of a knife. I drop into my seat without argument. Now that I'm pretty much a dead woman I may as well prolong what little life I have left.

The Judge looks disgruntled but sits back down. Diogo steps to the table and places his fists on the heavy marble. His arms bulge and strain against his shirt. He lowers his eyebrows and pins the Judge with a glare.

"You will commute her sentence and remand her into my care."

The Judge's mouth pops open in surprise. He sputters

for a moment before saying, "This is… is not possible. Judgment has been passed and her sentence declared."

"Do you imagine that you have more authority in this city than I?" Diogo's voice is frighteningly calm. Even in my short acquaintance with him I know that people don't question him. That it would be dangerous to do so. And I suppose from Diogo's point of view, it would be just as dangerous to allow questions. Unrest would arise among the ranks and threaten his position.

"But you've never stepped in before. Sentencing is my job," the Judge protests.

"Consider this a new precedent then, if you must. I am the highest Authority in this city and my word is law."

Still the Judge persists, not wanting to give way. "But what will the people think!"

"They will think what I tell them to think," Diogo says coolly. "As they must do every other day."

I choke back an angry exclamation at Diogo's arrogance. I despise the way he treats his citizens like cattle. Still, I prefer to survive if that option is on the table. I seal my lips and listen as the two men speak.

"I am fast losing what little patience I possess, Judge. You will commute the Desert Wren's sentence and remand her into my custody. Henceforth I will be responsible for her." Diogo drops a hand to his belt where he has two weapons clearly displayed, a gun and a long, sheathed hunting knife.

It's clear that the Judge wants to continue arguing. It's also abundantly clear that to do so would be extremely bad for his health. He bows his head in acknowledgment and turns his glare toward me. His words are clipped as he says, "Taran – Desert Wren. Your sentence is commuted. You are henceforth remanded to the custody of

Commander Diogo Fuentes, Warlord of the New Tucson Sanctuary."

He makes a note in his diary, stands to gather his items and leaves without another word, his robe swishing angrily behind him. I'm left sitting at Diogo's table, a little stunned and a lot nervous. Several hours ago I was eating a rushed breakfast of cactus juice and pheasant before setting out to climb the wall. Now I've essentially become the property of the single highest Authority in the city and beyond. The closest Sanctuary city is in New Sacramento. Which means that no one can threaten or contradict the man standing opposite me. He's the final word.

I try to wipe the look of dismay from my expression, fail, and finally say, "What now?"

He considers me. I suspect this situation is as new to him as it is to me. His home isn't filled with prisoners and he's not much of a people person that I can tell. I don't think he makes a habit of taking in stray criminals.

"You will obey my rules," he says sternly.

I try not to laugh but it bubbles out. I'm exhausted, hungry and his words seem hilarious. I can't remember the last time I obeyed anyone. Maybe my grandparents, but they'll be long dead by now. This thought sobers me. "No," I tell him, shaking my head. "You picked the wrong woman if you were looking for an obedient criminal."

He rubs a hand over his face before straightening. "The obedience is for your sake, Taran, not mine. You obey, you can live comfortably. You don't, and I will make sure you understand why obedience was the better path."

"Sure," I snort and look around. "So, am I supposed to be doing your dishes or what? Like some kind of slave?"

He glares down at me from his superior height. "You do not want to take a flip tone with me, girl. I am the man that stands between you and death. You should not be trying my patience."

I stare up at him, considering. Then I shrug. He's not wrong, but, "I don't know how to obey. I've been on my own since I was sixteen."

"What about your husband?" he asks. His tone is casual but his eyes and body language, they're anything but. He's invested in my answer. Wants to know about my husband.

I think about withholding everything, but there's not much point. He already knows I'm married, and he'll have to kill me if he wants a name. "I didn't live long under my husband's roof."

"When did you last see him?" Diogo demands, his body stiff, waiting for my answer.

"Five days ago," I tell him truthfully. I suspect our repertoire will become akin to a dance. He wants information and there is so much that I can't give him. Yet I don't want to lie. Lying can lead to giving more information than I intend if he starts untangling the truth from a web of lies. I must find a balance between the truth and protecting those that I care about, while somehow still holding onto my skin.

The truth about when I last saw my husband seems to strike him badly. His brow creases in annoyance and his muscles tighten. It bothers him that I have a husband I'm in contact with. I don't know what to say though. It would be far more unusual for a woman my age to be unwed than single. He seems to come to the same conclusion.

"When were you wed?" he asks.

"I was given to him when I was fourteen," I answer truthfully. "I resided in his home until I was sixteen."

He grunts in acknowledgment. "You left your husband's home ten years ago."

I want to make an acerbic comment on his ability to

handle basic math but suspect my humour won't be welcomed. Instead I nod. "Yes, that's correct."

"Why did you leave?" The question is deceptively casual, but I can tell that he desperately wants an answer.

"I don't wish to discuss my marriage any further," I say, clasping my hands in my lap. "I was forcibly wedded. The marriage failed. I'm sure mine isn't the only one you've heard of."

"No, but runaway wives are usually returned to their husbands." He eyes me speculatively. "You didn't return to your husband's home, yet you're still in touch with him."

I shrug but don't answer. I'm finished with his questions. I don't want him guessing my connections. And his questions are too close to an interrogation. I realize quickly that he's better at this than I am. If I continue to answer, then eventually I'll give him more than I should. Enough that he'll be able to trace my origins and become a serious danger to my loved ones. Best to give him nothing to work with.

When I don't speak, he straightens away from the table. His dark eyes are hooded. "You will give me what I ask for, Taran. In time, I'm confident that I'll gain everything from you, including a name."

I turn my head to look at him. "In time I'll be gone, Diogo. Either dead or free. Those are my options. Not whatever this is." I wave my hand impatiently around the room. "This is a game, and I refuse to participate."

"You'll do as your told." He doesn't come closer to me, doesn't threaten me, but the atmosphere in the room feels oppressively close. His entire focus is on me. Like I'm the mouse in his trap and he's decided to keep me for now, toy with me.

"I'll do as I wish." My words are foolhardy and we both

know it. I'm less than half his size and I have no recourse for the moment. I'm as good as helpless in the grip of his custody. Still, he needs to know that I won't be a willing participant.

He doesn't answer, instead turning away and striding into the kitchen. My stomach rumbles as I hear him shuffling around. When he returns he's carrying a plate stacked high with food. My eyes nearly pop out of my head as I take it all in. There's more food on that plate than I usually eat in three days. And the variety! My mouth waters as I take in the fresh fruit, meats and cheeses. I haven't even seen fruit in months, let alone this much of it all at once.

He doesn't tease me or demand answers in exchange for food, as I thought he might. Instead, he places the plate in front of me and drops into the chair next to me. For a split second I think about refusing his offer, but my hunger wins out. I've been hungry for so long, I don't remember what full feels like. I've taught myself to simply subsist on less so others can share and survive. I'm not the only one who does this. Many within my rebel circle of friends will give up rations to illegals, so we all have a better chance at survival.

I pick up a piece of papaya and shove it into my mouth, moaning as the first burst of flavour hits my tongue. It's the best thing I've ever eaten. I continue until I've plowed through the rest of the papaya and a banana.

"Where'd you get the fruit?" I ask curiously between bites. It's everything I can do to slow down long enough to ask.

"Some of it's grown in the city in greenhouses and the rest is imported from other Sanctuaries down south." The edge of his lip curls up as he watches me devour his food like I'll never eat again. I turn to look at him more fully. His face is really quite expressive, once a person gets past the harsh, serious lines. His lips are mobile, tipping up when he's amused or thinning out when he's angry. And his eyes, though so brown they're pretty much black, are constantly assessing everything around him, intelligence shining bright in their depths.

As I'm staring at his mouth, his lips part and he says, "While you're in my custody, you'll be assigned a guard to watch over and protect you."

I expected him to say something about my voracious appetite or my terrible table manners, since I'm shoving bits of food in my mouth faster than a Primitive can bite. I swallow the mouthful of pheasant I've just eaten and say, "Water please."

For a split second he looks surprised. Maybe at my lack of argument on his security measures. I don't know, and I don't care. I'm hungry and thirsty and that takes priority at the moment. We both know I'll try to escape at the first opportunity. He would be stupid not to keep close tabs on me. Especially since he has a city to terrorize and can't keep eyes on me at all times.

He fetches a glass of water and drops into the seat next to me, continuing to watch as I eat. I ignore him until I'm finished. When I eat a little over half the plate I push it away with a sigh and gulp the water down.

"Eat more," he says, pushing it back toward me.

"I'm finished." I sit back in my chair, leaning away from him. While I was eating he placed an arm along the top of my chair.

"You suffer from hunger, Taran. Given your size and the ribs I saw poking at your flesh, you've been hungry for a long time." His voice takes on an impatient edge, as though he's annoyed at my hunger.

I glance at him out of the corner of my eye. He's

frowning down at the plate. "Yes, Diogo. I go hungry sometimes. It's what happens in my sector. I'm not sure if you remember the food riots..." How could anyone forget the food riots? The lower classes tried to burn the city down in an attempt to get the government to ration food fairly. "But I'm not going to be able to assuage a lifetime of hunger in one meal."

He takes my words in and nods. Then he says, "From now on you will not be allowed to go hungry again. At each meal you will eat until you're full." His sharp eyes rove over my frame, before he adds, "And there will be consequences if I discover you giving away your food."

He's not a stupid man. Somehow he's figuring me out, and he's doing it fast. It's odd to have someone care about my hunger. The people in my circles look to me for guidance. Despite my youth, I sit on the rebel council as one of their top advisors. I am an authority where I come from, no one questions how much of my rations are given out to others. Yet, this man is attempting to care for me.

I wonder why? And will I like the answer?

NINE

DIOGO

I study the woman as she sits drooping in her chair, exhaustion creeping up to claim her. Long, dark eyelashes fan the tops of her delicate cheeks. Now that her hair has dried, it shines a beautiful auburn colour, falling down her back and shoulders in waves. She shifts to prop an elbow on the table and slumps into her hand, then winces as her chin touches the palm. She jerks her hand away and straightens, dropping the hand into her lap and cradling it with her other hand.

I frown and reach for her. "Let me see."

She automatically pulls her arm away, but I catch the hand. I flip it palm side up and use my fingers to uncurl hers so I can see the entire hand. The cut is clean now, her makeshift bandage missing. It's not terribly deep but it should still be cleaned with antiseptic and re-bandaged. Not left to catch an infection.

"Did this happen while you were climbing the wall?" I demand, tugging her to her feet. I walk her through my place, back into the bedroom.

She glares at me. "It's a little cut, Diogo. Why does it matter?"

I shove her back and point at the bed. "Sit." I command. She complies, though hesitantly, staring at the big bed before sitting gingerly on the edge. "I need to know about the injury so I can take care of it properly."

She stares up at me. "I cut myself on a piece of metal."

"When was your last tetanus shot?" Tetanus shots are still available, though not as plentiful as they once were.

"About five months ago."

It's not surprising she would stay up to date given her habit of climbing the wall. I grunt my acknowledgment as I head for the washroom, returning with the First Aid kit. I kneel at her feet and take her hand in mine. "You need to be more careful, Taran. This city is filled with scrap metal. You could be badly injured."

I swab the wound and wrap a gauze bandage around it. She sits silently, never once flinching as I prod the small wound. She's a tough girl. I feel a swell of pride that the Desert Wren has, in many ways, turned out to be just as I thought she would be, a good adversary.

When I'm done, she cradles the injured hand in her lap. "Why do you care?" she demands.

I consider her question. Consider not answering her. But she'll soon find out my intentions. Even if they haven't completely solidified, I have an excellent idea of the direction I want my relationship with this woman to take.

"You will stay with me here, keep me company until I decide otherwise." My voice is gruff and my answer unsatisfactory if the look on her face is anything to go by.

"I don't understand you," she says softly, frowning. "Why do you want me here? I'm a terrible roommate. I leave my stuff laying around, I snore, I eat all the food." She attempts humour to mitigate the tension that constantly swirls around us. Even though I won't reciprocate her humour, I do appreciate her sharp wit.

I stand, towering over her. She recoils on the bed, pulling her legs up protectively. I catch a glimpse of a strong, narrow thigh before she tugs the shirt down.

"You don't have to understand, just obey."

She scoots backwards and glares up at me. "And if I don't obey?"

"It's better that you do. I'd rather you not become injured or taken into custody when I'm not around." I shove a hand through my short hair, rubbing at my scalp and feeling the exhaustion of the day. I'd like to climb onto the bed with her, but suspect she'd lose her mind if I tried. I'm not quite ready to engage in that type of battle yet. "I've no wish to hurt you, Taran."

Her face flushes red and she bites her lip. It's clear to me that she wants to say something but is probably holding back because she feels vulnerable sitting on my bed, with nothing on but my shirt. She doesn't know yet that I've brought her here because I value her opinion. Her goals and her ethics. Though also attracted to her body, I want her voice, her words.

"Speak your mind," I say as gently as I can.

Words burst from her, like having permission is all the impetus she needs. "Why don't you want to hurt me?" she demands. "I'm nothing to you. I'm the exact sort of bug you keep squashing so you can preserve your precious order through the city. I'm a troublemaker, a constant thorn in your side. Worse, I've actively broken many of your laws. I've flaunted your Authority at every turn and taken advantage of every hole in your security. You should want me dead."

She's shaking with the passion of her little speech, caught somewhere between fear and anger. I watch her silently as the fight drains from her and she once more looks small and vulnerable against the heavy hide-stitched quilt of my bed.

"And yet I don't want you dead." I cross my arms over my chest and study her. The urge to take her in my arms and hold her as she rails at the world is strong. "I want to keep you close and protect you."

"But why?" she bursts out. "It makes no sense. You've executed people I consider friends on lesser charges than I've been sentenced for. Why do you want to protect me and not them?"

I sigh heavily. I understand her point of view. She sees me as nothing more than a brutal dictator. And I don't suppose she'll understand me any time soon. Not until she gets to know my character. The reasons behind my convictions.

"There must be sacrifices during war. The rebels that I've had executed are martyrs in a war that's bigger than all of us. They stand for idealism, democracy, values, but they don't stand for an organized, flourishing society. Without sacrifice, there can't be prosperity."

Tears sparkle in her eyes.

I understand her feeling of helplessness. "I'm sorry that you've lost friends, but I can't protect everyone, Taran. I wish that I could."

"Fuck you!" she hisses, her frustration bubbling over. "We aren't at war, there's no reason for these so-called sacrifices."

"You're wrong, girl. Look around you. The world of humans has fallen. We'll never recover what we've lost. The only thing to do is look forward and build on the ashes of our mistakes. Create a stronger race, rather than seek to recover what has died."

"We're not dead though, we're a species in recovery! Now is a time for us to band together, approach the world with kindness and acceptance, not this survival of the fittest atmosphere you've fostered."

"The age of civilization has passed," I tell her gently. "Without strong leadership and the ability to make hard decisions those few pockets of humanity that are left will collapse and die out. The world of our grandparents is long dead and I have no wish to cede what's left over to the Primitives. I will maintain order in this Sanctuary until I'm either dead or the city has been overrun and is no longer capable of sustaining itself."

"But who chose you to be our leader!" she snaps. "You make decisions for thousands of people without stopping to ask what the majority of us want."

"The majority of humans are cattle," I tell her coldly. "They have proven that their decisions will lead to death and destruction. The human race was given the opportunity in the late 20th century to thrive, but they chose self-interest over survival. Even once they were given the news of their inevitable destruction, they still buried their heads and plowed forward into the abyss of death. I've been left in charge of what's left. I won't make the same mistake, won't allow majority decisions to rule. My word is law and it has kept this city alive."

"But that isn't fair!" she cries out, twisting her hand in a pillow. "You judge us based on the mistakes of our ancestors. You don't give us the opportunity to rise again, better and stronger."

"You're wrong, Taran, that's exactly what I'm doing."

"We aren't better if we're a vicious, destructive people, run by a man that only understands war."

"We're alive, and that is the ultimate goal."

"I don't want to be alive in a world that looks like this!" she shouts passionately, now sitting up on her knees.

I envy her idealism. This is what attracts me to her. She's everything I can't be but want desperately to hold on to. She represents beauty, hope, passion. Perhaps I've set her up as a symbol. It doesn't matter. I want her and now, after spending time with her, I can't let her go. She's my perfect conscience.

I decide to back down. She's giving me exactly what I want. An argument for idealism. I find that I'd rather not crush that idealism or upset her while she's in desperate need of care. There's plenty of time for us to fight through our beliefs and for her to explain her way of living. It can wait until she's back on her feet with several complete meals in her belly. "Go to sleep, Taran."

As I turn to leave, she says, "I can't sleep in here. This is your bed."

I turn in the doorway to look at her. "I will allow certain rebellions from you. But when I give you a direct order, you'd better learn to obey." When she opens her mouth to argue I shake my head. "Just sleep. Gather your strength for another day. Another fight. I've no doubt you will treat me to many more of your opinions. For now, I give you my word that I won't touch you. You'll sleep safely."

I don't give her the opportunity to speak again. I leave the room, closing the door behind me. Should I put a lock on it? I'd rather not have a man in here full-time, watching her every move, but I'll have to leave her alone sometimes.

For now, I decide to just leave her to sleep. Until her guard arrives I won't go far. Won't risk losing her. I'm under no illusion that she couldn't disappear just as effectively as she hid from my forces these past several years.

I sit in one of the few comfortable chairs I own and pull my radio out. When civilization fell, we were left to pick up the pieces without the technology we'd come to rely on. Cell phones no longer work, the network being one of the first things to go down. Internet went down shortly after. The wealthier cities were able to repair and maintain radio towers. We also use leftover satellites from the few that still work to maintain communication with other Sanctuaries in other countries across the world.

I turn the radio signal to our private security network and call Jorje with a request. "Get someone to go back through our records, about twelve years ago. Find the girls brought in for Sanctuary, around 14 years old. Possibly given a husband. Possibly named Taran. When you find the information, have it brought to me."

In less than an hour the file is in my hands. I almost can't believe that we finally have something solid on the illusive Desert Wren. I glance toward the bedroom before opening the file. It seems almost too private. This is information she refused to give me willingly. I should wait until she's ready to tell me, or until I can get it from her myself. But I won't. Putting the puzzle of this woman together has become priority.

I open to the first page and am gratified to find that she gave me her correct name. Her last name is Langlois. French. Her place of origin is North, where Canada once stood. Her grandparents and a sister are listed as her only living relatives. Yet she was the only one brought into the city. Her grandparents were likely turned away at the gates. But where is the sister?

Reading her file is leaving me with more questions than

it's answering. I flip to the last page. Her active residence status. I scan the page until I reach her house of residence. Residence: Sanctuary, New Tucson West. Placed under the care of the family Gunther. I flip to the next page, blood pumping through my veins. The answer is right there, burning like an accusation. The 14-year-old Taran Langlois was wedded to the twenty-seven-year old Xavier Gunther.

The name hits me like a punch to the gut. I know exactly who Gunther is and now I have his estranged wife. The Desert Wren is married to the leader of the rebellion. This is why she was reluctant to give me any information. I stand, anger coursing through me. I'm not sure if I'm angry that she's married to a man who will be executed on sight if he's caught or that she's married to a man I've met. A man I both admire and despise. I want to strangle her. I want to fuck her. I want to make sure she never sees Xavier Gunther again.

I stride to the bedroom and throw the door open, banging it against the wall. I expect to confront a sleep-mussed woman. To lay down her new law and demand her capitulation. Instead I'm faced with an empty room. She's gone.

TEN

TARAN

The moment he closes the door I'm on my feet. He's seriously underestimated me if he thinks I'll stay here like a good little pet and obey his commands. Even before coming to the Tucson Sanctuary I wasn't exactly good at following rules. I would wander off when my grandparents begged me to stay close. I've always been inquisitive, with a deep-seated need to explore my environment and make it my own.

And then, as I grew, so did my convictions and my disdain for rules that felt arbitrary and unnecessarily cruel. Losing my grandparents was the final nail in the coffin of my willingness to listen and obey without trust. I'd lost faith in any kind of authority. I was a complete hellion by the time I was placed with Xavier.

I search through the chest of drawers, looking for something more to wear. I can't wear a single shirt and nothing else during my escape. I at least need shoes. I nearly whoop out loud when I find them tucked into a bottom drawer. It looks like he's gotten rid of my other clothes, but he left my shoes. I suppose it makes sense, there's no chance I'll fit in his shoes and new shoes aren't easy to come by.

There's also no way I'm going to fit into any of his pants, I decide as I hold a pair up to my body with a grimace. While his hips are narrow, his entire frame is much larger and more muscular than mine. I'm definitely several sizes smaller. Even with a belt his pants will fall right off and trip me up. I'm going to have to go naked under the shirt. I do manage to find a good quality coat with a leather exterior and some kind of soft woolly interior. I hold it against my face for a moment, enjoying the luxury of such cloth against my skin. I pull it on and roll the sleeves back as much as I can with the stiff leather. It swamps me, but it'll protect my skin.

I rush to the window, taking silent steps on bare feet. It opens under my hands. I was fairly certain he would insist on a window that opens. While I understand his choice of the largest tower in the city for his residence, I also can't imagine the man being cooped up all the time, without escape. He looked completely at home in the desert this morning, waiting for his prey, the open country surrounding him and the dusty air swirling around his large body. If I hadn't known he was Diogo Fuentes, Warlord of New Tucson Sanctuary, I would've taken him for an Outsider; a person capable of living and surviving without Sanctuary. They often reject cities in favour of making their own way in the world. A dangerous prospect. But in some ways, with my thirst for exploration and freedom, I find it an incredibly appealing idea. If I was bigger, stronger, more skilled, I may have considered taking the Outsider path.

If there was ever a screen in the window it's now long gone. I push the window open as far as it'll go and then lean up on my toes to look out and down. We're very high up.

Even higher than the wall. But there are small ledges on the windowsills all the way down. And several floors down from where I'm standing the building has a platform where I can rest.

The drop is sheer and the climb will be dangerous. I'm going to have to be incredibly careful. But I'm good at climbing, good at making my way through, up, over, and down all sorts of buildings. I've been finding shortcuts in and around the city since moving in. I'm an expert on all things structural in Sanctuary.

I take a deep breath and throw a leg through the windowsill, pulling myself out onto the ledge. I begin my descent. The climb is going to be long and I don't want to rush. My anxiety is high. I'm positive Diogo will notice me missing at any moment and come looking. The only way out of that bedroom is through the window or the door. I'm not sure if he was on the other side of the door when I left, but I'm certain he would've taken security measures before leaving me alone. This is my only escape route.

I luck out, about 10 floors down I discover a section of broken windows that I can easily reach. I drag myself toward them and carefully balance on the window ledge before dropping into the remains of what used to be an office. As I sink into a crouch to catch my breath I look around. There's a pile of old rusting chairs and rotting desks in the corner. Otherwise the place has been kept in good order and swept clean. My muscles are screaming and my hair and clothes are damp with sweat. When I stand again my legs are shaking and I have to take a few careful steps before I can go faster. I'm glad I don't have to complete the climb, it would've been torture to an already exhausted body.

I quickly find my way to the stairwell and run down as

fast as I can, hoping I won't run into anyone. Once more I luck out. I push the bottom door open and burst out into the street. There are only a few people around and they glance at me curiously as I leave the residence of the Warlord. The need to leave this area is pressing. I don't look like I belong. A single comment about a woman wearing nothing but a coat, a shirt and running shoes would have me arrested again.

I take off at a run, sticking to back roads and areas I'm fairly certain the elites would avoid. Though sector one is cleaner than the others, not piled high with debris like every other section of the city, there's still the occasional dilapidated building and scrap pile. The debris grows thicker once I leave the main square surrounding the Tower. I use these heaps to cover my escape. I've never been in this sector so I don't know a way through the checkpoints that isn't direct. I have no papers and nothing for bribery.

As I approach a checkpoint I sink back into the shadows against a building. There are two security officers covering a big metal gate with razor wire all across the top. This is going to be the most watched, most secure sector in the city, housing most of the Authority, judges and elite. I'll have to figure out a way of contacting the rebels to see if they can create a distraction for me.

I'm about to turn and make my way back along the wall through the shadows when someone grabs me and yanks me into an alley. I let out a quick shriek before I'm pushed up against the wall, a hand over my mouth. I beat at the arms pinning me and try to throw an elbow into his head, but he's faster. Anticipating each move I make, almost as if he taught me how to fight back if I'm ever grabbed.

Xavier.

I collapse back against the wall and squint into the shadows. His familiar blond hair glints in the sun and his teeth flash a quick grin, turning his already handsome face downright beautiful. As soon as he feels the fight drain away from me he lifts his hand and drags me into a hug.

"Taran," he says into my neck.

"Xavier," I mumble against his shoulder. He's holding me too tight, my ribs feel like they'll crack. But I don't mind. After the day I've had, I need the security of this kind of squeeze.

He holds me away from him and grabs my face, tipping it up to his as he scans me from head to toe. He frowns at my bare legs but doesn't comment. Instead he grabs my hand and starts down the alley at a jog. "We have to get out of here. They'll be all over the checkpoints once you're discovered missing."

I try my best to not fall behind. While not as tall as Diogo, Xavier is still taller than me. His legs outpace mine by a long shot and I have to run to keep up with him. Fatigue is hitting me hard though and my head spins with dizziness as short puffs of breath burst from my mouth. I feel like I'll sleep for a week as soon as my head hits a pillow.

"How did you know where to find me?" I ask, gasping for air and clutching my side with my free hand.

"The guy I have at headquarters said they had the Wren in custody. Said you were taken out with Fuentes and that the Judge was sent to his place."

I gape at his back. The Judge left Diogo's place just over an hour ago. I'd known Xavier had people inside the Authority, but he must've moved incredibly quick to get into Sector One and watch for me to make a move toward escape. But that's Xavier. Always planning, always ready for every scenario. "Thank you for coming for me."

He glances over his shoulder and laughs, his brown eyes sparkling with mischief. This is something I'd always loved about Xavier. His ability to find humour in the most grim situations. "I wasn't about to leave my best people smuggler in the hands of the Authority without checking in. You could've been sentenced to death."

"I *was* sentenced to death. Fuentes had the sentence commuted. But how did you know to get over here so quickly? Who's your inside guy?" Xavier's always held his information close, never sharing, not even with me, his closest associate and wife. He believes that information has power; the power to do good and the power to harm. He would tell me that he didn't want me getting hurt. I wondered though, was he protecting me or himself. Information can be extracted under torture.

He slows to a walk, his hand still holding mine in a tight grip. He caresses the back of mine with his thumb. "I can't tell you, especially now."

"Why especially now? What's happening now?" I look around and realize that we've made our way back around to Diogo's building. "What are we doing here?" I ask, tugging at my hand. I should be running as fast as I can in the opposite direction. Once Diogo discovers I'm missing he'll send people out right away to look for me.

Xavier stops walking and turns to me, pushing me back into the shadows. His face looks anguished, but his eyes have a manic spark to them. A spark I've seen many times while he was in the pursuit of a goal, letting nothing and no one get in his way. My stomach sinks. I'm not going to like his reason for bringing me here.

"I want you to go back."

"What?" I gasp, staring at him in dismay. Didn't he

come here to rescue me? To take me back home, to my sector. To the slums.

"I need you to go back to Fuentes. For some reason he's become obsessed by you, obsessed by the legend. We need to take advantage of this and set you up in his care as a plant."

"You. We!" I hiss at him, poking him in the chest. "What about me? I don't particularly want to die, Xavier. And I was steps away from a death sentence in there."

I'm hurt that he's willing to send me back into such a dangerous situation. I may be his separated wife, but I thought we cared more about each other than this. My mind flashes to Diogo. Even the few hours I spent with him showed me an entirely different character. A man that was protective, almost overly so. I clench my hand around the cut on my palm. He'd taken care of me, shown some small amount of tenderness. Xavier has always been too committed to the cause to put my needs above the rebellion. Above his own. And while I'm also committed to the cause, Xavier will decide what's best for the rebellion and manipulates circumstances to his advantage.

He frowns down at me. "We need this, Taran. No one on our side has ever been so close to the Authority. To Fuentes. You can be the start of the downfall of his leadership. Having you on the inside will give me the information I need."

"I know," I say on a sharp sigh. I step away from Xavier, trying to think. Having a rebel living in the same home as the Warlord is like a dream come true for our cause. Still, "I really don't want to go back, Xavier. He wants to keep me with him, in his home, like some kind of pet. Being that close to Fuentes, that close to execution. It makes me uncomfortable."

He waves his hand between us. "Your sentence was commuted, you'll be fine."

I stare at him with narrowed eyes. "How can you know that? What if he beats me, or rapes me? What if he decides to kill me and I've cut off my only avenue of escape?"

He looks guilty for a second before smoothing his features. "He won't, Taran." His voice is cajoling but my trust in him is waning. "I told you, I have someone on the inside."

"How high up?" I demand, frowning.

"High enough."

I'm starting to wonder if my capture was maneuvered by more than Diogo. If somehow Xavier had something to do with the setup, to get me closer to the Authority than he's ever had anyone. A piece of me, the piece that held out hope that one day I might be able to find some kind of life with my husband, dies.

But he's right. We do need someone in a position to keep an eye on Fuentes. To insinuate themselves among the higher ranks. Feed information to the rebels. Try to change the minds of those in charge. "He'll watch me carefully for awhile. He won't trust me. He'll either think I'm preparing to run, or he'll realize I'm in a good position to spy on the Authority. He's not stupid and he's not blinded by arrogance."

Xavier frowns at me. "You got to know him pretty well in just a few hours. Exactly how close did he get to you?"

I glare at him. How dare he suddenly act jealous? All he's ever done is use me to further his goals for the rebellion. Even our marriage had been orchestrated. He'd seen me, seen what I was capable of. Seen the fire and my hatred of authoritarian rules. He applied for the marriage and took me to the rebellion the moment the papers were signed.

He'd never intended us to have a real relationship, though we did try a few years ago. His ambition and my independent streak made it impossible.

I wasn't heartbroken or disappointed. Xavier had been too busy, too involved in his role as leader of the rebels to pay much attention to a young woman's emotions. Still, as the years passed, our feelings toward each other evolved. We grew apart, reaching for our separate goals. I'd sunk deeper into the rebellion, creating a place for myself. Setting up my own role, leading illegals to safety.

Now I wonder if part of him isn't jealous that I'd surpassed him as far as giving the rebels someone to flock around. In some ways, the idea of the Desert Wren has reached almost mythical proportions.

"I'll go back," I tell him, staring past his shoulder, toward the dying light at the entrance of the alleyway. I shift my gaze up to him. "But not for you. For the cause."

"Taran..." His voice is pleading, his face softening as he looks down at me. What does he see? A small, vulnerable woman about to go into the Warlord's lair by herself? Or his wife, the woman who should stand at his side but never could?

"How do I get back in? I scaled a good chunk of the building down, and I'm telling you right now, I won't be going back up the same way."

He chuckles and shakes his head. "No, we'll get his attention another way."

He pulls a radio off his belt and changes the signal. He lifts it to his lips. "I need backup in Sector One, near checkpoint six. We have a suspected rebel trying to leave the sector without papers. I believe she's the Desert Wren. Handle with extreme caution when approaching, she may be armed."

I gape up at him. The second he's off the radio I send my fist into his stomach. He coughs and takes a step back, holding his hands up. "Sorry, sweetheart, but we have to make this escape attempt look real. You can't just get caught loitering outside the Tower."

"Fuck you," I snap. "The idiot police will be coming after me with guns drawn. I'll be lucky if they don't shoot me first and detain me second."

He flashes a grin and lifts the radio to his lips. "The Desert Wren must be apprehended alive. Repeat, she must be taken alive."

I growl and take a threatening step toward him. He backs up another step and says, "You better start running little bird."

"I'll get you back for this!" I turn on my heel and start running in the opposite direction, away from Diogo's building. The sector is big enough to get lost in, but now, with security crawling all over it looking for me I won't be able to hide for long.

I sprint full tilt at an angle away from the checkpoint, zigzagging through the streets. It has to look like I was trying to leave checkpoint six, where I was supposedly spotted. Although anyone with half a brain will figure out I was never there once they ask a few questions. "This is such a stupid plan," I grumble.

I wish I knew the layout of Sector One better, but I've never had reason to be here before. I pass building after building, most are cleaned up and occupied. In the other sectors, every second building and house would be in complete disrepair, most uninhabitable. There would be plenty of places for me to run inside and get lost. But this sector has been better taken care of than all the others. Even the streets are cleaner, not full of trash and scraps. Fewer razed buildings.

I'm about to turn and try another direction when I hear the unmistakeable sound of footfalls behind me, hitting the pavement with echoing slaps. I don't hear shouting or police coordinating my capture as they close in on me. Maybe I'm only being chased by one person, maybe I can still get away. I'm fast and skilled, I might be able to outpace or outwit the person chasing me.

I cut through another alley and burst in behind an abandoned building, gutted to only its skeleton. Finally, something I can work with! I hurtle over a twisted metal frame, dart through an open doorway, and down a long hallway. The drywall has long since rotted from exposure, leaving only patches of walls and metal behind.

I can't tell if anyone is still behind me or if I managed to lose them. I need to find some place to hide so I can catch my breath and reassess my options. I run into a stairwell and start climbing. This is a dangerous exercise as unmaintained buildings crumble and collapse all the time. Most children have been told to stay out of abandoned buildings. I've learned to use them to my advantage.

I climb until I reach a blocked section of stairwell. I'm forced to backtrack down to the third floor, instead of continuing up. I don't pause, I throw my weight against the door, shoving it open. It hits something solid on the other side, but there's just enough room for me to squeeze through. Anyone bigger won't make it through that door. Anyone smaller won't have a chance if I catch them in a fair fight.

I forget for a moment, as I hurdle full tilt down another hallway filled with shadows, only the sunset pouring in through broken windows and missing section of wall, that I'm supposed to allow myself to get caught. The need to escape, to run free, is strong within me. My fight or flight instinct has kicked in hard. So when I slam into a big, unmoveable chest, which sends me flying backwards, I come back up swinging my fist wildly.

A hand clamps over my wrist. I twist to the side and hammer my other fist down on the inside of their arm, weakening the hold. I hear a growled "fuck" right before I'm released. I duck past him and take about two steps when I'm grabbed once more and thrown into a wall.

"Oomph!" The air whooshes out of me as my back hits hard. He brings an arm up under my chin and pins me. I try to kick out at him, but he shoves my leg to the side, tearing a cry of pain from me as his knee connects with my thigh. He tightens his arm against my throat until I'm struggling for air.

"Enough!" He shouts at me.

Diogo.

I can barely see him in the darkness of the hallway. His face is deeply shadowed. But his hold is painful and his voice is angry.

"Please!" I gasp. Dizziness is swamping me, threatening to carry me into unconsciousness.

His arm tightens and I fear he intends to snap my neck. Xavier was wrong, I'm not safe in the care of Diogo Fuentes.

"Caught you, little bird." His deep voice is the last that I hear as I'm taken on a wave of unconsciousness, succumbing to exhaustion and a restricted airway. "You're mine."

The intensity of my rage crashes through my veins. She left me. Without a backward glance, as though our brief time together had no impact. As angry as I was, I feared for her life once I realized she'd gone through the window. Now that I have her back, in my hands, I want to hold her, I want to squeeze her until she can't think of leaving again. Of putting her life in danger. I want to hurt her, crush her under my bare hands.

But I don't want to see her broken.

This thought pulls me back from the brink of killing her. Death and destruction have been my common friends for so long that I can barely see my way back to civility. As much as I portray the coolly intelligent commander, I am as much a part of this dead world as it is me. Only the strongest survive, and I'm among them. I feel the need to crush and destroy weakness. The woman beneath my grip is a contradiction. An anomaly. She's weak. A wraith in an uncivilized world. Yet she uses her ability to look small and unassuming as a strength, to blend in. She's strong in ways that I don't yet fully comprehend.

I catch her as she slumps against the wall and lift her up against me. I bury my face in her neck, against her hairline and inhale. She smells of sweat, dirt and freedom. She's like a wild animal, slipping through the bars, refusing to be caged, her need to be free outweighing her common sense.

I won't underestimate her again. She will no longer go unsupervised. She can't be trusted.

I gather her up in my arms and stride down the hall, careful to avoid weak points in the floor. Her strategy was a good one. Lose her tail in an abandoned building. She likely would've run to the top and either tried to leap onto another building or climb her way down. She must be incredibly talented when it comes to climbing. I should have her train my men in her techniques once she settles down.

"But you underestimated me too, little Wren," I murmur as I carry her, striding down the opposite staircase, the one I took up to the third floor to intercept her. I know this building inside out. I know every inch of Sector One. I knew that she would become trapped in the other stairwell and forced through the door onto the third floor. So, though it went against instinct, I'd allowed her to race out of my sight and up the stairs, knowing exactly where she would come out.

I carry her out into the street. The light from the sun is fading fast, causing a dusky hew across the buildings. Dust swirls in the slight breeze. An officer approaches me, one of the men from checkpoint security.

"Want me to take the prisoner to processing, Commander?" he asks, reaching for her.

I check the urge to kill the man where he stands, reminding myself that he's only doing his job. I don't like that he's looking at her, proposing to take her away. I tighten my hold. "She will remain in my custody. Have

Commander Cruz come to my private quarters with a guard."

I don't wait for his response. I set her in the back of the vehicle and tell the officer to take us to One Church. He nods his head and finally averts his eyes as I climb in beside her, pulling her against my chest.

As we drive, I consider my behaviour. I'm not acting like myself. I'm being driven by an obsessive need to keep and protect this woman. Her welfare has become more important than any other goal I've had. I know that my thoughts are insane, that my Lieutenants will question me if given the opportunity. But somehow, for some reason, I feel that Taran, Desert Wren, is the key to Sanctuary. I don't understand it. I don't give a fuck if no one else will agree. I just know that something has shifted and I'm helpless in the grip of this feeling.

She must be protected at all costs. And she must never leave my side.

TWELVE
TARAN

I'm awake in an instant, all of my senses going on alert as consciousness returns. Several things hit me at once. The first and most important is Diogo's presence. I can *feel* him in the room with me. I'm no longer wearing my shoes or the coat but I'm still wearing his shirt. I realize by the low-voiced murmurs that someone else is in the room with us.

I'm about to fly off the bed when Diogo's face swims into my vision and his hard hands grip my shoulders, shoving me back down onto a bed. My frantic gaze leaps around the room and I realize I'm back in his bedroom.

"Let me go!" I snarl up at him.

He ignores me, shoving his chest into me, pushing me deep into the bed. He's far too big for me to argue with. He twists and says to the other person, "Get it done and get the fuck out."

"Turn her onto her front and hold her still," the other man grunts.

"What are you doing?" I shriek angrily as Diogo flips me over as easily as he would a child. Then he puts his weight on my back and legs, pinning me to the bed. With

Diogo on top of me I'm unable to fight. I'm forced to suffer this indignity, whatever it is.

I can't figure out what's happening until I feel the first pinprick against my skin. Then I realize. I'm being tattooed with a new identification. He's using a needle and ink, digging the bluish black colour deep into my flesh.

"No!" I yell as he pokes me over and over, dragging the needle through and across my exposed skin. I try to twist away but Diogo shifts his hands until he's pressing my shoulders flat into the bed. I lay, my entire body tense, ready to fly the second they let go of me. I lose track of time as I'm forced to submit. I'm quivering from the sting and unrelenting tension by the time the needle is removed from my skin. Whatever he put on my back took longer than my first identification mark.

"Done," says the other guy. He stands, and I get a good look at him. Black hair and eyebrows, thick and dark, pulled down over disapproving eyes. His face is pitted with scars. He's looking at some kind of device when he says to Diogo. "She is now part of the Fuentes house."

The Fuentes house. Diogo has given me the mark of his own house, the most powerful in the city. Once I have an escape plan I'll need to run as far and fast as I can. I'll have to leave the city until my mark can be removed. I'll be too easily identified and returned to Diogo. He's given me the protection of his house but has also ensured that I can be more easily hunted.

"Fine," Diogo grunts. "Get out. Leave someone to watch the place. And Jorje?" When the man looks up, Diogo says, "Make him your best."

The man nods sharply, his eyes never straying in my direction and leaves without another word. A trained soldier.

Diogo pulls his hands from my shoulders and moves back, giving me space. I push myself away from him, curling my legs protectively underneath me. I reach over my shoulder, wincing when my fingers touch the heated spot where my new tattoo stands out against my skin. I twist around to look at it, ignoring Diogo's penetrating gaze. I can make out the top of a cage with a bird inside. Underneath is the name Fuentes. He isn't numbered like the rest of the houses, he gets to have a name. My heart pounds at the thought of being trapped by such a small thing. Then I remind myself that I can fly any time, I just need to be smart. Move out of reach and lose myself.

As though reading my mind, Diogo pinches my chin in his fingers and forces my gaze to his. "You will not leave again. I've caged you, little Wren, and I'm not letting you go." His voice is a command, but something about the words sounds so final. As though he's declaring an edict that will be followed through on at all costs.

I shiver and curl into the heavy blanket covering his bed, tugging it up my bare legs. His dark eyes follow the movement, but he doesn't comment. Instead he says, "Were you harmed while out of my custody?"

I frown at him. "You're a strange man, Diogo Fuentes. Why do you care what happens to me? I'm nothing to you."

He growls and snaps, "Answer the question, Taran. Were you hurt?"

"No," I snap back with a frown.

He nods and pushes himself off the bed. "Good. Now get some rest."

Though I want nothing more than to be alone, work through a strategy of spying on the enemy and then escaping, I feel the need to ask. "Why did you bring me back here? In fact, why did you bring me here at all? It makes no sense, Diogo. You've marked me with your house, given me your protection. Why? I'm your enemy."

"You are not my enemy," he says, frowning fiercely down at me.

I snort and roll my eyes. "Yet, we're definitely not on the same side. I offer Sanctuary to any and all that want it, flaunting your precious laws. While you..." I wave my hand at him. "Force us to live in a city that's more a prison than a society. You murder innocents and turn away most refugees."

"Our definition of innocent is different, but our ultimate goals are the same."

I gape at him in disbelief. "How do you figure?"

His face softens a little as he looks me over. I tug harder on the blanket, pulling it further up my body, as if covering all the bare skin will stop the way he looks at me, as though he wants to devour me whole. He makes me feel vulnerable.

"We both want the survival of the human race."

I chew on my lips. He's right. That's exactly what I want. I guess I never saw it as basic survival. Never really looked at the Warlord's motives for the way he runs our city. He was always a distant, shadowy leader. The enemy. The man who stands between humanity and civilization. Values. But he's right. Though we fight for opposing sides, our goal is the same. Survival.

"Your method of saving the human race is wrong," I say bluntly. "You make immoral decisions that have sweeping and lasting consequences. You choose a method of survival for all of us that some of us would never choose for ourselves. Would rather die than live with."

He's staring at me thoughtfully as I speak. Then he says, "You will not be allowed to die, Taran. Despite our opposing views."

I watch him, taking in his harsh features. His physical presence exactly matches his personality. He's uncompromising, brutal, strong and hard. The opposite of me in so many ways, even if our end goal is the same.

"What do you want with me?" The question comes out more of a plea. I don't understand why I'm here. Why he's so fascinated. I should disgust him.

"You will become my consort," he tells me calmly. "You will remain at my side while I'm leader of this Sanctuary city."

My body recoils as if it has a life of its own. My brain follows shortly after, screaming silently in horror. Why would the Warlord of the New Tucson Sanctuary possibly want me as his consort? "That's ridiculous," I snap angrily. "I can't be your... your consort, you don't even know me! We're the opposite in all of our thoughts."

He moves toward the bed, coming toward me, a persistent light in his eyes.

"I've known of you for years, Taran. Watched your reputation among the rebels grow. I took great interest in this woman, reported to be young and highly intelligent. I watched from the sidelines as you continued your work, bringing illegals in, negotiating for supplies and using the riots to your advantage. You've baffled my security forces over and over until I was forced to step in and run point on your capture."

"But I've been breaking the law for years! Why would you want me as your companion when I'm the opposite of everything you believe in?"

"Not all of our fundamental beliefs are opposing, Taran. Where we differ is in our ideas on the execution of those beliefs. But you are in perfect alignment with my ideals. We both fervently believe in the welfare of this city and wish to protect the citizens within. I value your enthusiasm and your driving desire to create a better world. The combination of your skills, intelligence and idealism will make you the perfect wife."

He kneels on the bed and takes my hands in his, pulling them away from the blanket.

"We'll murder each other," I say desperately and try to tug my hands from his. "It's impossible! I can't marry you." He clamps long fingers around my wrists and drags me forward until I'm falling into his lap. I shove an elbow into his chest, but he only grunts and holds me tighter.

"Stop fighting me, Taran." He pushes me backwards onto the bed and hovers over me. I'm painfully aware that the shirt I'm wearing has ridden up my thighs exposing my legs. I try to wiggle out from underneath him, but he locks my wrists together in one hand and forces them over my head. He pins my neck to the bed with his free hand.

"Why are you doing this?" I gasp. "You're insane if you think we can somehow live together. I don't agree with any of your philosophies. You run this city like a military base. You arbitrarily pass judgement and executions."

"Never arbitrary, Taran. Everything is done with a reason."

I want to believe in what he says, but his reasons for executions are indefensible. The punishment of death is too harsh for most crimes. "I hate the classes and ranks you've fostered in the city," I hiss up at him. "You play God in your tower, choosing who will live and who will die. Who will enter your precious city and who will be turned away to die in the mountains."

"I choose what's best for this city," he says, his voice perfectly even, as though he's unaffected by the emotion of the moment. If I could slap him, I would.

"You choose wrong, Diogo!" I shout at him.

Instead of responding with anger he cups my cheek and runs a thumb over the curve. "I know about your grandparents, Taran. I'm sorry."

Tears of anger fill my eyes. How dare he talk about my grandparents, like he has any right! "Fuck you!" I snarl, arching into him, trying to buck him off. It's like trying to move a boulder. "You killed them with your laws and your rules. They were turned away, defenceless to the elements and the Primitives. You're cruel and unfeeling."

His fingers tighten painfully around my wrists as he finally gives way to some of the emotion swirling between us. "I don't explain myself, girl," he says coldly. "But I will tell you this once so we don't have to discuss my stance on refugees again. It gutted me to create the laws that govern this city. I knew at the time that I was stripping away the civilization that humans built into our society hundreds of years ago. But we no longer live in a civilized world. Slowly this world is taking itself back. Humans are no longer at the top of the food chain. Only the strongest will survive while the weak die out. If we attempt to protect the weak, we'll die as well. Turning them away to a quick death is far more merciful than bringing down an entire city because resources disappear."

Tears are leaking down my cheeks and into my hair. I hear him, but I can't agree. "But what are we without civilization? What are we if we aren't fostering the things that make us human."

"We're animals," he says simply. "Fighting for our place in a dead world."

"I can't agree with that, we're better than that, more than that. Why bother surviving at all if we're nothing but disposable animals?"

"Exactly, Taran." His dark eyes hold mine as surely as he grips my hands. "You will stay with me, you'll be my companion. You'll bring my civilization back and teach me to be more again."

I gape up at him for a moment, processing what he's said. He wants me to help him find his humanity? Does that mean that there's hope for him, for our city? "I despise your laws, Diogo. Even if you force me into marriage, I'll work against you every opportunity I get."

"You won't have any choice except to obey." He says this as though there's no other option. The man doesn't know me at all if he thinks obeying is even a remote possibility. Even if we were marrying for love.

"I won't marry you." I tell him.

He chuckles, and I know why. If consent were needed, then there would be a lot fewer marriages in Sanctuary.

"You will." His voice drops and he looks down at my face, his gaze moving to my mouth. Is he... going to kiss me? I suddenly feel dizzy and short of breath at the very thought.

"But I'm already married," I say as a last resort.

He growls and tightens his grip on my wrists until I cry out in pain. I open my mouth to protest but he drops his head and takes my lips with his before I get the chance. His kiss is fierce and hard, quickly over. My lips are stinging with the force of his kiss. I'm stunned. Just that morning I was a rebel on a mission, climbing the wall toward the outside world, freedom at my fingertips. Now I'm the captive of the highest Authority in the land. The soon-to-be bride of Sanctuary's Warlord.

THIRTEEN
TARAN

As it turns out, marriages are not at all difficult to end. At least not if you're a Sanctuary Warlord. I stand at my wedding ceremony, wearing only a shirt, and smothering a yawn that's so wide I feel it right down to my toes. If Diogo didn't have such a tight hold on my arm I would probably collapse in a puddle at his feet and sleep through the ceremony.

After he kissed me, he left the bedroom, allowing me a few hours of sleep. Before leaving, he said, "The window has been bolted shut and the door locks from the outside now. You can rest easy knowing there won't be any escaping from this room."

"Thanks," I called after him sarcastically.

I'm not sure how long I slept for, but the sky was full dark when he pulled me from the bed, allowed me a few minutes in the washroom to freshen up and then escorted me back out into his gutted, concrete living room.

"You," I say distastefully when I realize the Judge is waiting for us. It's hard to feel at all friendly toward the man who, only a few hours ago, declared me a traitor and sentenced me to death. It doesn't seem unreasonable to hold a grudge.

He ignores me and says to Diogo, "Her marriage with Xavier Gunther, of the house Gunther, has been dissolved. I have prepared the paperwork for your marriage to Taran, Desert Wren, henceforth known as Taran Fuentes of the house Fuentes."

"Good." Satisfaction saturates that one word.

Spreading the papers out on the table, the Judge points to where Diogo needs to sign. I ignore them both, crossing my arms under my chest and glaring at the wall. There's no point in any kind of protest, women don't have choice in marriage. We're treated like walking uteruses. Or is it uteri? Either way, we're basically made to feel as though our single function is to act as baby-making machines.

The Judge straightens, gathering the paperwork. He turns disdainfully toward me and says, "Congratulations, Mrs. Fuentes."

"I don't recognize this marriage," I say coldly, pinning him with a hard stare. "The union of marriage is supposed to be consensual. This is as much a mockery as my trial was."

The Judge gasps, his eyes darting to Diogo. Then he steps toward me, but not close enough to touch. He lifts a finger toward my face and says, "You should be more grateful, girl. Commander Fuentes has saved your life. And now, he has given you his name and his family."

"Are you jealous, Judge?" I sneer, fisting my hands at my side to stop myself from launching at the obnoxious man. "Maybe you should've put your own name on those papers, married him yourself."

He draws back in shock, bringing his hand up to his chest while still clutching the papers. "Why you... you...!"

Apparently, suggesting the Judge may have a crush on the Warlord is close to blasphemy in his opinion. The small man draws himself up angrily and takes a step toward me, his fist raised. Who knows if he intended to actually hit me, or just wave it around because Diogo steps in, sliding his hand across my lower back and tucking me against his side. I shiver at the feel of his broad hand covering half my back. He could so easily crush me.

"You will watch how you speak to my wife, Judge." His voice is calm and cool, but the underlying steel is there.

"But...!" the Judge splutters.

"You will not be given another opportunity to speak respectfully. I'll have your tongue removed if you continue."

The Judge freezes and then nods his head. He turns on his heel and leaves quickly. I stare curiously after him wondering if Diogo meant what he said. Would he really cut off a man's tongue just for insulting me? I glance up at Diogo and decide he would.

"You aren't very good with people, are you?" I comment, stepping away from him. I feel bereft as his hand falls away but try to ignore the feeling. I've been alone for a long time, only able to snatch brief moments of human contact here or there. Unable to forge meaningful romantic relationships.

He grunts and walks toward the kitchen, picking up a lantern as he walks by it. I trail after him, looking around with more curiosity than I had before. He has gas lamps and candles out, lighting the area, giving the concrete building an almost skeletal look. The bare area is wide, many of the walls having been knocked out. I wonder if he did it himself. Without fresh coats of paint available, the walls would've fallen into disrepair like everything else in the world around us. Without human intervention, infrastructure is left to rot and fall.

But his place is clean and tidy, especially the sections he lives in, the kitchen, main area, bedroom and washroom.

"You have a generator?" I ask him. "Why don't you use it to generate electricity up here."

"I have a small thermoelectric generator. I try not to use it for more than the basics."

"Like hot water," I point out sarcastically.

He flashes me a grin as he reaches into a cupboard and pulls down some bread and fruit. "Woman, I get paid in hot water. If I were to lose my hot showers I would go on strike, resign and leave this city for the nearest hot spring."

I snort and roll my eyes at him. "If the rebels knew it was that easy to get rid of you, we'd have taken out your generator years ago." I tilt my head thoughtfully. "In fact, once I get this information back to them, you're done, Diogo. We'll run you out of town."

He drops what he's holding and pounces, gripping my shoulders and pinning me in place. I gasp and bring my hands up to his chest. I try to shove him away but it's as useless as every other time I've tried to escape his hold. He gives me a shake, rattling my teeth.

"Have you been in contact with the rebels?" he demands, his voice flipping completely from easy-going to fierce interrogator.

Oh shit! I need to learn how to hold my tongue. I stare up at him mutely, refusing to give him any information.

"You are my wife, Taran. You owe your loyalty to me. Tell me now, when you escaped did you manage to make contact with the rebellion?"

"Loyalty?" I burst out hammering down on his chest with a fist. "You don't demand loyalty, Diogo, you earn it.

You earn respect and trust and you're so far away from that we may as well be living on different planets. You won't get anything from me."

His grip becomes bruising and he backs me up until I hit the wall. I shiver and turn my head from his intense gaze, terrified of this side of Diogo. He's such a contradiction. Sometimes kind and gentle, then he becomes the ruthless Warlord I expect him to be.

"I can take what I want from you, Taran. You belong to me."

"You arrested me and forced me to stay!" I protest. "I don't belong to anyone but myself."

"Then consider yourself spoils of war, because you're my prize and I'm keeping you."

He lifts me right off my feet, pressing his body full-length against mine, holding me up. I can feel every inch of his hard body through the thin cloth of my shirt. He's all hard muscle through the fabric of his stiff uniform. I cling to his arms, not wanting to fall as his lips find mine. I open my mouth on a gasp and he takes advantage, thrusting his tongue against mine.

Just as I think to bite down and end this brutally passionate display, he takes my chin in a hard grip, forcing my jaw wide. As he plunders my mouth his other arm reaches around my back and presses me tight against his body. I lift my hands to his shoulders and push but I can't get any leverage, we're too close together. Not that it would make any difference, I haven't been able to make a dent in this man yet. Only my words seem to elicit any kind of reaction.

As soon as his hand relaxes on my jaw, I tear my mouth away and shout, "Diogo, stop!"

He ignores me, dropping his mouth to my neck and

exploring the exposed skin there. When his lips encounter the shirt he reaches between us, grips the neckline and tears it open a few inches, exposing my chest. Then he presses his lips against the skin of my collarbone, sucking it hard, biting, marking. I gasp and unconsciously bring a hand up to hold his head. Feelings rush through me, the high of his lips on my skin, being held tight against his body, his scent invading my senses.

Before I know what's happening he's pulling away from the wall and carrying me through the apartment. When I try to push away from him, he holds me closer against his chest, his hand cupping the back of my head. His other arm is still tight around my waist and my legs are dangling.

"Diogo, what are you doing?" I ask, panting to catch my breath.

I'm not stupid, I know exactly what he's doing. He's going to consummate our ten-minute old marriage. The thought should terrify me, does terrify me, but it's also exhilarating. Setting aside our opposing politics and the fact that he basically kidnapped me and forced me into marriage, I find him very attractive, almost overwhelmingly so. The combination of persistent dominance and protective man is appealing, even if he is a terrible human being.

His touch is far from disgusting. It stirs up my dormant libido, forcing me to wake up and take notice. My fingers itch to explore him and my mouth waters to taste him. I want to fuck this man, but I don't want this to be our defining moment. It's too soon, and we don't know each other.

He drops me onto the bed. It's dark in the bedroom and I can barely see him in the shadows of the room. "Diogo, no!" I yell as he drops on top of me.

He takes my hands and forces them over my head. Once

more I'm assailed with contradictory feelings. The need to fight is strong. Stronger than ever. As though I know I'm losing pieces of myself to this man who I barely know, and sex will be another connection that binds us together. Yet I'm also falling rapidly under the spell of his passion. I can feel his cock, thick and hard, pressing against the apex of my thighs. He's lost in his own passion, which is a heady prospect. The idea that this man, the most powerful in the city, wants someone as insignificant as me. Wants me with a passion he can't seem to leash.

"Diogo... please," I beg, trying to tug my hands down from his grip. He ignores me again, biting into the flesh just above my breasts. He uses his other hand to tear the shirt the rest of the way open. I moan as his hand closes over my breast, covering the entire mound in his palm.

"Please," I gasp, as I slip under his spell. "I'm scared!"

My words finally stop him, stop the man with a tiny piece of civilization left in his soul. He freezes against me, breathing heavily, his hands hard against my flesh. Finally, he looks up. I can see his eyes glittering in the dim light entering the room.

"Why?" he demands, his voice harsh with passion. "You want me. Your body responds to mine."

"It's too fast, Diogo," I manage to yank my hands from his grip and bring them to his shoulders, pressing against him. "I don't do... this."

"You're a virgin?" he asks, curiosity and awe warring in his voice.

"Of course not!" I snap. "Your people married me off at the age of fourteen, how would I be a virgin?"

His fist slams into the bed beside me and I try to roll away only to encounter his other arm, fist planted firmly in the mattress. The idea of me not having my virginity bothers him. I don't know why. I was a married woman for over ten years. I only fucked Xavier a few times before we decided there was nothing deeper to our relationship. Loneliness drove me into the arms of other men a few times, but nothing significant. No other long-term relationships.

"Are you a virgin?" I ask sarcastically, knowing he's not. When he gives me a scathing look, I roll my eyes. "Then why would you expect a twenty-six-year old woman to come to your bed untouched. We live in the time of the Great Fall, not the dark ages."

"Stop talking," he growls. Then sits up, straddling my hips, still pinning me to the bed. I want to wiggle out from underneath him, but I don't think he'll let me get far. He shoves a hand through his hair and glares down at me. In the shadows he looks massive, hulking over top of me. "I don't expect a woman of your age to be a virgin, Taran. But you need to never speak of the men who touched you to me. Especially your ex-husband."

He's jealous. The prospect is both daunting and exhilarating. If he's jealous that I've had other sexual partners, then that means this relationship he's looking to have with me is more than a political move. More than him just coveting the Desert Wren and wanting her idealism.

"We will have a real marriage, Taran," he says, staring at me with a penetrating gaze. Even in the darkness, his obsidian eyes glitter with intent. "Among other things we will go to bed together. Often."

I lick my lips and cradle my bruised arms against my chest, covering my bare breasts. He notes the move but doesn't say anything. "I know," I whisper, allowing some of my vulnerability to show. "But I need time, Diogo."

"Why?" he demands. "We're married. This is as good a

time as any to get to know your husband. Get to know what I want from you."

I'm getting a vivid picture of exactly what this man wants from me. "Please, Diogo. I didn't ask for any of this. I just want some time to adjust to the idea. You... you're a lot to take in. You're the ruler of this Sanctuary, practically a legend. You intimidate me. I want to get to know you as a man before we do... this."

As the words leave my mouth I realize they're true. I want to get to know the man behind the Warlord. I'm attracted to him, but I'm also terrified of him.

Finally, after long moments of just staring down at me, he rolls away and gets to his feet at the side of the bed. He walks quickly to the door, turning back to say, "This is only a brief reprieve, Taran."

As he leaves, I learn something about my new husband. He has honour.

I lock her in the room and walk away, climbing the flight of stairs to my rooftop retreat. I must leave her, or I'll turn back around, go in there and fuck my little wife into submission. She's more tempting than I ever realized. Touching her electrifies every part of me. It's as though I'm discovering a dormant side to myself, but it responds only to her. I want to hold her, dominate her, protect her. I want to keep her with me at all costs.

And her response to me. Fuck, I never imagined what a heady aphrodisiac a woman's response could be. Sex was always... just sex. It felt good, but for the most part it was unnecessary to my goals. But with Taran, I feel different. She's her own brand of beautiful, inside and out. And when she's next to me, taking my kisses and returning them eagerly, I lose my head.

Cool air caresses my skin and I feel instant peace, the dark city mapped out below my feet. This is my place of solitude where I can feel the beckoning hands of freedom. The quiet open air with the world stretched out peacefully below. I come here when I feel consumed by my role as leader. Now it's Taran driving me to this place.

As a child I was raised knowing I would rule a Sanctuary, like my father before me. I learned from him, gathered information, found my own city and toppled the leadership. New Tucson Sanctuary was an easy target, run by fools and beggars that believed in compromise, negotiation and democracy. Their leadership was going to collapse anyway, from a combination of lack of resources, civil unrest and Primitive attacks. My men and I decimated their security forces in hours. Faster than a Primitive horde could've wiped them out.

The city was left vulnerable. We picked up the pieces, established new laws, and I've ruled this Sanctuary ever since. I rule with an iron fist and a heart of ice. Human plight doesn't move me. Human existence does. And though I've taken a wife, a woman who will act as my conscience, I will not change my convictions. Humans can't flourish without direct intervention and guidance. The strongest must be hand-picked and encouraged to procreate.

A vision of my new wife, small and sprawled out in our bed, flashes through my mind. She might be small, but she is tough and mighty of mind. She will take me as I am and help me forge this new world. She will add her strengths to mine and we will rise up, stronger and wiser together.

But first, I must bring her to my way of thinking. I must destroy her past and usher her into a future with me. Starting with her ex-husband, Xavier Gunther. I will hunt him, and destroy him. The thought of ridding my city of a man that has caused countless problems and captured Taran's attention fills me with satisfaction. Gunther will be the symbolic execution that the Desert Wren was supposed to be. He will replace her as sacrifice, toppling the rebellion.

With the Wren on my side and Gunther wiped out of existence, there won't be much of a rebel leadership left to rise up against the Authority. My new wife may hate me for these decisions, but she won't have any choice. She now belongs to the Warlord.

My radio crackles, startling me awake. I reach for it automatically. Late night calls aren't unusual, but I'm glad I chose to rest separately from Taran. She needs to sleep and recover. I sit up, scrubbing a hand over my face and try to shake off the cobwebs of sleep. I glance out across the city from my place on the roof. It's still full dark, curfew is in effect and very few lights glow throughout Sanctuary.

I bring the radio up to my mouth. "Fuentes."

As I wait for the response I push myself up off the old military cot and stand, stretching out stiff muscles. I sleep up here on the roof more often than I sleep in my own bed. I crave the freedom of open air and stars. I also enjoy being able to see the shadows of my city laid at my feet. My kingdom. It's not perfect, but it's mine.

"Cruz here," Jorje identifies himself. "Primitives have been spotted in the desert not far from the Eastern wall. I'm sending a team to check on the report."

My heart picks up, beating hard in anticipation. These are the moments I live for. Taking out the enemy, protecting my city. War. We haven't had a good Primitive attack in over a year and I'm primed to take point.

"Hold for me," I tell him. "I'll be there in ten."

"Copy," he replies and ends the call.

I leave the roof, striding down the stairwell to my apartment. I shove the door open and go immediately to the lockbox holding my equipment. I drag on my coat and gloves and equip my belt with two hunting knives and my radio. I sling a rifle across my back and add more ammunition to the belt.

I'm ready to leave when I hesitate. I glance toward the bedroom. I've never had anything or anyone to answer to before. Not that I do now. Taran won't give a shit. Not yet. Her feelings are all geared toward anger and hatred. Still, I can't bring myself to leave without checking on her. Last time I did that she'd disappeared. Now the urge to make sure she's there and doing okay is too strong to ignore.

I open the door and cross silently to the bed. She's almost impossible to see in the dark of the room. The light from the lantern spilling in from the other room highlights her form, tucked safely in the blankets of the bed. I kneel and bring my face close to hers. Her lips are parted and her breath is coming out in long, even puffs. She's sound asleep, oblivious to the threat of approaching Primitives.

Unable to help myself, I brush the hair away from her cheek and tuck it behind the small shell of her ear. Her skin is smooth and soft like satin. I want to kiss those perfect lips, but resist. She's better off asleep, believing that she's safe in her Sanctuary.

I stand and leave the room, closing the door behind me. In the hall I stop to give instructions to my man, Garrett, stationed as a guard. He nods grimly, without making eye contact. He'll do his job or forfeit his life. I head down the stairs to the ground floor and out into the cool early morning air. The city is silent and unmoving, few sounds disturbing the night. Curfew falls between 11pm and 6am. All citizens must remain indoors during this time. Anyone caught outside is subject to arrest and interrogation.

I drive to headquarters, ignoring the guards that wave me through the checkpoints. They know me and my vehicle. They know better than to detain me.

I enter headquarters, nod toward the soldiers gearing up in the main room and walk directly to the war room. Jorje and the rest of my advisors sit around the table. "Report," I say, dropping into the chair at the head of the table.

Jorje starts speaking. "A couple of Primitives have been spotted by the Eastern guard. He says they're heading toward the wall in an erratic pattern. They aren't moving fast, don't smell fresh blood yet. Probably just stumbled on our Sanctuary and want to see what's inside."

I nod. That's the most likely scenario. Primitives move fast and with purpose when they sense prey nearby. "There'll be more behind these ones," I interject. Primitives don't travel alone or in pairs. They move in groups or hordes, spreading their disease as they go and taking the 'survivors' with them. The only thing that stops a Primitive is death, and even that's difficult to deal out to a being whose entire biology right down to the cells has been morphed into something already approaching death.

"That seems highly likely, though none have been spotted behind these ones," Jorje agrees. "Stragglers aren't common. If it is just the two then they'll be easier to pick off."

"Nothing easy about killing a Primitive," someone down the table says.

I turn my gaze on him. Stryker. A philosophical man

with a good head for battle strategy. He's never enjoyed killing of any kind. He sees the necessity in taking out the diseased half-dead that plague our land, but he believes that we're killing humans. People with family. People that can possibly be brought back if a cure is ever discovered. He's a good man, but he's wrong.

"We'll do our job," I say, acknowledging his words. "Keep the city safe." I turn my gaze to the men around the table. "Shriver and Ellis, take some people out and shore up the Eastern wall in case they make it that far. Stryker and Cruz, you're with me. I want ten of our best. Everyone else, you're on city patrol. Keep the police alert and watch for unusual activity."

We stand and separate. Stryker makes his way to my side while Jorje goes out to organize our men. I nod toward Stryker. "I want you at my side. Need your eyes, tell me if you think there's more out there we're not picking up."

"Yes, boss," he says, falling into step beside me. I shout to Jorje as we're on our way out of the building. "We'll take point. Your men can fall in behind us."

I don't hear if he responds, I'm already swinging into the jeep. Vehicles are limited. Even the military is forced to share the few that we have. There aren't enough mechanics or parts to keep them running. With each passing year, more and more fall apart and become obsolete. We need them for things like this, which means we aren't treating them well. We're either driving hell-bent across the desert chasing threats or making our way through city streets filled with debris. The guts of each vehicle are cobbled together with whatever's available and plunked inside of frames that are rusting from lack of paint.

"Seatbelts," Stryker says, sliding into the passenger seat. I snort as he pulls a seatbelt across his shoulder and buckles it in. He's lucky the damn thing even works anymore. "Seen your driving, man. Don't want to die before we get there."

"You're a princess, Stryker," I say, pulling out of headquarters and racing toward the main gate. There are two other gates, one closer to our goal, but they aren't big enough to take our vehicles through. Walking room only. Makes it harder for them to be rushed and forced open by either Primitives or illegals. Easier to guard.

"Fuck, man." Stryker stretches an arm across the frame where there used to be a window and squints against the air rushing at our faces. "Better a live princess than a dead man because you couldn't find the brake in time. Not sure you even know where to find it."

I grunt my acknowledgment. I don't have many vices but driving fast across the empty desert is one of them. A perk of being Warlord is that I get my choice of vehicles. When I drive one into the ground, it's quickly replaced. I should probably feel guilty about this indulgence, but I do a lot for my city and ask little in return.

We're waved through the front gates. The second we're through I hit the gas and peel out toward the Eastern section, keeping my jeep close to the wall. As the crisp desert air rushes through my hair and cools my exposed skin, I enjoy the brief feeling of freedom. The urge to just drive and never stop, leave the yoke of Sanctuary behind, is strong. Not as strong as usual this time. There's a woman sleeping in my bed, her lure stronger than the freedom of the desert.

As if reading my mind, Stryker shouts over the rush of the wind, "Heard you got married. What the fuck, man? Didn't even know you were dating." He snickers at his own joke. Dating is a dead luxury. People don't date anymore, they fuck for survival.

If Stryker weren't an older man that's seen more war than peace and survived, I wouldn't bother to answer. But I respect the man. His advice is sound and he never steers me wrong. "Did you hear who she is?"

"Some kind of prisoner," he grunts. "According to the gossip flying around HQ like a women's sewing circle, you told the Judge to hand her over to you."

I'm impressed that Jorje didn't speak up, didn't give the men more information about my new wife. He's a good man. Knows when to keep his mouth shut.

"She's the Desert Wren," I tell Stryker.

His reaction is swift and predictable. He whistles long and loud and slaps his thigh. "You finally got your hands on the little bird then. Fuck, she's been a problem for years. Been itching to get hands on her myself. What's she look like?"

I laugh. There aren't many that would get away with that question, but Stryker was in love with his wife. Abrielle died years ago, taken down in the horde attack that took out Sanctuary New San Antonio. He hasn't looked at another woman since. Just moved on to the nearest Sanctuary city and offered his considerable security services. Stryker and his team are in charge of wall surveillance and security, which is why the Wren is on his radar. She's been climbing his wall for years and he's been trying to get his hands on her for years.

"She's small, like the bird. Red hair, light eyes. She's young too, mid-twenties and cleans up good. Intelligent and driven. Everything we thought she'd be."

"Good," Stryker grunts. "You did good, Fuentes."

Stryker is the type of man to prize intelligence and character over looks. He's been chasing after her with an edge of admiration for her uncanny ability to hide from detection.

On more than one occasion he's commented that he thought she'd be well suited to strategy if he could finally capture her and turn her to our way of thinking, away from the brainwashing of the rebels.

"I see something," he says, voice serious. He takes out his binoculars and leans forward for a look while I race toward the spot he's pointing at. "Two Primitives. They've spotted your dust trail. They're running toward us at top speed."

Top speed for a Primitive can approach the speed of a large cat. They don't care about their own health, don't care about survival beyond the next meal, next bite, next fuck. They'll run themselves into the ground chasing prey. Run until their legs fall off, then chase their target on the stubs of their legs until they have nothing left to give. Reason is one of the first things to go in the brain of a Primitive."

"Get ready," I shout. "I'm going to turn, you'll get first shot."

I'd rather take the first shot myself, but I have to stop the jeep. We learned early on not to try plowing through them with a car. Not only do they dent and damage our precious vehicles, but they just get back up again and keep coming after us, even broken and bleeding. And the last thing we need is a Primitive launching themselves at us with a geyser of blood coming out of them. Better to take them out in one shot and not get near their fluids. Primitive blood by itself isn't as likely to turn humans as a bite, but it doesn't hurt to be as careful as we can.

I skid through the dirt cranking the wheel, sliding the jeep so Stryker has a clear shot at the Primitive in the lead. He takes the shot but misses, his aim knocked wide by the bumping of the vehicle coming to rest. I grin as I crawl out my window, reaching for my rifle. His loss is my gain.

The Primitive sees me and hurtles straight at me. I cock the rifle and pull the trigger. Its head explodes and it flies into the dirt carried forward by the momentum of its run.

"Down!" Stryker yells.

I hit my knees in the dirt as his bullet goes whizzing right past me. The sound of the bullet impacting something has me looking over my shoulder. About ten feet away another Primitive goes down.

"Thanks, old man." I climb back to my feet, resting my rifle on my shoulder.

"Don't thank me yet, idiot," he growls, holding his binoculars up to his eyes. "As predicted, the rest are on their way and you left our backup in the dust."

"More for me." I bare my teeth, pull out my knife and reload my rifle.

I throw the blanket off my legs and stand. Something feels... off. I approach the window and look out over the city. Dawn is just arriving, lighting the city in a golden path. The beauty of the natural world slowly encroaching on what was once human territory always steals my breath. Especially when I can view it from high up. Though I detest many of the things that have come out of the Great Fall, I can't entirely fault the planet for taking back its own. For reclaiming the surface that humans had spent centuries destroying.

I check the window, just to be sure. Yup, Diogo did indeed have it nailed shut. I pick at the nails for a few minutes trying to see if there's any give. Of course, there isn't. I'd need some tools and more strength than I possess to get them out. I turn and head for the door, seeking out the reason for this strange feeling I have. Like something's not right.

It's absurd, I've been here for less than a day, how should I know what's right or not in Diogo's world? Yet, he is my caretaker now... my husband. If something happens to him, it's entirely likely that I'll revert back to police custody and the Judge will resurrect my charges and the death sentence.

I open the door and step directly into the path of a man nearly the same size and fierceness as Diogo. I jump back and clutch the edges of my shirt together. His eyes follow the movement and then quickly move past me to fix on the wall behind me.

"Can I help you, Mrs. Fuentes?" he asks coolly.

I look him over. Uniform, weapons, cold, angry look. He's a military man. There aren't nearly as many as there are police. The city's military is made up of men with certain skills that will benefit the Authority. These men are handpicked by Diogo. I've spent my career in the rebellion avoiding men like this. The city police are a joke compared to the precision and brutality of the military.

"Where is my..." I hesitate. Calling him my husband will probably get better results, but I can't seem to bring myself to say the word. "Where is Commander Fuentes?"

His eyes flick briefly to mine and I see the same look of death shared by most of his brethren. "Commander Fuentes was called away."

"Well aren't you helpful," I say sarcastically. "So you're here, to what, guard me? Make sure I don't run away while his lordship is out?"

His lip twitches in annoyance at my blatant lack of respect. I don't care. Diogo hasn't earned any from me. Kidnapping and forced marriage will get him nothing but scorn from me. And this man is his puppet.

"I'm here to attend you, Mrs. Fuentes."

Uh huh, attend my ass. This man is nothing more than

an over-grown, super deadly babysitter. "What's your name?" I demand, heading toward the kitchen, still holding the two halves of Diogo's shirt together.

He doesn't move, but he follows my every move with watchful eyes. "Garrett," he grunts. He doesn't give me a last name, a family house, or a military designation. Interesting, he either doesn't want me to know or doesn't identify with anything. Maybe a mixture of the two. There are plenty of us orphans floating around the Sanctuary cities. Maybe Garrett identifies purely as military. They've become his family. I wouldn't be surprised if Diogo picked men with an eye toward those in need of family. They'd be more loyal to him.

"Are you hungry, Garrett?" I ask, rifling through the cupboards. Even though I ate my fill only a few hours ago, I'm starving again. My stomach is growling and the urge to eat, which I've spent so long suppressing, is rising up.

Garrett ignores my question as I go through the cupboards, finally deciding on a can of peaches. It seems like such a treat. A rarity and an extravagance. I wonder if Diogo was saving them for something. I decide I don't care. I want them so I'm going to eat them. That's the price of taking on a captive wife, she gets to eat all the food and steal all the hot shower water.

I dig some more until I find a can opener and smile happily as I open the can. The tangy scent of peaches and syrup tease me. My mouth waters and I can hardly wait to finish prying the lid off before I'm digging in with my bare fingers. I sigh in contentment as I shove the first wedge into my mouth. Sticky syrup drips down my chin and over my fingers. I don't care. I'm so pleased with my discovery that I'd tip the entire can upside down in my mouth if I had a bigger mouth and didn't think I'd choke.

I devour about half the can before finally slowing down. I glance over to see Garrett watching, his eyes glued to me. His gaze trails down my front and I realize in my hurry to get at the peaches I let the shirt gape open again. This little soldier is going to get himself into big trouble if he keeps staring at me like that. I suspect his commander wouldn't be impressed. Still, if I can use his distraction to my advantage then I will.

I smile at him, showing my teeth. I lick the syrup off my lips and say, "You sure you don't want any, Garrett?" I deliberately purr his name. I don't have many feminine wiles but the few I do have are in full force. My mission is to get information and this boy looks ripe for the picking.

Before he can answer, the door to the stairwell slams open and Diogo strides in. His face is set in fierce lines, his wide shoulders tense. He's wearing big leather boots, a thick, heavy-looking coat that covers his upper body, and jeans with a belt. A massive curved knife is strapped to his belt and a rifle is slung across his back. Blood is splattered over him, covering his torso and jeans.

His gaze sweeps over us. Me in the kitchen barely dressed, toes curled against the bare concrete floor, Garrett standing a few feet away. His head is now twisted to the side, looking at Diogo. I can't see his expression, but if I had to guess, the tension running through his body would indicate fear.

"My god, what happened to you?" I demand, nearly shouting. The sight of Diogo like that, covered in blood is like a punch to the gut. What if he's been hurt? I don't think he has. I don't see any injuries and the path of the blood spatter would indicate it came from someone else. But what if it comes from a rebel? Someone I know. Emery or Xavier, any of my friends.

He ignores the question, turning his deadly gaze on Garrett. "Get the fuck out."

Garrett hurries away without another word, clearly relieved that his boss isn't immediately swinging that big ass knife at him. Diogo turns toward me, making his way slowly over. He reaches for the rifle strap slung across his chest and pulls it over his head. He drops it on the table as he passes and continues toward the kitchen.

Waves of aggression hit me as he approaches and I back slowly away as he stalks toward me. His eyes are hot, angry and filled with lust as they rove over my body. I feel his intensity right down to my bones. My stomach swirls and my blood feels like it's flowing heavily through my veins as I respond to him on a visceral level. I clutch at the counter behind me, the half-finished can of peaches forgotten.

He walks right up to me and pinches my chin between his fingers, tipping my face up to his. "You will *never* again appear as you are dressed now. I am the only one that gets to see you like this. Understand?"

My heart thunders in my chest as I'm faced with Sanctuary's Warlord. The man that kills for the thrill. That rules the city without a conscience. I'm stunned by the vehemence of his words and though part of me wants to argue, wants to point out that I couldn't have known Garrett was out there when I left the bedroom, I realize that, in this moment, the best path to take is submission.

"I understand," I whisper.

His gaze takes on a satisfied glint, though they still glitter hard obsidian at me. "If you ever think to flirt with any of my men then I will kill them, Taran. No questions, no second chances. You belong to me. I won't share you. Understand?"

I nod helplessly in his grip.

"Say it," he demands.

"I understand, Diogo."

The words barely leave my mouth when his crashes down on mine in a brutal kiss. He buries his hands in my hair and when the sharp, metallic scent of blood hits my nostrils I realize that he's wearing blood-soaked gloves. Disgust wars with desire as he crushes me against his body, pressing my bare chest to his bloody coat.

I struggle to push him away, tearing my lips from his. "No, Diogo, don't!"

My denial seems to spur a fire in him. He grips my hair in a fierce hold and forces my head back up for his kiss, this one more punishing than the last. My lips press hard against my teeth. I have no choice but to open my mouth or be cut to ribbons. He thrusts his tongue deep, sweeping the recesses with a fervency that stuns me. His tongue is hot, persistent, filling my mouth completely and choking me.

Just as dizziness hits and I think I'm going to pass out from the roughness of his possession, he lifts his head. My reprieve isn't long though. He picks me up off my feet, turns on his heels and strides for the bedroom. I let out a shriek of protest. He doesn't hear me though. He's blinded by lust, passion and blood. He wants to fuck away the aggression of the kill and he's going to do it, right now.

He drops me on the bed. I land on my back winded. When he reaches for his knife, pulling it from the sheath, I panic. I must've read him all wrong. He's going to murder me right here in his bed!

I try to roll away, but he grabs me, flips me back over and clamps a hand over my neck, pinning me. I gasp against his tight hold and bring my hands up protectively when he angles the knife toward my body. He knocks my hands aside and proceeds to finish what he started, cutting the fabric all the way down my front. He resheaths the knife and looks down at me, his eyes glowing with possessive energy.

"Wife."

I should slow down, be gentle with my new wife. She's small and I took her by surprise. I'm not usually an aggressive beast when I take a woman to my bed. Yet, with Taran, I feel different. Feel the driving need to imprint myself all over her. I want her to feel every part of me inside every part of her. Want my scent to linger on her skin and in her hair. Want her to remember who she belongs to.

She won't understand this intense need of mine though. She's already confused by how fast I've pursued her. Doesn't understand why I want her so bad. She doesn't realize that she's been a myth to me for long enough that I built a pedestal for my little bird. A pedestal with a cage on top. And finally meeting her in person, confirming all my beliefs of this incredible woman, I want to ensure that she never leaves my side.

I've been protecting this city for so long, sacrificing so much of myself, that it's time I finally take a prize. My little wife is the best prize I can think of. She's staring up at me with panic in her eyes, fearful of my raging desire. She should be afraid. These feelings are new to me too and they make me unpredictable.

But I don't want to hurt her, so I force myself to slow down, to sink into her stormy gray gaze. Her beautiful, unique eyes centre me. Reach deep into my soul and hold me still.

"Taran." I say her name, awe in my voice as I gaze down her naked body. She is beyond perfect, with feminine curves despite her tiny stature. She flinches as I reach for her, but I only slide my fingers across her ribcage, mourning the bones that are clearly visible. I'll spend a lifetime giving her everything she's ever wanted for. Every day she will eat until she's stuffed. Light candles and lanterns whenever she wants and use heated water.

I lean over and press my lips to the skin between her small breasts. She brings her hands to my shoulders and pushes, but her strength is slight compared to mine. Still, I gather her hands in mine and hold them together against her stomach. It's best if she can't struggle this first time, best if I can take care not to damage her.

I reach down with my free hand and unbuckle my belt then tug it away from the loops of my jeans. I wrap it around her wrists, binding them together. I tug until its tight enough to hold her but not tight enough that she'll lose circulation. I pull the leather back through the buckle and secure it. She's staring up at me with injured, accusing eyes.

"For your own safety," I explain before tipping her bound hands up over her head. Now that her hands are taken care of I feel better about slowing down enough to explore her. I trail my lips across her jaw toward her ear, tilting her head to the side so I can access the tiny shell.

"Diogo..." Her moan is a half-hearted protest. The shiver that wracks her body tells me everything I need to know. She enjoys my touch, though she tries to resist. Doesn't understand this pull between us.

I understand, I've understood from the beginning, before I ever met her. I'm attracted to her light and her idealism. I want every part of her, brain, body, spirit. Even her rebellious streak appeals to me, the man that creates and enforces rules. Her ability to defy and flaunt those rules makes her an enigma in a world of tightly leashed chaos. And she is attracted to me as well, despite her protests.

Taran wants the strength she senses in me. She craves the stability and protection I can offer her. Even though she despises my methods, she can't argue with the results. I was instrumental in creating the Sanctuary that we now live in, and I protect the citizens within my city walls. For a girl that has no one to call family, hasn't known a stable life since she was born, I represent safety. Even if she hates that craving, hates reaching for the man who has captured and enslaved her.

I trail kisses down the side of her neck, savouring the sensation of her soft skin against my lips, against the rasp of my chin. She smells like heaven, like fresh air and freedom. She squirms underneath me and I wonder if she's wet for me yet. I find the spot between her shoulder and neck and bury my teeth into the flesh. She cries out and her hips jerk into mine as I suck her flesh, tasting her skin, marking her.

She's driving me wild, bucking her body up against mine and crying her pleasure in my ear. Those guttural moans are like music. It pleases me that my wife enjoys my touch. I mark the same spot until I know she'll carry my bruise for the world to see then I move on, trailing stinging bites from her neck down to her breasts. I take one of the peaked nipples into my mouth, testing it against my tongue, rolling the tiny bud and enjoying the sensation of the hard yet resilient flesh in my mouth.

"Oh god, pleeease!" she yells in my ear, bringing her legs up to clasp my hips.

She drops her arms, still bound, to wrap them around my head and hold me against her. She arches her back, thrusting her nipple deep into my mouth. I bite down, marking the delicate flesh of her breast. She cries out, even louder, and jerks her hips against me.

She is more than I can resist. I'm now confidant that my little wife wants me as much as I want her. Our union will be one of mutual pleasure. I reach down between us to open my zipper, my hand lingering over her pussy. The temptation is too much for me. I touch her, burying my fingers in the heated warmth of her. She is wet and welcoming, accepting the slide of my fingers through her labia before I find her centre. She moans again and widens her legs as I sink one finger into her passage. She's tight, almost too tight. But she'll take me. Her body is meant to accommodate mine.

I lean back and finally free myself from the constriction of my jeans. She's rolling her hips against me, asking for my possession. I'm nearly out of my mind with lust for her. She's so fucking perfect. I've never met anyone like her. So honestly passionate in all of her actions. She wants me though she doesn't want to want me.

Her wholehearted response drives me wild, taking my breath and my ability to think.

I replace my fingers with my cock, and reach up to hold her head, forcing her gaze to mine. Her eyes are glazed, but they search my face. I thrust, pushing into her. I'm stunned by the heat of her clasp. She's too tight for me to push all the way in all at once. She makes a garbled sound and tightens her arms around my neck, dragging my head down to hers. I press my forehead against hers and stare at her lovely features, twisted in concentration as I take several shallow thrusts, going in deeper with each one. Her body stretches, taking me in.

I can see the merging of pleasure and pain in her eyes, in the grimace on her features. She lifts her legs higher along my hips and I wish that I'd taken the time to remove my clothes. I want to feel her skin against mine. I want to slide against her with no barriers.

After a few more thrusts she picks up the rhythm, countering with her own hips, pushing them back against me, taking me deeper. I can see the build of pleasure in the way she tilts her head back against the pillows, closing her eyes, savouring our connection. Her mouth is shaping a perfect O as small puffs of breath escape her. Her fingers slide through my hair on the nape of my neck, tangling in the short strands and tugging me closer against her. She wraps herself around me like a vine clinging lovingly to its host.

I'm in heaven. I can't imagine anything better. Didn't know this depth of feeling existed. If I was dangerous and protective before, now that I'm claiming her, I'm going to be unreasonable. I want nothing to touch this woman. Nothing but me. I don't care that my thoughts are unreasonable, that they're contrary to the cool logic in which I conduct most aspects of my life. I want to keep Taran forever, and I'll do whatever it takes to ensure that happens. Even if it means protecting her from herself. Caging her.

I growl into her throat as I feel my body tightening, the familiar sensation of coming hitting me hard, so much more intense. I grip her hard, clutching her to my chest as I thrust into her. I hope that she's alright, that she isn't hurt during my wild release. I can't stop.

I shout into her hair as I come, shooting semen deep into her body. Satisfaction floods through me, a primal reaction to making her mine.

She's panting in my ear, still clinging to me. I don't know if she orgasmed, didn't have space in my head to care. But now, I want her to feel pleasure at my hands, know what I can give her.

I tip her back onto the bed, slide my still hard cock from her body and drop down between her legs. I push two fingers inside her and am greeted with another musical moan and the short thrust of her hips up into my hand. Her body is well-lubricated and I find her G-spot right away, pressing my fingers hard into the soft wall of her pussy.

I lick the inside of her thigh, nipping the flesh before moving to her centre and eating her. I mean to go slow, to enjoy her, but I'm consumed once more by the essence that is Taran. I'm devouring her, sucking her into my mouth, tasting her, swallowing her. She gives herself up willingly, flinging her bound hands over her head and riding my face, bucking into me, forcing herself onto my tongue.

I swipe the slippery nub of her clit with my tongue, forcing her to take the rough invasion. Her shrieks fill the air and she rolls her face into the side of her arm as her body explodes under me. Fluid gushes from her, soaking my fingers. I drop lower and lap at it as it flows from her body. Her fluid and mine combined, pushed from her as her body contracts with the force of her pleasure.

I watch her face intently as she comes down. The drowsy happy look is perfect, something that I will hold in my memory. Especially as I know that soon she'll remember. Remember who I am. Who she is. Remember that I am her enemy. The enemy that makes her body sing.

EIGHTEEN

TARAN

He moves up my body, carefully brushing my hair from my face before unwinding his belt from my wrists. He gently rubs my wrists where they'd been bound. I'm still stunned by the force of my orgasm. I've never really come with a partner before. I enjoyed sex, but I don't think I realized how much I was missing. Or maybe I was never attracted to the men I fucked the way I am to the dark Warlord.

Though I'd rather not admit it, or rather it not be true at all, I find Diogo very attractive. His face is strong with a tough jaw, a sharp blade of a nose and full lips over a week's growth of beard. He's handsome in a weather-beaten way with lines around his eyes and a near constant frown. His body is big, maybe too big. His size is easily recognizable and intimidating. Though I'd seen him before, knew he was massive, I'd never gotten close enough to really see the scope of his size.

Now, as he moves away to sit on the edge of the bed and remove his clothes I finally see him naked. I gasp as he reveals a body covered in scars. I sit up, drawn to him, drawn by the intimacy we shared. Yet still I hesitate, my hand hovering over the back of his shoulder. He turns his head, gives me a warm look and takes my hand in his, pressing it against his skin. I'm a little surprised by how hot he is.

I run my fingers over his shoulder and down his back, sliding my hand over his ribs. He doesn't have a house tattoo that I can see. I guess he doesn't need one. Everyone knows who he is. He lifts his arm, closes his eyes and sighs contentedly as I caress him. It feels strange to share such a moment of tenderness with a man I barely know. But I suppose in times like this, where life expectancy is low, forging a future with near strangers has become the norm rather than the strange.

I touch the scars on his side, pausing to stroke a pattern of small puckered, pink holes in his flesh. At first I think they're bullet wounds but then change my mind. The skin around them is shiny and stretched. They're burn marks. And they were done deliberately. As though someone had seared a hot poker into his flesh.

"My father was a demanding man," he says gruffly.

He shakes off my touch and stands to remove his jeans. I look away, flushing. Then I peek again. That thing was inside me. I want to see what it looks like.

My mouth falls open and I'm sure that my slight flush has turned into a full on scarlet beacon when I see the size of him. Warlord Fuentes is extremely proportionate. I look away quickly. But that sight is now burned into my mind. His penis is long and thick, very intimidating, even flaccid as it is now. It hangs down his thigh as though prepared to take another piece of me.

I tug off the tattered remnants of my shirt and climb quickly under the blanket, pulling it up to my chin, covering my nudity. His eyes glow in amusement as he watches, but he doesn't say anything.

"Where were you?" I ask him, trying not to sound as desperately curious as I am. I want to know why he came to me covered in blood.

He searches my face, then sits on the bed beside me. I move over as much as I can to give him room but not seem like I'm obviously trying to avoid touching him, which I am. Sort of. I don't know. The man has me confused.

"Primitives outside the wall." He settles into the bed beside me, tugging the blankets from my stiff fingers so he can slide under them. I jump as his thigh brushes mine.

"Did you kill them?" I ask timidly. At least he wasn't out killing rebels.

"Yes," he says shortly.

I chew on my nail for a moment, thinking. "How many?"

He gives me a sharp look. "About ten."

A small horde then. Soldiers skilled in Primitive combat could easily take them down without too much fuss. Did take them down. It's been awhile since there were reports of Primitives near the city. I'm not naïve to the fact that there might have been more and that the military may have kept it from civilians to prevent panic. Still, Primitive attacks are difficult to keep quiet. People talk about them, and gossip and fear circulate among the people.

As if reading my mind, Diogo says, "News of the Primitive attack doesn't need to get out."

I frown at him, edging my way closer to the other side of the bed. "People should know, Diogo. So they can prepare. We both know that where there are a few Primitives there are usually many more behind them. They move in packs. Really big packs."

Of course he knows all this, but saying it out loud makes it seem more real. Primitives multiply as they move, as they find more victims. I shiver, imagining my grandparent's fate, knowing that Primitives are only one of many scenarios of how they might've met their deaths. It doesn't matter. They'd be long dead by now. People without Sanctuary can't survive, not unless they're extremely tough, like the Outsiders.

"You don't have to worry about the city being attacked, Taran," he says. His voice, while steely, isn't unkind. "There's no need to cause a panic with baseless gossip."

"It's not baseless." I turn to him, anger burning in my eyes. "We have as much right to be prepared for an attack as you do. What if your military intervention fails? What if we're overrun?"

His gaze sharpens on my face. "This isn't just about the Primitives is it?" he asks, divining my thoughts. "You don't like that I'm asking you to keep this quiet because it means that the Authority is likely keeping other things from the Sanctuary citizens."

"And are you?" I ask tartly.

He drags me down onto the bed beside him, rolling me underneath him. His big body crushes mine into the mattress, yet I'm not uncomfortable. The cage of his arms wraps around me and I give into the sensation of contentment. It's been so long since anyone has just held me. It's not a crime to enjoy these little moments, even if I'm taking them from an enemy. Maybe if I tell myself I have no choice, I'll feel better about my easy capitulation. I'll save my fight for another day. When I have half a chance of winning.

"We keep many things from the inhabitants of Sanctuary. It's called strategic information distribution. We tell them what they need to know for their safety and the safety of this Sanctuary. Humans are incapable of survival as a whole without strong leadership and that leadership has decided on the old cliché, what they don't know won't hurt them."

"That's ridiculously arrogant!" I snap, digging my fingers into the flesh of his arms. A small punishment.

He smiles grimly. "Perhaps, but it's effective."

"But the people need to know," I argue. "What if they decide to climb the wall, or go hunting or something, without permission from the Authority? They could easily run into a Primitive horde. They'd be sitting ducks if they didn't have the military training you have."

His eyes harden along with his voice. "If they're going over the wall illegally then they deserve whatever happens to them."

Even though I know his stance on these subjects, know his laws, I still have trouble reconciling the brutal leader with the man that just took my body to heaven and back. "But they wouldn't go over the wall at all if they knew there was a threat out there. Why sacrifice citizens needlessly?"

"My point still stands, Taran. If they go over the wall illegally, with or without certain information, then what happens to them is in their own hands. Including arrest and prosecution, which is more likely than a horde attack."

"What if it was me? I've gone over the wall often, probably more than you even knew," I demand staring up at him accusingly, eyes burning. I try to push him away, slide out from underneath him, but he's a solid block of man, pinning me firmly to the bed.

He tightens the cage of his body over mine and drops his head until I'm forced to look into the hellish obsidian gaze. "You will *never* go over the wall again, Taran. Will never put yourself in danger like that again."

"Or what?" I ask, knowing full well that I'm pushing a man who shouldn't be pushed. But it's best if we get this out of the way now. Find out where the other stands.

"Do you think your cage will only consist of a couple of nails in a window and a full-time guard?" he sneers down at me, his lips twisting cruelly as he speaks. "I can shrink it to the size of a cage. Just big enough to hold one small woman."

"You wouldn't do that," I say confidently. If there's one thing I've learned about Diogo since meeting him it's that he doesn't want to see me in pain. That he will actively avoid things that will cause pain. Unless he's doing it himself, and even then, I've caught him checking his strength a few times.

"Don't test me, Taran," he growls at me, "and you won't have to find out what I'm capable of. You make me feel... unpredictable. It would be dangerous to push me."

I believe him, believe that he's unpredictable. In all my sightings of Diogo and everything I'd heard of him, I'd never heard anything like this. Never a wife. Never this protective of a single human. In fact, his entire philosophy centers around ensuring the continued existence of our species, which often means sacrificing individuals. For him to become so fixated on one individual, me, is unprecedented.

But I still don't believe he'll put me in a cage, or I hope he won't. I'll die if my world shrinks any more than it already has. Part of my fascination with climbing around abandoned buildings, with scaling the wall and sitting on top, is the freedom of having a world at my feet and a sky over my head. In a chaotic world where survival is by no means guaranteed, it feels like the closest I can get to heaven while I'm still alive. I'll do whatever it takes to protect my freedom.

Diogo brushes the hair from my head and his voice softens as he says, "Stop thinking so much, Taran. I will take care of you, give you the things you need. You have nothing to worry about."

"What if the things I need are different from the things you're willing to give me?" I want to tell him that I don't need his protection, but this is the safest I've ever felt. I feel secure in his arms. For now, at least. I nod and look away, unable to handle the knowing tenderness in his gaze.

"Go to sleep," he says gruffly and rolls off to the side, stretching out next to me. He's so big his body takes up more than half the bed. I'm forced to curve against him if I don't want to fall off. He wraps an arm around my shoulders and pulls me further into the heat of his body, tucking my head against his shoulder.

"I'm not tired," I say and immediately yawn. At least, I didn't think I was tired. I'd slept my fill last night while Diogo fought Primitives. But now, after the heat of our passion and my conflicting emotions, I feel the lure of sleep once more.

"Then lay with me while I sleep," Diogo says, closing his eyes and stroking my arm lazily with his hand. "I'm not ready to let you go."

And I'm not ready to leave him yet. A small fire has ignited within me for this man. I need to see where it burns before it's time for me to go.

I wake up still wrapped tightly in Diogo's embrace. His arms are so tight around me that, at first, I think he must be awake. But as I turn my head to look at him I realize he's still deeply asleep. His hands are big and warm against the bare skin of my arms and his breath is coming out in deep, even gusts, tickling the hair on top of my head.

I watch his face, tracing the hard lines with my gaze. We lay that way for long enough that the sunlight marks a path across the floor. I think it must be late afternoon, though I'm not sure. I decide that I've waited long enough for him to wake up, and he's not showing signs of doing that any time soon. I gently lift his arm, looking for any kind of response. When none comes, I slide out from under his grip and set his arm back down. As I crawl off the bed a slight frown mars his brow. I hold my breath, waiting for him to wake up, but he only rolls onto his back and throws an arm across his eyes.

I open the dresser and rifle through his clothes. I come up with another shirt with buttons all down the front. This one is blue. I put it on and button it up. At least if he keeps destroying everything that I wear, he'll just be tearing up his own clothes. I smile at the thought of him running out of shirts, forced to wander around the city bare-chested. None of the city women will complain.

I reach for the door and then hesitate. Last time I ran into one of his guys out in the main area, Diogo got pissed off. He doesn't like me showing skin around his men. I shrug it off and open the door, stepping out. Not my fault that the Warlord hasn't provided a decent wardrobe for his new wife.

I open the door and peek around. Garrett, or whoever might've replaced him, isn't lurking about. Hands on my hips, I ponder this development. For a guy that values security as much as Diogo does he's pretty bad at keeping an eye on his new wife. I could take off if I really wanted too and part of me thinks that's a fantastic idea. Not my slightly sore woman parts, or my full belly. But the part of me that knows this fairy tale won't end well. The dictator and the rebel? We have no future beyond a few stolen moments, despite what Diogo thinks.

Xavier wants me to stay. Thinks this is the perfect opportunity to plant a spy in the enemy camp. What Xavier is neglecting to realize is that Diogo isn't stupid. Driven, single-minded and brutal, but also incredibly intelligent. He knows that he's sheltering a rebel under his roof. Not just any rebel, but one completely invested in the cause. Diogo won't pass on any vital information, either by accident or on purpose, thinking I've somehow become loyal.

Oh well. I'll just make the most of my situation. Eat Diogo's food, enjoy some great sex and wear his clothes until I decide it's time to return to reality. Return to the slums of Sanctuary to pick back up where I left off. Unless the city policies change, I'll always have a purpose. There'll always be illegals clambering for food or looking for safe passage.

I decide to pass my time waiting for Diogo to wake up by exploring his home. Five minutes later I've found a locker, the food pantry again and the table. Apparently Diogo believes in sparse living. An interesting fact considering he's an elite and obviously has access to the better things in life. That he chooses to live like the less privileged is an interesting thought that I'll unpack later. For now, I sink down onto my knees in front of his locker and examine the lock. I'm certain that I can pick that lock in a heartbeat. I'm also pretty certain the locker contains weapons. The rifle he was wearing is no longer on the table, which means he must've gotten up after I'd fallen asleep and locked it away before coming back to bed. And I didn't notice any other place in his apartment where he keeps weapons. If I had, I probably would've shot him immediately after he first brought me up here.

Now that I'm less inclined to murder Diogo I decide to leave it for now. There's no point in tipping him off to my lock picking skills until absolutely necessary. I push myself off the floor, dust off my knees and move to the door I noticed earlier. I expect it to be locked, but it opens easily when I give it a shove.

Shaking my head, I go through the door and up a flight of stairs. "Honestly, Diogo. It's like you're inviting me to escape," I mumble to myself. Maybe he just really likes the chase. I grin, thinking about the devastating kisses he likes to bestow when he's pissed off.

My smile turns to astonishment as I step through the next door and onto the rooftop. My heart pounds and a rush of pure exhilaration sizzles through my veins when I realize that this is the best view of the city. Even better than the view from the wall, far better than the view from the abandoned buildings I like to climb. I walk to the edge of the roof and pull myself right up on top of the ledge, standing on my toes so I can get the best view of the city I possibly can. Breathtaking is an understatement. I can see the wall curved out around the edges of the city, its metal branches sticking out here and there. It should be ugly. It represents oppression and death. Yet it's also somehow beautiful. Just like everything else, shrubs and vines are slowly encroaching up the sides of the monstrosity, claiming it. Long after we're gone nature will take it back completely. Dismantle it and drag it back down to the Earth as though it never existed.

I stand with my legs wide and my arms stretched out, my gaze wandering the city below, taking in the buildings, the checkpoints, the people. From up here it looks like a kingdom, dying and flourishing at once. I can understand why Diogo has chosen this building as his home. It isn't just the power of symbolic placement, he loves to watch his kingdom. Clock in the workings and plan his next move. Probably clear his mind like I'm doing now.

With a sigh, I drop down off the ledge and back onto the rooftop. I flinch as a rock bites into my bare foot. I'll have to mention shoes to my negligent husband when he finally rolls out of bed. I wander around the roof, exploring. I find a cot and smile knowingly. He probably sleeps up here when the weather permits, stretching out beneath the stars. Though I don't know him well yet, I sense a solitary spirit, a man who craves freedom as much as I do. Only he chooses to control the world around him in order to achieve what he thinks is freedom, while I escape the cage to fly free for a few hours at a time.

I gasp in surprise when I realize that what I thought was

a shed is actually a greenhouse. I touch the glass panels that run the length of it, awe making my touch extremely gentle. Nowadays windows are made of cobbled together sand, which is blasted with high heat. Very few actual glass panes still exist. Yet Diogo somehow got his hands on enough to create a greenhouse.

I pull the door open, once more shaking my head at his carelessness. Does the man lock anything besides his weapons? He needs to work on his priorities. Most people have access to some kind of weapon, but not everyone has a greenhouse. They're so rare, in fact, that I would think he should have a full-time guard on this one. Of course, it's unlikely anyone knows it's up here. Except for Diogo, and now me.

I step through the door and into the humid environment within. Looking around I realize what care he's taken with these delicate buds. Probably growing them from seeds into beautiful, full plants. As I wander the short rows I try to guess at what I'm seeing. Fresh tomatoes, cucumber, some other things I don't recognize. Herbs, I think. We have community gardens to help sustain food rations, but the plants tend to be specifically bred for hardiness and desert living. Water is carefully rationed and there isn't much left over for the gardens. Apparently Diogo lives by a different set of rules.

Tentatively I reach out and rub the leaf of a tomato plant, avoiding the big, juicy looking red bulbs. I don't want to accidentally knock one down and ruin it. I bring my fingers to my nose and inhale the aromatic scent My mouth waters and tears spring to my eyes.

I'm about to sink my face into the plant to take in as much of the delicious fragrance as I can when I hear a tiny chirp. I think it must be coming from outside but then it happens again, and I hear the flutter of wings. My heart pounds as I trace a path to the very back corner of the greenhouse, steeped in shadows. There, up high on a shelf, I discover a bird's next. Sitting on the edge, looking at me suspiciously, is a tiny desert wren. Her feathers are ruffled and she's eying me angrily. I realize she must have eggs in her nest.

"Are you trapped, darling?" I ask her, searching all around. Then I see it, a small section where a pane of glass is missing. There's plastic covering most of it, maintaining the integrity of the humid interior of the greenhouse, but with just enough space for a small bird to fly in and out of.

A splash hits my hand and I jump. I bring a hand up to my face as I realize I was startled by my own tears. I didn't know I was crying. The beauty of the greenhouse and the little bird has shaken me. What does Diogo see when he comes in here, when he shares this space with the wren? Why did he keep her, a bird that shares the same name as his elusive rebel enemy? He's provided Sanctuary for her, a safe place to hatch her chicks. Yet she's still trapped. That window can be closed at any time, on the whim of a Warlord.

TWENTY

DIOGO

I wake abruptly from a deep sleep with the certain feeling that something is missing.

"Taran."

I'm on my feet and throwing on my jeans within seconds. I was a fool to think that I would wake when she did, that she wouldn't take the opportunity to run. My gut twists as I realize that the only place she could've gone is the roof. There's a man outside my apartment who would've detained her and sent her back to me if she wandered out there. And she's smart enough to know that. I swear viciously as I imagine her scaling down the building again, slipping and falling. My gut burns with the thought of her twisted dead body laying on the ground far below.

I fly through the door, throwing it open so hard it hits the wall. I take the stairs three at a time and burst through second door onto the rooftop. I don't pause, I hurl myself at the ledge, clutching it hard, my throat closing as I look down the side of the building to the ground.

"Diogo." Her soft voice comes from behind me.

I turn sharply, relief punching a hole through me as I take her in, standing there safe and sound a slight frown puckering her brow. Clutched in her delicate hand is a bright red tomato.

I'm nearly driven to my knees at the sight of her. She's safe. I should've realized she wouldn't run again. Not this soon and not without a plan. She'll recover first from her last attempt and then create a strategy that will ensure more success than the last time.

Hard on the heels of relief is anger. She should not leave my side, should've waited until I was awake before wandering off. She puts herself in danger at every turn. And though I know logically that I'm not thinking reasonably, I can't help this driving need to chain her to me so nothing can ever happen to her.

Wordlessly I reach for her, taking hold of her and dragging her into my body. Startled, she drops her tomato and brings her hands up to brace herself against me. I bend to her, taking her lips in a desperate kiss. I try to moderate the anger and frustration, but I know I'm bruising the delicate tissue with my inability to hold back from her.

Needing her closer I pick her up off her feet and press her against me. She gasps into my mouth, giving me the opening I need to explore the interior, stamp my territory with lips, tongue and teeth. She clings to me. I hope it's passion she's feeling because I'm not capable of slowing down.

I shove her back against the wall next to the exterior door and lift her shirt. My shirt. Sweeping her body with my hands, I memorize every soft part of her. I reach between us and free myself from my jeans. I remember that I should've checked to see if she's wet just as I drag her leg up to my hip and slam myself home with a primal growl. I relax as I glide through her slick channel and fit myself to the hilt deep in her body. She lets out a shriek and stiffens. Even wet, this position is a lot for someone her size to take.

I drag my lips from her skin long enough to mutter against her throat, "Taran, tell me you're okay."

Her body relaxes against mine, then she reaches up and wraps her arms tight around my neck, dragging my head further into her neck. "I'm okay," she whispers back.

Thank fucking God, because if she'd said no, I don't know if I would've stopped. The last thing I want is to hurt my delicate wife, but I lose my head around her, lose my control with every touch. Even the sound of her voice is like a lightening bolt to the system. Everything in me recognizes her as my mate.

Clutching her against my chest, I wrap one arm around her waist and start thrusting up inside her, fucking her with even more intensity than the first time. Now that I've experienced paradise in her body I can't live without it. I want to spend a lifetime with her.

Her cries fill the open evening air around us, driving me insane. I love the husky guttural sounds torn from her throat as I slam into her over and over, using her wetness to lubricate the motion. Her sweetness invades my nose as I bury my face in her hair. I groan against her, feeling the edge of orgasm closing in. Too soon. I want this to last forever.

She's pushing back against my arm, arching in abandon, throwing her head back as she rides my cock. Lifting herself and dropping onto each thrust until we're moving in unison. She cries out as I pull from her body and drop to my knees in front of her. She sways unsteadily and reaches for me looking to follow me down.

I push her back against the wall with a hand wrapped

around her hip then lift her leg over my shoulder giving me access to the sweet part of her I crave. I bury my nose against her and inhale deeply for just a moment before settling in to lick and suck her tiny clit. She squeals her pleasure and tightens her leg on my shoulder. Small hands bury themselves in my hair and she clutches me to her, mindless with passion.

I eat and drink her, getting high on her taste and her scent. She's the best meal I've ever had. Her hips jerk against my face and she screams as her orgasm overtakes her. I hold her shaking, boneless body up against the wall and eat her through another orgasm. She yells her pleasure again, gasping desperately for breath.

Standing, I gather her in my arms once more, lift her high and drag her down my body, impaling her. She slides easily onto my cock, taking me right to the hilt. Then she reaches for me, grabbing my face and dragging it to hers for a long lingering kiss. I feel drugged by her, helpless to resist her siren's lure.

I slam into her, rougher than before. I want to bend her over and fuck her from behind, driving deep and hard into her, but I don't want to break our connection. I'm about to come and I'll be fucked if I do it anywhere but inside Taran.

She takes my bruising thrusts and screams for more, clutching me against her. I crush her to my chest and bury my tongue deep into her mouth just as I bury my cock as far as it'll go inside her. Orgasm rips through me, shuddering down my spine, gripping my balls and soaring through every part of me. I come inside her, pumping semen with each thrust. Satisfaction rides me hard as I mark her.

When I finally stop, I realize she's clinging weakly to me, relying on me to hold her up. I walk toward the cot, slide myself gently from her body and lower her onto the bed. I follow her down, holding her against me with an arm wrapped around her stomach. I slide my other arm under her head, cushioning her neck.

After our breathing evens out she murmurs, "Are you mad at me for coming up here?"

"No," I say in her ear. "This is your home now, Taran. You're free to explore and make yourself comfortable."

"But you seemed angry when you saw me and grabbed me." She passes over my statement that this is her home now.

I sigh deeply, my breath moving the hair on the back of her head. "You unbalance me, Taran. I have a little trouble controlling my emotions around you."

"I'm... sorry," she whispers.

"Don't be, I welcome this feeling." I harden my voice so she knows I'm serious. "Having someone I care enough to protect within these city walls will motivate me to work harder, create a home where you'll be safe."

She rolls toward me a little, looking over her shoulder, her grey eyes stormy and enigmatic. "Do you mean that?"

"Of course." I tighten my arm around her waist and drop a kiss against the back of her shoulder.

"What about my happiness, Diogo?" she murmurs. "Does that matter to you?"

I don't answer right away. Can't. We both know that she's asked a complicated question. That my needs and desires will clash with what she wants. I search within myself and find that I don't like the idea of her unhappiness. Not if there's anything I can do to remedy the situation.

I answer slowly. "In time, happiness will come to you, Taran. I'll make sure of it."

She seems to think this over, a tiny frown puckering her

forehead. She nods slowly, "I don't know why I believe you, but I do."

"Because I don't speak of things I have no intention of doing."

She flashes a smile and my heart stutters in response. Her smile lights up her face, already flushed from sex, making her more beautiful in that moment than I could've imagined. Her hair is a chaotic auburn halo around her head. The impact of her wild beauty is such that I find myself memorizing every part of her and filing it away for when we're inevitably parted by work or other commitments. Though I'll likely find a way to keep her as close as possible until this intense obsession wanes a little.

"And what about your happiness, Diogo?" she asks hesitantly.

A glow spreads through me that she cares enough to ask. I could be just a captor to her, just the man that fucks her until she finds a way to leave. Instead, she's making an effort to get to know me. The man inside the Warlord.

Instead of answering I kiss her. We've barely known each other two days. I can't tell her that I truly suspect my happiness lies entirely with her. That I was the walking dead before she woke something within me, bringing it alive. Now my heart beats for her and my happiness is tied to hers.

But this emotion is too intense, too soon to burden her with. So I say, "You don't need to worry about me, Taran."

She sighs and rolls away. I suspect she's looking out at the horizon. The top of the wall is barely visible from our vantage point, but beyond that, the Santa Catalina mountain range lays long and majestic, a shimmering mirage in the dying evening light.

We lay that way for a long time, relaxed, pressed

together on the small cot. When her breath becomes even, gusting against the arm propping her head up, I think she's fallen asleep. Then she speaks, her voice small and lost.

"Did you name me after your Wren? Did you always intend this? To bring me here and make me your wife?"

He doesn't answer for a long time and I think he either didn't hear me or doesn't want to. Then he says, "No."

"Seems odd that you have a desert wren in your possession at the same time as you captured another and forced her into a cage."

He stiffens against my back and I worry that I've offended him. Still, I'm not one to let uncomfortable truths die.

"Coincidence." The tone of his voice is a warning that I shouldn't push anymore.

Of course, I push. I roll over to face him and push up on my elbow. I'm halfway draped across him, my legs tangling with his. He's so big he takes up almost all of the cot.

"Do you intend to let her and the chicks go once they hatch?" I demand.

"Of course," he says, and the growl in his voice suggests I've offended him.

But I know him, have watched him rule this city for as long as I've been here. He doesn't let his citizens make choices for themselves. He's decided a dictatorship will serve them best. I don't believe that he's going to just let those birds fly free. "And you'll let the hatchlings learn to fly on their own? Even if she pushes them off the roof before they're ready to go?"

"Taran," he snaps.

"The answer is important to me, Diogo." I press my hand against his chest. "Please?"

He sighs and shoves a hand through his hair, nearly toppling me over with his elbow. "I'll block the section of the greenhouse she leaves through when they're ready to fly. She can teach them using the shelves in there."

"Those aren't high enough!" I protest. "They won't learn properly."

"They'll have to make do." He sounds annoyed now.

"And once you decide they can fly, you'll open the greenhouse and let them go?" I persist.

"Yes, that was always my intention, Taran. Even before I met you."

I shove away from him and stand, pushing his shirt down my thighs so I feel less exposed. "Not good enough, Diogo," I say passionately. "You can't cage a wild animal and expect them to understand freedom when it comes. They'll die in the wild if they don't learn properly."

He sits up, studying me. Despite his casual posture I know how fast he can move when he's motivated. I take a few steps back.

"You can't cage her. She won't thank you. More than likely she'll kill herself trying to escape. You're far better off just providing her sanctuary while allowing her the freedom to live the way she's meant to."

"And what if she dies?"

"That's a risk I'm willing to take."

He stands, steps right up to me and says, "Well I'm not."

He takes hold of my arm and pulls me toward the door of the building, slamming it ominously behind us.

Two flawless days together have convinced me of one thing; I'm in imminent danger of falling in love with the enemy.

Diogo has shown me what happiness can look like. Not the fleeting happiness of eating something rare and delicious. Not the unsubstantial happiness of a sunrise over the desert. It's not even the moment of deep satisfaction when I lead refugees to safety and find them Sanctuary. It's not the feelings I had for my family, that constant feeling of comfort, knowing that I'm loved unconditionally.

No, this is something different, something more. This feeling is far more dangerous. It's sharp, terrifying, almost painful, but utterly exhilarating. It's something I've never really experienced in this desperate life of survival. Of watching each day pass with the relentless gnawing feeling that death is just around the corner.

Hope. I feel hope for myself, for the future. It's like standing on a ledge and reaching out for something that I know could hurt me but is completely worth the risk.

I study Diogo where he sits across from me. We're on the roof sitting cross-legged, both of our arms elbow deep in soil that he's had stored for planting more of his precious seeds. He's showing me how to grow plants from seeds. I'm enjoying the sensation of the rich, moist dirt sifting through my fingers. I've never really liked dirt before. Everything is dusty in our desert Sanctuary. It gets in the hair, teeth, clothes. It coats every surface where windows aren't available to keep it out. It creeps, encroaches on everything. But this dirt is different. It'll nurture life, help create the food we need to survive.

Diogo is looking more relaxed these past two days. We've avoided discussing his position in the city and my objections to that position. We've insulated ourselves from the world and created a safe haven for just the two of us. I should be planning my escape, a future without him. I should be pushing him to give me information on his military and their movements. But the truth is I don't want to know. I'm content just taking this time out. I've never done anything like this. I've never taken even a single day to myself. The slowing down of time is a precious feeling so I'm taking this fleeting moment of happiness and squeezing it to my chest. Sharing it with Diogo, my husband.

"Now you dig a little well in the centre of the soil," he explains patiently, lifting my hand from where I'd buried it deep into the warm, slightly damp dirt. He shapes my fingers into a little bowl and then cups his big hand around mine. He turns our hands over and digs at the dirt, creating a hole.

My breath catches at the exquisite feeling of his touch. Those long, skilled fingers slipping between mine, guiding my hand with gentle precision. I shiver as an image of him running his hands down my body floods my mind. His touch is possessive but also tender when he explores each curve, taps his fingers against my ribs and hipbones, dips his tongue into my ears, my navel, the arch of my foot, everything… as he learns every facet. He's even explored my knees and my toes, explaining that he wants to know every part as intimately as he knows himself.

"Yesterday we dug rows in the dirt," I say, my voice husky and my face flushing with the after-effects of memory. "Why are we digging a well today?"

He flashes me a smile. I suspect that Diogo doesn't smile. I've certainly never seen it on the rare occasions I've seen him at a public ceremony. Grim lines fan out from his lips and eyes, marking the fierce seriousness that he's become known for. Yet, over the past couple of days, his beautiful, hard lips have stretched more and more, tilting upward at one corner. Just for me.

"Yesterday we were planting carrots. Today we're planting something different. Your favourite."

"Tomatoes!" I exclaim, grinning at him.

"Tomatoes," he agrees.

I feel happiness as I finish digging the little well and then watch as he places a couple of seeds in the dirt. Then he reaches across the pot, takes my hand in his and uses my fingers to cover the tiny seeds, or 'put them to bed' as he calls it.

"This plant is yours now." He strokes the back of my dirty hand with his long, soil-covered fingers, sending sparks shooting through my veins. I cling to each precious word. "You'll take care of it, Taran. You'll water it each morning first thing, and then again before bed. Maybe more if it's a hot day. You don't want the soil to get too dry or it'll become hostile to your seedling. It won't grow as big or strong as you want it to."

"Like children," I murmur.

"Or any living creature. We all need sun, water and air to survive."

I can feel the light dimming from my eyes and I look away. "We also need food, Diogo. Not just one or two sectors, but all of us."

"Don't," he says, his fingers tightening around mine, refusing to let me go.

I try to crush the desperate feeling rising up inside me. I suspect we're reaching the end of our truce, but before we can ruin the serenity with a fight, Garrett crashes through the door, throwing it back until it cracks against the wall. I flinch back, expecting an attack while Diogo reaches for his knife, which is lying on the ground beside us. I barely have time to blink and Diogo is on his feet, standing protectively in front of me, the knife held out in front of him, low and ready to take out an intruder.

"Commander, your radio!" Garrett gasps, trying to catch his breath.

"Left it inside," Diogo growls. "What's going on?"

"Primitives," he says grimly. "Inside the city. Moving around the West side of the wall, toward the slums."

"Fuck!" Diogo snarls. "There're thousands of people packed into the slums. If we have a Primitive outbreak over there, the city could fall."

I sit crouched on my hands and knees, stunned by this news. In the years that I've been in this Sanctuary I've never known Primitives to be able to get through the wall and inside the city. Despite his harsh method of leadership, Diogo has to be commended for his ability to keep the walls strong and the Primitives out.

"Tell Jorje I'll meet him at checkpoint 37 outside the western sector. I'll be there in ten minutes. If his team arrives before mine he's to engage immediately. They are to exterminate any Primitives on site." Diogo doesn't say a word to me as he follows Garrett through the door and back inside the building. I leap to my feet and follow them down the steps, my bare feet slapping against the concrete as I run after them.

"Where do you want me, Commander?"

When we enter the apartment, Diogo goes straight for his weapons locker. "Stay here," he says gruffly. "If anyone but me enters this suite you have my permission to take them out."

Garrett falls silent, but I see his expression. He's disappointed that he won't get to join the Warlord for this battle.

Diogo pulls weapons from his locker including a sidearm, a rifle and a bullet belt. I swallow as he pulls a heavy coat on and begins strapping his array of weapons to his belt. He slings the rifle over his back crossing the strap over his chest. His gaze flickers up to mine as though he can hear my silent screams of fear and anxiety.

I know it's pointless, but still I say, "Take me with you, I can help."

He turns away, striding toward the door, completely ignoring my plea.

"Diogo!" I beg.

He pauses before swinging the door open and glances back at me.

"I lived in the slums, I know them. Those are my people, my friends," I cry desperately. "I can help! I'm trained with most weapons and I'm accurate with a rifle."

He says nothing as his eyes travel down my body. I'm wearing a small shirt and a pair of pants, both perfectly fitted to my frame and made of good quality material. I'd checked the stitching when he first presented the clothing to me, it was perfectly even, made by a sewing machine.

Such machinery is a luxury, so he must've had the clothes specially designed. His eyes stop on my bare feet and his face softens for just a second.

"Please, Diogo," I beg. I can't stand the thought of my friends being in danger. Or of him being hurt. I feel this driving need to watch over him, protect him as he rushes into battle.

His eyes flash back up and his face is wiped of all expression, serious and stony once more. Wordlessly he leaves. I stare after him, fighting the urge to follow, knowing he would just send me back or Garrett would stop me from going.

As if sensing my feelings, Garrett comes to stand next to me, placing his hand on my shoulder. I look at him, surprised. Diogo would cut that hand off if he saw it on anywhere near me, let alone touching a part of me. Still, I sense only the desire to comfort.

"He's good at his job, Taran, he'll come back." He gives my shoulder a squeeze before letting go and stepping back a safe distance.

"And my friends? What about them?" I ask, a shiver running through my words.

Garrett doesn't respond.

TWENTY-THREE
TARAN

Four hours later and Diogo is still gone. I'm worried sick and pacing the floor round and round the table. Garrett hasn't moved from where he stationed himself at the door. His sharp eyes flick from the door to me as I move past. He hasn't tried to comfort me since Diogo left, hasn't said a word. Finally, I decide that pacing isn't doing any good and turn toward the stairs up to the roof. Just as I reach them though, Diogo comes through the entrance.

"Leave," he growls at Garrett, who immediately disappears through the still open door.

"Diogo!" I gasp, hurling toward him.

I stop short of throwing myself at him though. I'm still not so comfortable with him that I'm willing to initiate physical contact. I edge around him so I can look at him while he pulls off his rifle, unbuckles his weapons belt and drops it on the table. He's splattered in blood again, this time across his upper body and neck.

"Blood," I say dismally.

He doesn't look at me. He unclips his coat and shrugs out of it, draping it over the back of a chair. He bends to examine it, as though trying to decide how to get the blood out. Although, I'm starting to suspect this man knows how to deal with blood if the past week is anything to go by.

"Whose blood?" I demand, taking hold of his elbow and trying to turn him to face me.

He straightens to his full height and looks down at me. Standing this close, his icy demeaner separating us emotionally, he seems enormous. The muscles of his arm ripple as he flexes and looks down to where my fingers are uselessly tugging on him. Still he doesn't say anything to me, just eyes me with a gaze that feels like being stabbed by obsidian chips. After the intimacy we've shared I'd hoped for more.

"Zombie?" I persist, the word accidentally slipping out.

Out of respect, the people that are taken by the Primitive disease are known only as Primitives, but for years now, since the first outbreak, the urban legend swirling around the living is that they're zombies. The living dead. They have all of the characteristics. The flesh rots on their bones, their personalities are erased and replaced with mindless obsession, the driving hunger. And lastly, the ease in which the disease is passed from one person to the next through a bite.

"Don't say that word again," Diogo says coldly, stepping back, away from me.

It hurts that he won't touch me, won't talk to me. For two days he couldn't keep his hands off me, acted like a man that couldn't get enough. Yet now I get the distinct feeling he wants space.

"Is it primitive blood?" I persist.

"Why do you need to know so badly?" he asks sharply.

I stare at him. He's holding something back, something he doesn't want to tell me. That's why he's putting distance between us. "Diogo," I snap. "Whose fucking blood?"

"Human," he growls, his gaze dropping away.

My mouth falls open. He killed a human? But how? He went out with the intention of ridding the city of the Primitives. Now he's telling me a human was injured.

"One of your men?" I ask, gentling my voice. There's always a possibility when he and his men deploy that there might be loss of life. It can't be easy.

"Civilian," he answers, crushing my theory.

"How?" I cry.

"She was attacked, bitten." His voice is low, tired. "I had to put her down. It was kinder than leaving her to turn. I'm wearing her blood because I stayed with her through the end."

Shock courses through me. "Who was she?" I ask quietly.

"I don't know," he admits. "Someone from the slums. In the wrong place at the wrong time."

I hate his answer. It's too careless, doesn't hold enough account of the loss of individual life. It doesn't matter that he stopped long enough to see her death out to the end. He killed her. Killed a woman without a name. Maybe a friend. Maybe Emery. My gut twists at the thought of my dear friend dead.

"What did she look like? 50ish? Long gray hair. Curly. Blue eyes? Maybe wearing a knit hat." I ask hoarsely.

His eyes sharpen on me. "Who are you describing, Taran?" he demands.

"Just tell me!" I hiss angrily, curling my hands into fists.

"No, she wasn't the person you're describing. This woman was younger, blonde."

My shoulders slump in relief and I rub a hand over my face. I feel almost as exhausted as Diogo looks. I'm happy that the woman he killed isn't Emery, but the gulf between us seems to be growing as part of my heart remains in the slums with the city's poor, refugees and rebels.

"Don't," Diogo mirrors the same word he used right before Garrett interrupted us with news of the Primitive attack.

I shake my head and look at him sadly. "Even if I didn't know her, she was still human, Diogo. She was still a desperate woman in desperate circumstances that didn't deserve to die."

"I didn't attack her," he snaps, frowning at me.

"No, but you finished her," I say tiredly.

"I did what I had to do."

"Why did you have to do it?" I demand.

I know I'm not being totally reasonable. That we have to kill the Primitives before they can kill us, and that taking out a human who will most likely turn is more humane than leaving them to experience the gut-wrenching agony of having their body transform into the living dead. Once the transformation happens they'll still have to die. But logic has no place in my heart. I'm sickened by the idea of Primitives getting in the city, running amok through the slums, Diogo following close behind, cutting down the zombies and my friends alike.

He doesn't answer my question. Instead he watches me closely and says, "Why are you so upset, Taran? There are hundreds of thousands of people in this city. The likelihood of you knowing that woman is slim."

"What if it was me?" I finally cry out. "It easily could've been. I crawl and climb all over this city, but especially through the slums. I'm also particularly fond of the wall where they would've come in. They could've easily found me alone and attacked."

His expression softens to one of understanding and I

almost hate him for it. I don't want his understanding. I want to know that we're going to be okay, that we might still have the future I was envisioning a few short hours ago.

"You will never be that vulnerable again, Taran," he tries to reassure me. "That'll never be you."

"You can't know that!" I snap, pacing back a few steps. "You can't predict everything. What happens if the city is overrun? If Garrett is attacked and taken down, and I'm left on my own to face a horde. What if I'm bitten?"

"Stop it," he says sharply, reaching for me.

I step back again. "Just tell me, would you kill me?"

"Taran!" He says my name sharply.

I want to ask him more questions, figure out what makes him tick. Figure out why I'm different to him. But he takes hold of my shoulders and kisses me, slanting his mouth over mine. At first, I think he's trying to shut me up, maybe punish me for badgering him with difficult questions, but then he's lifting me, crushing me against him, his hands roving over my back, up and under my shirt.

The feel of those broad hands against my skin is like a match to parchment. I come alive, my desperate need for him matching his for me. He lays me back on the table, tugging my arms over my head so he can reach down and drag my shirt up my torso, then up my arms and off my body. His lips find mine in another intense kiss while his fingers search out the buttons on my pants, fumbling them open before dragging the fabric down my legs.

He doesn't get undressed, doesn't explore my skin with his lips as he's been doing the past few days. He tears open his own jeans, drags me to the edge of the table, pushes my legs wide and slams into me. I gasp and reach blindly for his shoulders as his big body forges a path through my soft, slightly damp passage. I'm not nearly wet enough for this rough entry. Yet something about his desperation calls to me.

I lift my legs and bring my knees up, tucking them under his arms. I reach for him, beckoning him down to me. He drops his shoulders until I'm able to clutch them and pull myself up against him, fitting myself to his body and pressing my lips against his.

The touch of my mouth slows him down. He responds to the tentative thrust of my tongue, easing himself from my body before thrusting forward, his cock finding easier passage this time. Instead of pain I feel only pleasure as he fills me, sparking my nerve endings. Soon I'm writhing against him, bucking my hips in an effort to rub my clit against the thick hair of his groin. He realizes what I'm doing and presses me back against the table. Licking his fingers he reaches between our bodies and starts stroking my clit with hard, even strokes until I'm crying out on the table and gripping fistfuls of my own hair.

"Come for me, Taran," he growls.

"Yes, yes," I pant, undulating my hips in an attempt to take more of his cock, fill my body with more of the delicious pressure. "I want to come!"

"Now, baby, do it for me now."

His words are a powerful aphrodisiac that sizzles right through me, taking me over the edge. I cry out and arch my back, panting as I ride the crest of an orgasm. He takes his fingers from my clit, grips my hips and drags me just over the edge of the table, slamming his cock so deep into my body that I shriek and come again, exploding as he takes his own pleasure, fucking me until he's spent. Until his seed shoots deep into my body, bathing the walls of my vagina.

I've barely started to come down from the high of two incredible orgasms when he picks me up off the table, holds me tight against his chest and strides toward the bedroom. I murmur a weak protest at being moved that he completely ignores. After depositing me in the bed, he stands back and removes his own clothes. I watch greedily as he reveals a broad chest and shoulders, a trim waist and hard muscles.

"Stay here." He leaves the room, returning after a moment with an open can of peaches and a fork.

I smile happily. Despite my earlier angst, Diogo is back to treating me like his cherished wife. He seems to anticipate all my needs. He understands my need to eat more often than is strictly necessary. I'm still not used to having food at my disposal, I want it near all the time. Want my belly as full as I can get it.

As if reading my mind, he forks up a peach and guides it to my mouth, holding the can underneath to catch the excess juice. I bite into the sweet fruit, moaning as the delicious tang explodes on my tongue. I don't know if I'll ever get used to canned peaches or if they'll remain my favourite. Along with tomatoes, of course. Diogo slides in next to me on the bed, propping himself against our pillows and laying his head next to mine. He takes a big bite of peach and then feeds me next. I eat enthusiastically.

Finally, when the can is empty and we're both sated, he sets it aside and gathers me against his chest. I yawn sleepily, my eyes fluttering closed against his skin. He pets my head, running his fingers over my hair.

"Diogo?" I murmur, not opening my eyes.

His hand stills. "Yes?"

"Will you find out who she was? If she had any family?"

I wait anxiously for his answer, not lifting my head, not looking at his expression. Finally, he answers. "Yes, Taran, I'll find her."

"Thank you," I whisper, feeling safe once more.

TWENTY-FOUR

DIOGO

I lean back in my chair, tossing the file folder on the table in front of me. Nestled inside is the brief history of a woman who was once faceless to me but will now haunt my memory. And deservedly so. I am the last person she saw before she closed her eyes forever. I will honour her with remembrance. For Taran. And maybe for myself.

Victoria Greystone. Blond hair, blue eyes.

Twenty-seven years old. Married to Alphonse Rodriguez. Two children registered to the couple. Mary Rodriguez, 5, and Sebastian Rodriguez, 7.

She lived in sector six near the West wall. I found out from her grieving husband that, on the day of her death, she was gathering herbs along the wall. Plant-life tend to grow rampant up the wall and in abandoned buildings and, despite the danger of crumbling structures, people will enter the buildings or climb sections of the wall in search of their next meal.

I feel relief, while studying Victoria's profile, to discover that neither she nor her husband were illegal. Both had sanctioned entrance into the city. It would be a shame to deport her husband immediately after he lost his wife.

When I go home that evening I don't discuss the things I learned about Victoria with Taran, and she doesn't ask. She seems content in her belief that I'll do as I say and I'm pleased that she's come to this conclusion. She wanted me to know about the woman I was forced to kill. Wanted me to feel the loss of Victoria's life. I'm not sure if I understand entirely why, but I'm not disappointed with the knowledge I've gained.

Usually I distance myself from the victims. Whether they're Primitives, illegals, criminals, or, like Victoria, a victim of circumstance. I don't need to know who they are or what makes them tick. I've been content with my life the way it is for a long time. But there's something about Taran that's opened me up. She wants me to appreciate life, and I want to see life through her eyes. If this is the way to do it then I'm willing.

When the Desert Wren first hit my radar she was simply a fly to swat. A criminal that would eventually be caught and brought to justice. Then, gradually, as I heard of her exploits, my admiration grew. I tried to work out how she was committing these crimes, and more importantly, why? She persisted on an altruistic path that could only end in her death, either through the dangers of climbing the wall, wandering the desert, or by execution. Yet she got nothing out of saving refugees. Nothing that I could understand anyway.

But now, as I learn about Victoria and her life, rather than just remaining with the brief glimpse of her death, I'm starting to understand. To Taran, these are individuals. Not just citizens. Everyone has a story and in their own way, each story is beautiful. Deserves to be given the chance to flourish instead of cut off in death.

Though I understand Taran's point of view, I'm not sure if I'm ready to embrace it. I need the distance between myself and the citizens of Sanctuary so I can effectively do my job. If I worry over every individual I won't be able to protect them all.

Yet, Taran believes this way of thinking is flawed. She does care about each individual, yet she's brought many, many people into the city illegally. She's provided food and shelters for legions. Perhaps she's succeeded where I've failed.

"Diogo?"

Her soft voice reaches through the darkness, sleepy and confused. I left our bed, bothered by these thoughts and made my way up to the roof.

"Over here, baby."

She makes her way slowly to the cot where I'm sitting, facing the city, watching the glow of the few lanterns still visible in buildings throughout mine and the neighboring sectors. I hold my arms out to her and she sinks down onto my lap, curling up like a small animal and burrowing against the warm shelter of my chest.

I wonder if she'll ask me what I'm doing, why I made my way up to the roof alone in the dark. She surprises me by saying, "Do you know what tomorrow is, Diogo?"

I frown into the shadows, searching my brain for the answer she's looking for. Her birthday? No, she told officers during her initial intake that it was April 27th. Her intake date was March 3rd.

"Sorry, sweetheart," I murmur against the top of her head.

She tips her head back and looks up at me, her eyes sparkling in the darkness. "Tomorrow is November 2nd."

Ah, yes. An important date for the citizens of New Tucson Sanctuary. The day they acknowledge and celebrate the passing of their loved ones. "Day of the dead."

"Yes," she says, her voice strengthening. "I need to go, Diogo."

I'm amused that she thinks she would be allowed to go, with or without my permission. The only way she leaves this apartment tomorrow is with me at her back. "I don't go," I say bluntly.

"Just because you never have doesn't mean you shouldn't go, Diogo." Her voice is cajoling, and I feel myself weakening. In our brief time together Taran hasn't asked me for anything that wasn't important to her.

"I won't be welcome," I warn her.

Though I can't see her grin, I can feel it.

"We'll wear masks. Lots of people dress up for the Day of the Dead," she says excitedly. "No one will recognize you. Please, Diogo, I've never missed it. I need to do it for my lost loved ones."

"Alright," I capitulate, wondering how many weapons I can fit on my person without raising suspicion.

Tomorrow, we're going to party with the dead.

The evening shadows flicker and dance in the candlelight surrounding Taran as she bends over the desk I found for her, putting the final touches on her mask. She looks both hauntingly beautiful and macabre. She used a combination of charcoal and white and red paints to create a skeletal look. A thick layer of black surrounds her eyes, followed by white to represent the skull and red for her lips. She painted a small heart on her cheek.

"Beautiful," I say, walking further into the room. She smiles into the mirror as I approach and drop a kiss onto her head.

She turns in her seat to look up and me and gasps, jumping back. I grab her arm before she tumbles out of the seat and steady her.

"Diogo!" she says aghast, half reaching up toward my face. "Is it real?"

What she's seeing is a war mask. The top facial half of a skull; twisted, pierced, grooved and ravaged by time. Fifty years ago my grandfather killed the Primitive it belonged to, one of the first to arrive in North America. The first skull of many my grandfather took. The first Diogo Fuentes, named after a Spanish conquistador, had been a General in the Mexican military before the fall of the Americas. My father told me that the General killed himself rather than risk turning after he'd been attacked by a Primitive. But there were no witnesses to the incident so it's more likely he'd been turned and spent his final years roaming the Yucatan with his horde.

"Yes, it's real," I tell her.

She stands, staring up at me in wonder and fear. She reaches up to run her fingers over the cheekbones and teeth. "Yes, I can see now. The pitting where he stabbed himself in the face, piercing the bone." If a person survives the brutality of a Primitive attack long enough to turn it's common for the first person they attack to be themselves. "The poor man."

I grunt my disdain. The Primitive that'd owned this skull had been among the first. The ones responsible for many deaths, for taking down an entire dominant civilization. I won't feel sorry for such a creature.

"He was human, Diogo," she says chidingly, divining my thoughts. "He had a family, people who cared about him and who he cared about. Please, have some respect for the dead. That's what this day is about. Paying our respects."

"Once they've turned they're no longer human, Taran. I lose all respect for them. They're simply targets."

She gasps angrily and pokes her finger into my chest. The gesture is cute on someone her size. "They are our family, Diogo! They didn't choose the bite, nor the terrible things that happen to them after. Their flesh being torn and stripped from their bones, their bodies desecrated..." She shudders as her voice drifts off.

"You've seen them, haven't you, baby?" I ask, lowering my voice. "Up close."

She nods and lets out a choking sound. "Yes. We saw a horde when we were following the last survivors down from Old Canada. They were everywhere. We were forced to hide under the ashes of a burnt-out cabin, wait them out. It took days. The things I saw, Diogo. It's haunted my dreams from that moment on."

My heart goes out to the young Taran who witnessed disgusting acts of cannibalism, sex, and murder. Primitive's revert back to their most primitive behaviour, which creates a mess of impulsive, angry beasts with one goal. The next victim. The next meal.

I run my hand down her hair, cupping the back of her neck and pulling her against me. "You have a big heart if you're able to forgive the same animals that took your youth."

She presses her face into my chest for a moment, before looking up at me. "There's nothing to forgive. They're a shadow of their former selves. They deserve pity and remembrance. Not disdain."

I rub my thumb under her cheekbone, blending in a smear of charcoal where she'd rubbed it against my chest. "I have to kill them, Taran. It's easier for me if I don't treat them like humans."

She studies me in the firelight, her head tipped back, rich auburn hair waving down her back. "You're much different than I imagined you'd be, Diogo. You have a conscience."

I don't tell her that she's become my conscience. That without her I can't feel. Instead I hold her against me for several long minutes, enjoying the sensation of such an exquisite creature in my arms. Finally, I let her go. "It's time to leave, especially since we're walking. The procession will be starting."

Taran had insisted we leave my jeep behind, saying it would be too recognizable. She doesn't want me discovered at this sacred event. Not when I've been responsible for some of the deaths being celebrated today. My heart warms for her even more with every moment of thoughtfulness she directs toward me.

She nods and reaches for the notes we'd made earlier. Little scraps of paper, each representative of our dead. She has a whole pile of them. I have one. Paper is difficult to come by, but somehow the celebrants of the Day of the Dead always manage to scrounge some. Us included.

We step out the door and I'm surprised to see many of my neighbors taking to the streets, masks in place, dark clothing draping their bodies. "I didn't know people from this sector join the activities."

Taran nods and tugs me in the direction of the nearest checkpoint, following a group of people that look to be some of my soldiers.

"Even elites have lost loved ones," she says. "This is a day for everyone, regardless of fortune."

A few minutes later, as we reach the first checkpoint I see a throng of people slowed down by the city police checking their papers. I frown as we're forced to wait for several minutes. It's possible that we'll miss some of the event. Then it occurs to me that the more crowded sectors will be even worse.

I take Taran's hand and pull her out of the line, striding with her toward the front. "No, Diogo!" she hisses. "They'll know who you are."

I ignore her as I approach the policeman. Just as he

reaches for the papers of the next person in line, I push myself through and step in front of him.

"Hey," he snaps. "Get back in line."

I stare icily down at him, my eyes no doubt glinting behind the mask. He shifts uneasily and takes the papers I hand out to him. He glances down and then goes sheet white. His head snaps up, he gives the papers back and stammers, "Commander, I'm sorry, I had no idea..."

"I want you to open these gates." I cut him off impatiently. "And once you do that, you'll radio to the other checkpoints and tell them to open up, on my authority."

The man's mouth hangs open for a second before he snaps it shut. "But Commander, how will we check identities and track movement?"

"You won't," I tell him. "Tonight, you let everyone through. You can close the gates again after midnight and ask for papers then."

The man nods his understanding and waves us through. He stops the people right after us so he can unlock the gate and call out to the crowd, letting them know they're free to proceed.

Taran slides her hand across my arm and rests it at the elbow, allowing me to lead her forward, toward the main city gates. "That was a generous gesture, Diogo," she murmurs from beside me, gripping a handful of the long black coat I'd insisted she wear. There's no disguising her tiny stature, but I'm hoping that obscuring her figure and face will make her completely unrecognizable. "You know you'll be giving the refugees, the city's undocumented, free passage?"

"This is a day for everyone," I say, repeating her words.

Giving the refugees free passage is well worth the skeletal grin she bestows on me and the tightening of her fingers against my arm. "Soon we'll have you switching sides."

"Over my dead body," I tell her, putting my hand over hers and trapping it against my arm.

"I hope not," she whispers, her voice all but carried away on the evening breeze.

We pass through one more checkpoint before reaching the heart of the city, the main gates. This checkpoint is wide open, allowing all citizens to pass through freely. The closer we get to the gate, the thicker the crowd, but it's definitely moving forward, everyone keeping a respectful order. We join the procession as it heads toward the burning pyre; a wooden tower built next to the gate.

Heat blasts us as we take our turn stepping up to it. I let Taran's hand go and press her to go ahead of me, my hand at her back. She steps away and tosses her handful of paper into the flames, watching solemnly as they burn. She turns away and steps to the side, rejoining the procession as it heads back into the city. After the last person has given up their dead, the city gates will open for just a moment, taking away the ash into the desert.

I step forward and drop my paper, watching as the breeze picks it up, tosses it and then throws it into the dancing flames.

"I'm sorry," I say, turning away as the flames seize Victoria Greystone's name, burning it to ash.

TWENTY-SIX

TARAN

A sob catches in my throat and I'm blinded by tears as I toss the names of my loved ones into the fire. For the first time since arriving in Sanctuary I've released my grandparents. It was too hard to admit that they'd died out there in the desert or in the mountains so I'd hung on to them, even as hope dwindled. I'd climbed the wall and snuck refugees in, searching each face for the dear ones that haunted my dreams. But now, on this Day of the Dead, I'm ready to let them go.

I sniff and swipe at the tears gathering on my lower lids before they can fall down my cheeks and ruin my makeup. I glance over my shoulder, searching for Diogo's towering form, but the crowd has swallowed me up and pushed me along, making space for the others that still need to burn their dead.

I open my mouth to call out for him, knowing that he'll be freaking out when he realizes he can't see me. But before I can shout I'm grabbed by the arm and pulled through the crowd. I yelp as my foot tangles in some debris, but before I can go down, strong arms clasp me under my armpits and I'm dragged back up.

"Be careful!" A voice snaps before the hand yanks me into the alleyway of a nearby building.

"Xavier!" I gasp.

He doesn't say anything, just continues to pull me through the dark alleyway before stopping. I open my mouth to speak, to ask him how he's doing and what he's doing, when he slams me against a wall. I hit so hard that the breath is knocked out of me and I collapse forward. He catches me and pins me against the wall making a sound of annoyance.

"What...?" I gasp, trying to catch my breath.

"You married the fucking enemy, Taran!" he snarls in my face, shaking me hard. "What the fuck are you thinking? He's going to kill you, kill us all, and you *marry* him? You were supposed to be our spy."

I gape at him, unable to form a coherent response. I've seen him giving passionate speeches, seen him mildly annoyed when a follower doesn't follow his command to the letter, but I've never seen him this wildly angry. I'm saved the need to say anything though, when a woman's voice reaches us through the darkness.

"Xavier! You put that girl down right this instant."

Xavier lets go of me and I sink to the ground as Emery rushes over and wraps an arm around me. I stare at her shadowy face for a moment, taking in the delicate skull she's painted on. Then I throw my arms around her and hug her tight. "Emery!"

"Now you remember us," Xavier growls bitterly from beside us.

"Oh, hush," Emery snaps, cradling me against her. "You

know as well as I do that Taran had no choice in her marriage to Commander Fuentes. Women are property in this godforsaken Sanctuary."

"She doesn't have to enjoy it."

"Stop it!" I hiss up at him. "And keep your voice down. If Diogo finds you here with me he'll kill both of you without even pausing for an arrest."

"A bit possessive, is he?" Xavier mocks. He's not even bothering to disguise the bitterness in his voice. Is he jealous? That would be ridiculous though, he never bothered with me before. He barely stopped long enough to pay attention when I was his wife, standing next to him, and that was only when I was doing something pertaining to the rebellion.

"Yes, he is," I say hotly. "And protective. He'd be furious if he knew someone grabbed me and dragged me into a dirty, dark alley and then slammed me against a wall."

Xavier takes a step toward us and then lowers himself into a crouch. His eyes are glittering like hard jewels as he says, "You're fucking the enemy while your people are dying. You were sent in with a mission and you're failing. Our new people smuggler damn near got caught. Alonso failed in his attempt to take your place and bring refugees through. He barely got away with his skin and the refugees were turned away at the gates."

I gasp in denial as his harsh words batter me. But he's right. I've been enjoying my time with Diogo while my friends have been suffering at the very hands that caress my skin and bring me alive. Still, I'm a single person, not a saint or a martyr.

"I'm sorry, Xavier, I never intended any of this."

Before he can respond, Emery interrupts, taking my

face in her hands and turning it toward hers. "Of course you didn't, love. None of this is your fault. And despite what Xavier says, you aren't responsible for every living person begging for a place Sanctuary."

I smile and say, "Thank you, Emery." I take one of her hands from my face and squeeze it. "I want you to know that I haven't forgotten. I'm still just as much a rebel as ever. But I'm working on the inside now."

"Good," Xaxier snaps. "We finally get something that makes sense. What do you have? Military movements, police reports? What does Fuentes have planned for the city?"

"I'm sorry, Xaiver. I have no intention of spying on him. Besides, he won't give me any of that information. He's not an idiot."

"Then what fucking use are you?" Xavier snaps. He stands and paces away from me.

I stand with him, Emery's arms falling away from me. I follow him as he walks deeper into the alley. "I can work on him, Xavier. I can change his mind about the refugees. I can convince him to open checkpoints and relax his guard when it comes to the citizens. He's not a bad person. He'll come around."

Xavier whips around and grabs me by the shoulders. "You think so?" He lowers his face to mine, his breath punching my lips with each word. "He killed one of us. Walked bold as day into the slums and stabbed her through the heart, then cut her head off."

I flinch in his hold as I hear the brutal truth but I lift my head and stare back at him, holding my ground. "I already know. He told me. She'd been bitten."

That shuts Xavier up. His hands dig into me until finally he thrusts me away. "She could've been saved."

"You know better than that."

"Fuck!" he shouts.

Then an answering voice shouts from close by, "Taran!"

I whirl on the spot and squint toward the head of the alley. Just as a large silhouette appears at the mouth, Emery hurtles toward us, grabbing hold of Xavier and dragging him away from me. Xavier follows her, saying to me in a low voice, "I'll be back for you, Taran. The Wren needs to rejoin her people. It's your duty, not your choice."

If there's one thing a rebel is good at, it's disappearing. They melt into the shadows well before Diogo reaches me. I stare after them, torn. Xavier is right, my duty lies with the rebellion. I was an important part and no one can do my job quite as well as I can. But I also believe I can do more at Diogo's side than standing with the opposing force and shouting at a concrete wall.

"Taran." Diogo reaches me, gripping my arm, worry saturating his voice.

"I'm alright," I say, looking up at him.

"They didn't hurt you?" he demands.

"No," I whisper. He doesn't need to know about all the grabbing Xavier did.

Diogo's voice loses the concern and ice invades his tones as he says, "Who were they?"

I think about answering, about telling him I don't know them, but Diogo is smarter than that. He's figuring out that I was brought into this alley for a reason. Diogo is persistent when he wants something, he won't give up until I tell him. So I stare silently up at him.

He doesn't say anything else, doesn't demand I talk. Instead he silently marches me through the streets. As we approach the first checkpoint he hands his papers over and snarls at the guard, "Shut them down, check all paperwork, detain anyone suspicious."

"Diogo!" I gasp as he drags me through the closing gates. "You'll trap the refugees." The men, women and children living illegally in Sanctuary will be caught up in a net. One that I caused. "Please don't do this!"

He whirls on me, taking my arms in a tight grip and dragging me up onto my toes, his skeleton face gazing furiously down at me. "Then tell me who they were, Taran. Tell me how to find them."

I gape at him. I can't do that. He'll execute Xavier if he gets his hands on him. But he'll expel any illegals that he catches tonight, ultimately sentencing them to death by turning them out of the city. He's given me an impossible choice.

When I don't give him an answer, he drops his hands from my arms, takes my hand in a tight hold and drags me the rest of the way home. He walks so fast that I have a stitch in my side by the time we reach his building. He seems to sense me slowing down and, just as we reach the first flight of stairs, swings me up into his arms. I don't really want to touch him right now, the combination of the mask and his anger searing through me. Still, I wrap my arms around his neck not wanting to fall. He climbs up all 20 floors with me held tight against his chest.

He nods at Garrett and then wordlessly enters the suite, kicking the door shut behind him. Instead of putting me down and demanding answers, like I thought he would, he carries me through to the bedroom and throws me on the bed.

I squeak as I land in a heap. He starts removing his clothes as I get warily to my knees. "What are you doing?" I ask, crawling back until I hit the headboard. I have nowhere to go, nowhere to hide. With each piece of clothing that hits the floor I feel the seething aggression pouring from him.

He doesn't answer my question. Instead he finishes disrobing, everything except the terrifying mask, and then reaches for me. I flinch away, but since I'm cornered, he easily takes hold of me and drags me to the edge of the bed. He starts removing my clothes with the same quick, easy precision he'd applied to his own.

"Diogo, no!" I slap at his hands, but he pushes them aside and continues divesting me of my clothes as easily as if I were a child.

When I'm naked and quivering on the bed, trying to cover myself, he finally pauses and looks at me. His voice is deep and cold, almost the voice of a stranger. "You are my wife, you don't say no to me."

"Diogo, please slow down," I beg, backing away from him, from the fierce monster that has possessed my husband.

He grabs hold of my ankle and flips me over onto my stomach. I'm so surprised I barely manage to catch myself, my hands underneath my shoulders, when he opens my legs wide. I try to glance over my shoulder, but before I can see what he's doing, he's on top of me. Oh god, he's going to fuck me.

I open my mouth to beg him once more to stop or at least slow down, but he enters me roughly, forcing a strangled scream from my throat. I wasn't ready for him so it hurts, but he stops when he reaches resistance. I don't know how much of him is inside me, but I'm forced to lay unmoving beneath the heavy bulk of his body as he pulls partway out and then thrusts back in.

I cry out again. My body is starting to respond, expecting joy at his hands, and easing the entry a little. It doesn't know what my brain knows. Diogo isn't trying to give me pleasure. He's fucking me because he doesn't know what else to do with me. He's furious but he can't do to me what he'd do to anyone else that denies him.

Tears gather in my eyes. "Diogo," I moan.

He keeps thrusting, forcing the entire length of his cock into me. Then he pauses, leans across my back, gathers my hair in his fist and drags my head up. "Was he your ex-husband?"

"Who?" I ask, all coherent thought out the window.

He wenches my head to the side and bites down into the back of my neck. I yell in shock as pain shoots through me. The pain recedes though and is replaced by an unexpected shot of desire. I lay unmoving, gasping, as the amazing sensations flood down from my neck, settling in my pussy. Finally, he lets go, pulling his teeth from my flesh and says in my ear, "The man you met tonight, was he your ex-husband."

"Yes!" I gasp. How did he know?

"Xavier Gunther," he snarls and thrusts hard into me, fucking me with strong, fierce strokes. I dig my fingers into the blankets underneath me and take each thrust as he forces himself into me, hitting my cervix and sending waves of pain and pleasure through me.

He slams himself home one last time, this thrust harder than any of the others, his hips slapping against my ass. I can feel the warm wetness of his seed bathing my passage. Tears leak from my eyes and drop down onto the bed as he pulls out from me. I feel bereft at the loss.

"Consider him dead."

As leader of the rebellion, Xavier was always a dead

man. But now that Diogo has focused on my ex-husband, he'll hunt him until he has nowhere to hide and he'll use the most brutal methods possible to make his vow happen. People will die. I've seen it before. This is the Diogo Fuentes everyone fears. This is the man I was too stupid to fear until now.

"Did you plan to meet him tonight?" I demand furiously, dragging pants over my legs. "Did you set this whole thing up? Convince me to take you out tonight with the intention of seeing Gunther?"

She rolls onto her back and sits up, flinching as her tender pussy touches the bed. She grabs the blanket and drags it up her chest, covering herself. Her makeup is badly smeared into a ghoulish mask that no longer resembles the sugar skull she'd painstakingly applied earlier. I ignore any guilt over her bruised flesh. She brought this on herself. She should be dead for this betrayal. Yet I can't bring myself to harm a hair on her head.

"No!" she denies vehemently. "I had no idea he'd be there." Then she pauses, thrusts a hand through her hair and looks up at me with those beautiful, haunting grey eyes. "I suppose I could've guessed he'd be there. He's attracted to crowds and he would've been on the lookout for me."

"Why?" I demand, my voice coming out in a snarl. "Why would he look for you?"

She swallows and presses herself back against the wall. I

drag the mask from my face in order to lessen some of her fear. But it's not the mask causing it. My actions have proven that she should be afraid of me.

"I was one of his best rebels," she explains. "You know that, Diogo. You knew what I did before you captured me. It's only natural for him to seek me out. Find out about my welfare, see what I – "

She cuts herself off and looks guiltily down at the bed.

"See what you've found out?" I finish for her. "Spy on me, feed information to the rebellion?"

She nods and then raises her eyes to mine. "But we both know that there was nothing to tell. We don't talk about that stuff."

I sit down on the edge of the bed, my back to her. Perhaps it's a foolish thing to do, give an enemy my back, but I can't bring myself to believe that Taran is violent. Not unless she's defending herself.

"And if you had information to give?" I ask her, not really wanting to know the answer. I don't want to hear the words of betrayal on her lips. This woman who's obsessed my mind, enslaved my body and shown me what love looks like inside myself. Yet she's right. She's a rebel, and I'm the city Warlord. We're automatic enemies.

She doesn't speak right away. I feel her shifting behind me, then the light, tentative touch of her hand sliding up my back. She places it on my shoulder and rests her head on top of it, kneeling behind me, her body pressed to mine. Warmth seeps through me, draining some of the anger.

"I don't know," she whispers honestly.

I'm satisfied with her answer. She didn't lie to me. Didn't tell me what she thought I'd want to hear. She searched inside herself and gave me her truth and though this evening has changed things between us, it has also given me a new and deeper understanding of my wife.

I take her hand from my shoulder and pull her around, twisting with her and laying her gently on the bed. I stand and blow out the candles before laying with her, holding her against my side. "Sleep, Taran."

She snuggles into my side. A moment later, her voice reaches me through the darkness. "What are you going to do?"

I stand in the deep shadows as the rebels begin arriving, filing through the bowels of the abandoned building they chose for their meeting. The rebel meetings move around, something my men and I have long been aware of. Though I'd given my people instruction to track the rebels and discover their whereabouts, meetings are rarely interrupted by an outside force. The residents of the slums are hesitant to speak, and I've never given the order to threaten them with harm... until now.

With Taran's life and loyalty on the line, my hunt for Xavier Gunther has become a vicious game of cat and mouse leading to this moment. My men and I stormed through the sections of the city reserved for the poorer classes and illegals, banging on doors and terrifying the residents. We met with little resistance except for a few dissenters, calling out their disparagement of the Authority. Once I'd had these people publicly arrested, the other citizens fell into place, quietly giving up information.

They're a guarded people, the rebels. Almost all of them have a similar look, untidy, unkempt and starving. I wonder if Taran looked this way when she lived among them. I know she didn't eat enough, but otherwise her health and hygiene are good. She brushes her hair and teeth daily and insists on washing her hands before meals. She practically lives in the shower when she's not in the kitchen eating, but I suspect it's the hot water that draws her.

I rarely get the opportunity to visit the slums, and when I do, I complete my business quickly and leave. The experience this time around has been interesting. I've met with a variety of people, from angry dissenters to shy residents, to illegals cowering in their homes, expecting to be evicted from the city.

I used their terror against them, offering citizenship in exchange for information. When faced with the choice, most had given in. They have families to think of, wives and children. They gave up everything they could, spilling the beans on their neighbors, the rebellion, weaknesses in the city's defences, even the rebel leaders, most of whom are actual citizens. The only thing I hadn't gotten out of them was information on Taran, their Desert Wren. Their loyalty to her withstood every threat. She was the one that led them into Sanctuary, provided them with safe haven. Gave the clothes off her back and food from her mouth. Nothing I or my men said could convince them to betray her.

She should've been the rebel leader, not Gunther. They spoke of him with indifference, easily giving up his identity and anything else they had on him. Though he organizes the rebels, he isn't well loved among the common folk. It would seem that he has a philosophy of future thinking and grand plans. He's willing to sacrifice the individual in a bid to move the rebellion forward, a chance at overthrowing the city Authority.

In short, my opponent has weaknesses I can exploit. His

philosophy isn't far off from mine. The difference is I have no thirst for power. No need to prove myself. I just am. His desperate search for followers, clawing his way to the top of the rebels, will also be his downfall.

He's organized this meeting at the request of his followers, to address the issue of their missing people smuggler and the recent outbreak of Primitives in the slums. I crouch on one knee as the throng of people gather on the floor below me. They're in the lowest level of the parking garage and I've placed myself on the floor above them. Murmurs reach my ears as more people join. I'm surprised to count maybe 70 people when Xavier finally arrives.

He makes his way through the crowd and climbs up on a concrete barrier and then steps over onto the roof of a car so he's above the crowd.

"Quiet," he shouts, holding his hands up and then lowering them to indicate the volume should decrease. Though the din quiets somewhat, whispered voices can still be heard throughout the enclosed space.

I snort my derision. Anyone that calls themselves one of the people, a rebel, would know to become part of the crowd. The rebels are looking for someone who understands them, takes up their cause because it's one they're familiar with. Instead they get Gunther, a man that holds himself above them and calls himself one of them. This is why the rebellion will ultimately fail. They need a real leader, much like the woman who remains trapped in my tower.

"We're gathering here today to discuss the recent sighting of Primitives," Xavier shouts over the crowd. Some of the whispers die away and people jockey in position to see him.

"We want to know what's happened to Taran!" a burly man in rags shouts back.

"Yes," says a woman standing next to the man, holding onto his arm. "Taran is dear to all of us and we want to know what's happened to her."

Xavier tries to keep his expression neutral, but even I can see his face twisting in annoyance from my position above him. "Taran is fine. But we need to focus on the issue at hand – "

"How do you know she's fine?" Someone else shouts. "Did you see 'er?"

Xavier paces as he responds. "Yes, I've seen Taran. She's alive and well. She's working with me on a project. I'm keeping close tabs on our girl."

I stiffen at the way he speaks of my wife. I want to jump down onto his makeshift stage and confront him, tell him exactly who Taran belongs to. Instead I force myself to relax and listen. Taran is safe in my keeping. No one can touch her.

"I heard she got arrested!" A concerned woman's voice rises above the crowd. "They'd execute her if they got hold of her. She's too dear for us to allow that to happen. We have to do something, we have to get her back."

"No one's doing anything!" Xavier bites out viciously then stops speaking for a moment as he tries to reign in his temper. I don't like the idea of Taran around someone like this, a too quick to anger wannabe leader.

Before Xavier can speak again, a woman pulls herself up onto the hood of the car and holds her hands up. She has long grey hair and a knit cap. I wonder if she's the woman Taran described. People fall silent, as if recognizing someone they respect.

"I can assure you, Taran is perfectly fine. I saw her five days ago at the Day of the Dead ceremony."

"Then why hasn't she returned to us, Emery?" A voice rises above the crowd and a teenage boy pushes his way forward. "She's never taken off before."

Emery's face softens when she glances down at the boy, though her voice remains brisk. "She's on important business, Eric. She'll return as soon as she can. She loves all of us, she won't want to be away for long."

I feel some discomfort at this statement. It's not my intention to ever let Taran return here, to her roots. She's better than the slums. She's beautiful and intelligent. Yet these people have come to rely on her presence and support. I don't see how her two lives can be reconciled, the rebel leader vs. the Warlord's wife.

Xavier pipes up again, "There you have it, our Desert Wren is perfectly fine – "

Once again he's cut off when someone says, "Her name is Taran! She ain't no bird. The fucking police call her that, not her friends." He spits immediately after saying his piece, as though cursing the police force.

I grin. He's not far off. Most of them are a bunch of inept bumbling idiots. That's why I take only the best into my crew. Men with an impeccable record, focused, capable of doing the hard work I often insist of them.

"That's enough!" Xavier says furiously, finally losing his temper. "Taran is gone and she's not coming back any time soon. You'll be the first to know when our beloved bird has returned to the coop."

I raise my brow at his deliberately nasty dig. I see why Taran's marriage to this man didn't last. He's a self-centered power fiend, whereas she's kindness and grace personified. They would've clashed on every level. I wonder if she left him or if he left her? And how I can ask Taran without upsetting her. I haven't had a lot of experience with the more delicate side of women, but something tells me she won't take kindly to any suggestion that she was a deficient wife. She's already pissed off about my relentless campaign on her precious rebels.

"Now, back to business." Xavier claps his hands to get the attention of the surrounding people. "We need to be on guard. There are more police and military in the slums than ever. They say they're protecting us from the Primitives, but we know better."

A murmur rises up. The few snatches I can hear seem to indicate a real fear among the rebels. "But how do you know there aren't more?" one person asks, while another says, "We need protection if the Primitives come here." And another, "Poor Victoria was attacked and killed."

"Victoria was killed by Diogo Fuentes," Xavier shouts coldly. "She didn't deserve to die that way. We need to stop the Authority in this Sanctuary, bring it down, start over with an elected leader."

"And who exactly will that be? You?"

Xavier glares at the person who spoke. "Or someone else. It doesn't matter. What does matter is that we reinstate a fair system of government."

"But what about the Primitives?"

"We can't lose focus of our goal just because of one attack. Who knows, maybe the military let the Primitives in to distract us."

A collective gasp rises up and I have to control my anger. How dare he suggest such a thing?

"That's enough," Emery says sharply from her place on the hood of the car. "The city guard have family too, and they know how dangerous the enemy is. They would never allow them to come inside these walls willingly."

Not my guard, but someone else might. Someone like Xavier if he felt he had reason. A catalyst to turn the tide of public opinion even more in his direction. Bring the police into his neighborhood; tighter curfews and document checks, more arrests, harsher sentencing. Clashes between police and slum inhabitants would increase; the rebel force would grow in numbers and strength. People would feel more oppressed and want to organize. My opinion of Xavier goes up. Perhaps he's smarter than I thought.

Before the meeting can degenerate further, Xavier raises his voice above the crowd and gives the people gathered a series of quick, sharp suggestions on how to protect themselves from possible invasion from either the Primitives or the city police. Most of his advice is solid, things I would also suggest in case of emergency.

Xavier is an interesting man. He has faults, but they almost make him a better leader. He doesn't seem to prize comfort or connection, the two things that can make a person weak. Comfort makes people lazy, while connectivity and relationships slow them down, make them more vulnerable to attack. It's the human condition to seek each other out, find common goals and bond. Even I'm not immune to such things. Taran has become my Achilles heel, as proven by my presence at this rebel meeting, an event that could easily end with my death if I'm noticed. The people below are not my loyal followers, but my harshest critics.

The one thing Xavier isn't is charismatic. I'd always assumed he must have some way of speaking to people and crowds to get them to listen but he's abrasive, abrupt and rude. His followers only listen because he makes sense. But they don't love him. He lacks the passion and fire of history's greatest rebel leaders.

It's almost too bad Xavier is my enemy. If he's any good in combat he'd make a great asset to my team. His cold-blooded, analytical approach to the rebellion is exactly what I look for in my soldiers. The ability to make harsh decisions and carry them out.

He wraps up the meeting. "We're done here. Leave the building in small groups so you don't attract attention. Make sure you're home before curfew. And next time, only the essential people need to come out to a meeting. If you have nothing of value to contribute, then stay home. Risking the rebellion isn't an option."

An annoyed murmur rises up as people shuffle around and head for the exit. I'm amused by Xavier's brusque manner. Much like myself, he's no good with people and he doesn't seem wholly comfortable addressing a room. I wonder if it was his thirst for power that led him to this role or if his ability to plan accidentally elevated him. It doesn't matter. Soon he'll be arrested.

I wait.

He waits.

Each aware of the enemy close by.

I'd managed to get five of his followers to give up the location of this meeting. It seems too much to ask that they all hold their tongues rather than running straight back to their intrepid leader with the information that Commander Diogo Fuentes knows. It's a brave move, continuing with the meeting, despite knowing I could have the building surrounded with my men. Destroy the entire rebel faction in one swipe.

"I know you're here," Xavier snarls, his voice echoing in the shadows.

The assembled crowd has gone and only the two of us are left. I climb up on top of the concrete barrier and drop down onto the car he'd been standing on earlier. I land in a crouch and then straighten, staring down at Xavier. Xavier reaches for his gun, startled at my move. Then drops his hand, his expression of surprise at my action melting to annoyance. By standing above him, I've chosen the power position. Just like him, I understand the intricacies of war.

"Are you going to arrest me?" he demands.

I laugh grimly. "No, Gunther, I'm only here to talk. This time." I leave the threat hanging between us.

"You won't get another chance," he taunts, his hand dropping back to his weapon.

"Don't be stupid," I tell him. "I've always known where and how to find you. How long did it take me to find you this time when I put the pressure on? Less than a week. I could've crushed this ridiculously small rebellion at any time."

He frowns, his mind trying to work out my motives. "Then why didn't you arrest me when I started becoming a thorn in your side?"

Again, I laugh at his small thinking. This is why Xavier will never become leader of this Sanctuary or any other. He might have the skills, but his ability to think into the future and use all of his resources to their full extent is abysmal. "You were never a thorn in my side, Xavier. The Desert Wren was a thorn, and I've neutralized her. You were only ever a means to an end. I needed you to stir up the rebels, to keep them occupied and focus attention on relatively minor issues."

"Minor issues!" he snarls back at me, stalking around the front of the car, pacing in agitation. "Food shortages, unclean water and lack of space is all minor to you?"

"In the face of real problems, yes, these issues are minor. Despite the shortages, there is still food, which means there is still survival. Unless the city takes in more people than it can handle. Which is why I was forced to take out your people smuggler."

"We'll find another one," he snaps.

"Not one so effective. You must admit, she was very good. The way she can climb and her earnest belief in doing good. She's really a treasure." I'm being heavy-handed, complimenting his former wife. But I need to see what kind of feelings he still has for her.

Instead of discussing Taran though, he turns the conversation back to the rebellion. "In what way are you using the rebels to your advantage, Fuentes? We've caused nothing but headaches for you and your people."

"You think too small, Gunther. The rebellion gives the poorer factions within this Sanctuary something to hold onto, something to focus on besides human misery. If they realized how truly hopeless the future is, then they'd give up. They would stop working, stop hunting, stop fucking. They'd stop living. And the human race needs every survivor it can get."

"Why are you telling me this?" he demands.

"Because before tonight I believed you were the one to unify their hopes. Someone to band around and generate ideas. Instead, I've discovered a leader that can do little more than muddle through the emotions of his followers rather than sway their common opinion towards projects. I'm disappointed. I'd hoped for a real enemy."

He tosses a frustrated hand in the air. "You don't know me, Fuentes. You don't know what I'm capable of."

I jump off the car, landing in front of him. He reaches for his sidearm, but I grab him by the neck before he can pull it and I twist, slamming him against the car. "I know you're capable of seeking out my woman, *my wife*, and frightening her. Do you think I didn't see the haunted look in her eyes when I found her, crouched in that alleyway on the Day of the Dead?"

I see the satisfied look in his eyes before he gets smart enough to drop them and mask his expression.

I squeeze my fingers tighter until he makes a choking sound. Still he doesn't bring his hands up. I would win a fair fight with him, no contest. He knows it, I know it. He won't challenge me unless he has a chance of winning.

"You will stay away from my wife." I stare into his eyes, showing him the pitiless death that constantly resides within me. "If you touch her again, if you even look at her, I'll make your death last for weeks. It will be the greatest public spectacle this city's ever seen."

He stares back at me, the defiance in his face melting into realization. "You love her," he croaks out.

I drag him forward and slam him against the car with all my strength. He groans in agony as the back of his ribs crack under the pressure. I lean in close to him. "Yes, I love my wife. Which makes me more dangerous than you can imagine. You need to understand the lengths I will go to in order to protect her. You need to agree to stay away from Taran."

"You're going to kill me anyway," he rasps, trying to keep the fear from his face. "Why should I promise you anything?"

"Yes, I'll kill you. But not yet. I'll give you months, maybe even years if you back away from my woman and stay in your sector. Be a good little rebel and do your job. Stray into my territory again and I'll take great pleasure in gutting you and playing with your intestines."

His eyes flick past me and a spark of hope ignites within them.

I growl, "If even a part of you values life, yours or theirs, you'll tell them to stand down. I have men surrounding this building. If I don't come out alive, then every person who was here tonight will be hunted and executed."

He searches me, looking for the truth. I don't bother to convince him. I always speak the truth. He can learn the hard way if he chooses. I've been prepared for death from the age of four, since I first came to understand who my father was. And though I'd like to spend more time on this Earth with Taran, I understand that death will someday claim me. Maybe that day is today. A rifle is pressed to the back of my head and the fetid odour of an unwashed body invades my nostrils.

"Stand down!" Xavier chokes out.

The rifle drops away and when I glance over my shoulder I see men, maybe three of them, melting back into the shadows. It's smart of Xavier to have a private guard. He's made enemies as he's climbed the ladder of the rebellion, both within his own sector and outside of it.

"Now, tell me you'll stay away from Taran," I demand. "And we can all go home tonight."

"Fine," he snaps. "I'll stay the fuck away from her. You're welcome to her, she was a shit poor wife anyway. She couldn't cook to save her life and she fucked half the rebellion. Good riddance."

Rage washes over me and before I even realize what I'm doing, Xavier is on the ground at my feet, his neck crushed in my hand. He claws for life as I choke it from his body, his gloved hands scrambling against my forearm. I drag him up and hold him off the floor, his feet dangling and his eyes bulging.

"I *will* kill you, Xavier Gunther. This is a promise." I throw him away from me and turn as he crumples against the shell of the car.

I stride from the building, signaling to my men on the outside to disperse.

There's one more thing I have to do before leaving the sector. I nod to my men and get back in my jeep. The address I've been provided isn't easy to find. Buildings, houses and streets aren't as clearly labelled as they are in the higher-class sectors. Debris litters the streets and people group together in the roads, hurrying home before the curfew siren sounds. I pull up to my destination, a quiet ramshackle home in a residential neighborhood surrounded by other homes falling to disrepair. Except for this one, 58 Maple Drive, I can't tell if they're inhabited or if they've been abandoned. Light glows through the window of this home.

One of the screws on the 8 has been lost and it hangs down below the 5. Both numbers threaten to fall under the force of my fist against the door. The side of the house has been spray-painted. One of the tags is an eagle, the symbol of Authority, painted red with a cross over it. I smile grimly at the image as the door swings open.

Emery Bailer gasps her surprise, clearly not expecting the Warlord of her city to be standing on her doorstep. She gapes up at me, her eyes round, her mouth slightly open. She's wearing the same hat she was wearing earlier over long dark hair streaked with grey. Her clothes are tidy but worn, a long dress over denim pants, a jacket, and thick socks.

"May I come in?" I ask.

She nods and steps to the side. We both know she doesn't have a choice but to let me in. She stares at me as I enter her home, suspicion and fear lighting her intelligent gaze. She's gracious though, turning to me and saying, "Can I get you anything, Commander Fuentes. A glass of water or a meal?"

Her offer of a meal is extremely generous considering who I am and the scarcity of food in her sector.

"No," I say shortly, looking around for any clues to my wife. "Taran lived here."

She doesn't answer right away. It wasn't a question. My crackdown on this sector has included any and all information on Taran. And though I'd gotten very little information on my bird, I did learn that, before her capture, she lived here, with an older woman. After seeing Emery speak of Taran at the rebel meeting I realized that she must've been the one Taran lived with.

I raise a brow at her, staring down with grim intent, telling her without words that I require an answer.

She sighs and says, "Yes, Taran lives here."

Her defiant use of present tense isn't lost on me. I don't respond though. Taran won't be coming back here. She'll remain with me. This is an unassailable fact.

"Show me her room."

Emery hesitates, her features tightening, before she turns to lead the way down a dilapidated hallway. Paint is peeling on every wall, baseboards are broken or missing and the floor has warped over time. The house is cluttered but clean. Emery has chosen to surround herself with mementos and memories of the old world, before the Great Fall. I doubt many of her keepsakes work anymore. She's creating a sad museum collection inside her home while desperately hanging onto the past. A common, but ultimately useless habit.

Emery opens a door at the end of the hall revealing a small and airy room. The junk that clutters up the rest of the home is missing from this room, leaving it with an open feeling. As Emery turns away, I stop her.

"How long has Taran lived with you?"

She narrows her eyes and chews on her lip, debating whether or not to answer. I can't blame her. In her eyes, I'm the enemy, and giving me any information goes against her values. On the other hand, she can be arrested if she doesn't give me what I want. I won't hesitate to take her down to the station and have her interrogated if she proves difficult.

But something tells me that, despite Taran never mentioning the woman by name, they're close so I try a diplomatic path instead of my usual sledgehammer approach. "Ms. Bailer, I'm not here to threaten you. I'd just like to get to know my wife better."

She blinks rapidly and glances down before she finally says, "Ten years."

I do the calculation. "When she left her husband."

She glances back up. "It didn't really happen that way. She was such an independent little thing, but she was still young, and Xavier was too busy to give her the care she needed. I'd grown fond of her. Her transition to my home was an easy one that all parties agreed on."

I can't imagine letting Taran go. Even as a young woman, her feistiness and energy would've attracted me. I'd like to believe, had I been the one to marry the girl, I'd have given her the opportunity to grow up and then pursued a romantic relationship when she was ready. Xavier clearly doesn't have a way with women. Or maybe it's just Taran he doesn't understand.

"I'd like to spend some time here, in her room," I tell Emery.

She nods and waves me inside. "I'll give you a few minutes. Though there isn't much to see. Taran doesn't really hold onto things. That one has always fluttered on the wind, drifting this way and that until she has a job to do and then she flies with purpose. Never had a need to hang on to worldly possessions the way I do. She puts more stock in people than possessions." She gives me a small smile and leaves.

I enter Taran's sanctuary with Emery's words in my mind. What she says definitely fits the Taran I've come to know. She's passionate and caring, but not once did she ask for a material good. And she easily could have. As the wife of a Warlord she should be outfitted with the finest clothing and goods. I don't believe it's even occurred to her to ask. Even if it does she still won't care. Emery is right, Taran flows with the wind, settling where she lands.

I touch the hand-sewn quilt on her bed. It's a beautiful pattern of patchwork stars in different shades of grey and pink. It's faded and frayed in places. She's had it for a while. I wonder where she got it from, if someone made it for her. If they did then it would be someone that cared about the girl. This quilt was obviously made with love.

An old chest of drawers contains some ratty clothes in Taran's size. Nothing catches my eye, so I close the drawers and move my gaze around the sparse room. On the floor, next to the bed, I find a book. I pick it up and sit down on her bed. I don't know what I was expecting, but it wasn't a dog-eared, yellowed romance novel, a bare-chested man on the cover. I check the publication date. 2003. I'm surprised that a book printed 70 years ago is in such good shape. It must've been well stored before my little bird got her hands on it.

I grin at the condition it's in now. She must've read it over and over. Books are hard to come by. Long before the Great Fall, books ceased to be mass-produced in paperback. The rise of technology usurped traditional book stores. She probably picked it up somewhere and cherished it for its uniqueness and the imaginative escape provided within its pages.

I stand and tuck the book into my pocket. I leave the bedroom, satisfied that I've gained some clues to the inner thoughts and emotions of my wife. Emery meets me by the door as I prepare to leave, a worried frown marring her features.

She hesitates, chewing on her lip, and then finally asks, "Will you bring Taran back for a visit?"

"No." My answer is immediate and unequivocal. There's no reason to bring my wife back to this sector. It can only remind her of the life she's left behind, and her job now is to look to the future at the side of her husband.

Emery blinks back tears and nods. Then she lifts her chin defiantly. "She doesn't deserve this."

I study her for a moment, seeing an optimism mirrored in Taran. A belief that all can be good and well if we work toward that ideal. They're both wrong, but I like that there are still people that think that way. I'm glad that Taran had this woman influencing her life, encouraging her.

"Life isn't about what we deserve, Ms. Bailer," I say softly. "But what we do with the things we're given."

She stares at me thoughtfully, her eyes shining with unshed tears. "Perhaps you're right, Commander. But if we do good things with the situations we're dealt then we might aspire to better."

I smile. She's a brave woman to insult me so subtly to my face, essentially accusing me of doing the opposite of good things with what I've been dealt. I like her.

"I will take your words to heart and keep my good thing close, learn from her and be better." I stare down at her. "She has become my conscience. I won't let her go, no matter what she means to you and the people here."

She inhales sharply and lifts a hand to her chest, rubbing. She stares past me, the door held open in her hand. I'm no longer welcome in her home. I've gotten what I came for. But before I leave, I tell her, "I'll treat her with respect."

Her voice follows as I stride down the path toward my jeep. "You'd better."

THIRTY

TARAN

"How are the babies doing today, Skye?"

I've come up to the rooftop to check on and water my tomato plant. A tiny sprout has made its way through the dirt, making me dance in excitement. Now, I'm sitting on the ground underneath the bird's nest, doing what Diogo taught me and picking the dead leaves and flowers off the plants. It seems like sacrilege to do such a thing to the plant, but he insists that it helps them grow bigger and stronger. I dragged the strawberry barrels over to Skye's nest so we could chat.

I laugh as she looks over the side of her nest and chirps at me, making high-pitched sounds as though actually talking to me. She's probably warning me off, though she's been less hostile to my presence the more time I spend with her in the makeshift greenhouse. "So, you want them to hatch sooner rather than later? That seems like a solid plan. It's a bit late in the season, but who am I to judge. I'm not a momma bird."

Chirp. Chirp. Chirp.

"Well, I guess I've never met another bird I wanted to

have hatchlings with. And other reasons best not discussed in front of tiny egg ears." I touch my finger to a green strawberry. My mouth waters as I imagine the burst of flavour once it ripens. The last time I ate a strawberry is when they were smuggled in with a group of refugees coming off the train. I was given a handful by the grateful people as a thank you.

"And what about now?" Diogo's voice startles me. I turn my head to look over my shoulder. He's standing in the doorway, the dying light of the sun setting against his back. "Have you found someone to have a baby with now?"

Though his tone is light, I can still sense the intensity surrounding his question. The way he says it, as though he means not just himself as a candidate, but someone else. Who could he possibly mean? My ex-husband?

Diogo turns to light a lantern sitting on the bench by the door, crouching to strike the match against the concrete floor. His figure lights up as he straightens and walks toward me, settling the lantern beside me. I hadn't noticed how much I needed the light until he gave it to me. I'd been squinting into the shadows, doing my best with the plants. Lamp oil is always a luxury. One I try to do without if I can manage.

He goes down on one knee next to me and tips my chin with his gloved hand until I'm forced to look at him. "Well, Taran. Do you want a baby?"

I try to speak, to say something flip to his words because they're too serious. Do I want a baby? What woman my age doesn't want a baby? The idea of holding something so sweet and innocent, of breathing in its scent as I hold it to my breast. Rocking it to sleep like I've watched the other women do. But then...

"We live in a dangerous world, Diogo. The first thing

we have to teach a baby is not to cry. Not to make a single sound. And too often the correction must be harsh so the child learns faster. To save its life if it's ever confronted with a Primitive. It amazes me that women keep having babies at all. Not with the risks they face. And not just the Primitives. Food shortages, tainted water supplies, vaccination shortages, riots. There's just too much that can kill a creature as small and helpless as a human baby."

"And yet some of them still survive," he stays, studying me closely. "The lack of birth control is an issue that has aided the human cause."

"Only someone like you would think that way." I don't bother to hide my disdain of his statement. "Not only is the baby coming into an uncertain world, but the woman having the baby is at much greater risk than women fifty years ago. How many people are trained for caesarean sections, or able to deal with pre-eclampsia? Women are dying in childbirth at a rate that hasn't been seen in almost 200 hundred years. Or dying in botched abortion attempts because they choose not to have the baby. No, thank you, Diogo. I don't want any part of that."

His brows slowly lower until he's staring down at me with a dark expression, his harsh features set in serious lines. "You won't have a choice, Taran. You will have our child when we decide the time is right. You will have nothing to worry about. You'll be given the best medical care we have in this city. And if that isn't good enough then I'll travel to another Sanctuary and find a better doctor."

His conviction, his insistence on my safety in all scenarios, is breathtaking and *almost* romantic. I have to remind myself that I disagree with almost everything he's saying. The way in which he chooses the birth of our first child without my input, his ability to gain access to medical care for someone he cares about but not the lower classes, and his suggestion that he'll just kidnap a doctor if the going gets rough.

"And you're going to decide when we have a baby? And what, you'll just let me know? Do you also intend to choose the sex? Maybe a mini boy warlord, like yourself, or a girl that you can sell off to the highest bidder when the time is right."

He sighs, reaches out to take my face in his hands, says, "I don't want to fight, Taran." And then he kisses me. I forget my ire under the magnificent pressure that starts at my lips and then travels, building a fire in my belly. If Diogo knew how easily he can ignite this feeling, how he makes my knees go weak and the fight drain from me, I'd be in big trouble. He'd have me wrapped around his finger all the time. By the time he ends his kiss, finishing up by nuzzling my nose with his, I've completely forgotten what we were arguing about, or if we were arguing at all.

"Mmmm," I mumble, reaching for him, intent on dragging him in for another kiss. We haven't had sex in the greenhouse yet. Now seems like a good time to add this place to my rapidly growing list of places we've had sex.

Diogo takes my hands in his and pushes them back. Then he moves away, putting distance between us. I narrow my eyes. He hasn't rejected any overtures from me yet. Usually at my first tentative touch he's all over me. Even if he doesn't have time, has a meeting or something to get to, he finds a few extra minutes to satisfy both of us.

"I have some questions for you." He stands and pushes a hand through his hair. He paces away a few steps and then paces back. In this tiny greenhouse he looks like a cooped-up giant. Some sections slant inward forcing him to stoop. "About your ex-husband."

"I thought you didn't want to fight?" I say with a frown.

"We won't fight, but I need to ask you about Xavier and I need you to answer truthfully."

"I always answer you truthfully," I snap, pushing to my feet and shaking a soil-covered finger at him. "And we will definitely fight if we talk about Xavier. You get jumpy when Garrett holds a door open for me. I can't imagine you being even close to okay while we're discussing a man I once went to bed with."

"Well that answers one question," he snarls, pacing away from me toward the door. "You fucked him."

Hands on my hips, I turn to face him fully before answering. "First of all, we fucked together, not *I* fucked *him.*" I ignore his growl of anger as he paces back toward me. I step lightly out of his way but still follow up with, "And secondly, I was forcibly wed to the man by your processing department. I didn't have a choice in the matter. I had no idea who you were or that we might have a future together, so you can stop being an asshole just because I had sex with the man."

"Stop talking about sex with Xavier and I won't go and immediately kill him."

I press my lips together to stop the next sentence, but it bursts out anyway. "He's not the only one I've had sex with. Are you going to murder them all?"

"Shut the fuck up, Taran!" he snarls, and then turns around and punches a hole in the wooden frame next to the door. My mouth falls open as splinters of wood litter the floor. "He said you fucked half the rebellion."

"He said that? Seriously?" I yell furiously. "Fine, you

can go kill him. I'll wait." He stands still with his head down, but I can see his lips twitch. Some of the tense anger drains from him as his shoulders relax. "Better yet, just maim him. Maybe stab him until he knows better than to talk about his ex-wife that way."

He turns back to me a real smile stretching his lips. "You're something else, baby. You know that?"

"I know that," I reply cheekily. Then soberly add, "You know, I only slept with two other men besides Xavier. Both were brief flings. I was lonely and the human connection felt good. What you and I have is so much... more, but it doesn't erase my history. I won't regret the things I've done, Diogo."

He shakes his head. "I won't pretend I like hearing that there've been other men in your life, but I understand. Even surrounded by people, Sanctuary can be a lonely place. You want to feel alive, even if it's only for a few minutes."

I smile. He gets it. We aren't nearly as different as I always imagined. We have some fundamental issues to work through, but Diogo Fuentes, Dictator and Warlord, isn't nearly as terrifying as I thought. He's human.

"What did you want to ask me about Xavier? We got sidetracked while fighting about my ex-husband."

He laughs. "You need a spanking, sweetheart?"

"Promises, promises." I bat my lashes and crook my finger at him.

He shakes his head. "Business first, pleasure later."

I sigh my disappointment. "Okay, ask away. But I think you'll probably get mad and start another fight."

He ignores my bait. "How long did you live with Xavier?"

I shrug. "Not very long." Then I think about it, wrinkling my nose in concentration. "I lived with him for a few years after we were first married, maybe two. Then only a couple of months when I was twenty-two. We decided to actually try to make our marriage work."

"Did he fuck you when you lived with him the first time? When you were just a kid?" he demands. He's vibrating with tension again and I can tell he's trying to keep a tight leash on his temper.

"Not that it's any of your business, but no, he was never interested in underage girls." I feel the need to point out, "It's your policy that married me to him at the age of fourteen. He had every right to have sex with me if he wanted to. It wouldn't have been a crime in the eyes of the law. Your law."

I'm satisfied with the visible flinch he gives.

"We need children, Taran. It wasn't an easy decision to allow women that age to marry, but they have a good chance at fertility and delivering healthy babies." I'm about to argue, to tell him that, in a dying world, forcing women to have children instead of giving them the chance to decide for themselves is barbaric. He doesn't give me the opportunity. Instead, he says, "I'm bothered by the thought that you could've been forced to have sex and bear a child at that age. I will have the law changed. I'll raise the age of marriage to 16 unless otherwise requested by both parties."

I'm stunned speechless for a moment. He's going to change a law because of me? Because of what *might've* happened when I was a teenager. The brief moments of happiness I've been feeling over the past week explode out of me into full-fledged hope. If Diogo is willing to change such an important law just for me, he might be willing to at least listen to my other suggestions. We might actually have a future together. My eyes tear up and my throat begins to close with the scratchy feeling that I get when I weep.

Still... "Make it eighteen, Diogo," I say through my tight throat.

He laughs and reaches for me, pulling me against him. "Seventeen. End of negotiation."

THIRTY-ONE

TARAN

After slaking our lust in a few passionate encounters, one in the kitchen and one in the bedroom, we spend the rest of the evening making slow, sweet love to each other. We hold each other, touch and explore. He lays back on the cot outside the greenhouse, his arms behind his head and allows me to run my hands and lips over his body. I explore each ridged muscle, licking and biting a path slowly down. I enjoy the way his body tightens beneath mine as he fights with himself not to grab me.

I settle between his thighs and take the hard length of his cock in my hands, marvelling once more at the size. He's such a large man. Not only in physical presence, but also in determination and fortitude. Despite our differences I've come to appreciate certain aspects of him and his leadership. I show my appreciation to the one part of him that wants it most, running my tongue down the side before fisting the base and wrapping my lips around the head.

"Fuck, Taran..." he groans pressing the heels of his hands into his eyes.

I continue, taking him slowly into my mouth and sucking him as deep as I can, maybe half his length. His width fills my mouth. I swirl my tongue around him, exploring each ridge, before running my tongue over the pulsing veins. After a minute I'm forced to surface and take a breath. I grin at him.

He grabs me by the arms and lifts me until I'm straddling him. "Hey, I wanted to finish that!"

He taps me low on the belly, just above my pussy. "I'll be coming inside you, baby. Right there."

My cheeks grow hot and I have to catch my breath as he lifts me again, pushing me down on top of his cock. I reach out to grip his shoulders, slowly rocking my hips as I accept his length, inch by inch. The full feeling as he slides deep inside is both incredible and a little painful. He gives me time to adjust though, letting me do it in my own time.

Finally, I'm seated on him, his cock completely sheathed inside me. He grips my hips, wrapping those huge hands around my body and caressing my ass. Then he helps me slide up and down, my own lubrication easing the path he's forging. I'm swamped by sensations. The building pressure inside me becomes almost too much as we rock together. I can't move my hips anymore, I'm too lost in the feelings sizzling through me. Diogo takes over, pulling me down to him, laying me across his chest, as he takes me by the hips and pushes me down on him, fucking me from underneath.

"Going to come!" I cry desperately against him as the orgasmic pressure rises to an unbearable degree.

"Come for me, Taran," he drops his head and murmurs against my ear, then bites me, sinking his teeth into the lobe.

I shout my pleasure for him, filling the night with my

cries. He slams my hips down on his, once, twice, three times more. Then stops, stiffening underneath me. He slides his arm up to my waist, wraps it around and holds me tight. The other goes around my neck, pinning me in place against him.

He's holding me so tight I feel like we're fused together. His breath stirs the hair on top of my head while mine skitters jerkily across his chest. Gently he rolls me to his side. The cot is very small, probably not meant for a man of his size, let alone the two of us. Still, he sees to my comfort first, reaching for the blanket and covering me before tucking me against his side.

We lay that way for so long that I think he's fallen asleep. We sleep up on this roof almost as often as we sleep in his bed together. Sometimes I wake up to him carrying me up from our bed. He craves the outside, craves the open space. And I do too.

I'm starting to drift off when he speaks, his voice low in my ear, "I've fallen in love with you, Taran."

I jerk my head up to stare at him. He's watching me intently, his eyes glittering obsidian in the darkness. I don't say anything for a moment, and when I do finally open my mouth to speak, he stops me.

"Don't say anything. If you don't or can't love me, then I don't want to hear it. It won't matter either way, you're still my wife and you'll remain with me. And if you do love me, then I'm not ready to hear it yet." He moves his head, staring up at the stars, a small frown wrinkling his forehead. "Loving you makes me dangerous enough. If you were to love me back I would destroy this city to keep that love. I'm a selfish man, Taran. A taste of your love will never be enough. I'll want to keep it forever."

I think about his words for a moment. They're like him, brutal with an edge of cruelty, but still beautiful. In their own way. I kiss his arm where I'm snuggled against him and whisper, "Okay, Diogo."

THIRTY-TWO
TARAN

I knew our peace, the moments of shared understanding, wouldn't last long, but I'd hoped for longer than a day. That we'd have long enough for our fledgling relationship to settle in. I should've known better. Nothing good in Sanctuary sticks around. Strawberries get eaten or die, with none to replace them. Baby birds grow up and fly away. Food shortages run rampant in the lower classes. Children get sick without medicine, parents get desperate, and the city police show their brutality when there's any unrest. The bad is as predictable as the sun.

Diogo and I wake on the roof, wrapped in each other's arms, his radio crackling nearby. He rolls off the cot while I catch the blanket to my chest, stretch and squint in the general direction of the sun, still low in the horizon and hidden by buildings. I'd guess it's early. Not even 6am yet. Diogo pulls his pants on, leaving them unbuttoned as he reaches for the radio.

"Report," he snaps.

I've come a long way with our Sanctuary's Warlord. I find his deep voice, clipped with annoyance at the interruption, sexy as hell. Maybe I find it, and him, so attractive because I know he's cold with everyone else but he turns into a fiery, possessive beast where I'm concerned. After spending a lifetime watching out for myself and everyone around me, the way Diogo treats me is alluring. He takes protective to a whole other level.

But his job, it's going to be a wrench in our relationship. It's been the driving force placing us on opposing sides from before we even met. And I can tell that whatever he's hearing on the radio is no different. I try to catch the words, coming out at a fast, clipped pace. Half the words are acronyms that I don't understand.

What I do understand are the words, "rebel faction" and "sabotage." I gasp, pushing myself up to a sitting position. I shove the tangled mass of my hair away from my face and lean over to search the ground for my clothes. When I don't see them, I remember that Diogo carried me up here naked. I tuck the blanket around my chest and stand, going to Diogo's side.

He's not trying to have this conversation away from me so I'm not going to pretend I'm not eavesdropping. He reaches for me, almost absently and tucks me into his side as he talks, his hand splayed over my hip.

"Have the team leaders gather in my war room. Bring Stryker in, he's leading the guard on the wall. I'll be there in ten minutes."

The radio crackles in acknowledgement.

He looks down at me, his eyes hard and unreadable as he studies me, searching for something. I know what he's going to ask before he even asks it. "Do you have any knowledge of a rebel plot, Taran? Something big?"

I chew on my lip, trying to decide what to tell him. I try to pull from his hold as I think, but he sets his radio down and tightens his arms in a cage around my body. He stares down at me, waiting for an answer. Loyalty to my people wars with loyalty to my husband. I'd never imagined being in such a position. I'd always just whole-heartedly given myself to the cause, choosing my friends from among like-minded rebels.

"Answer, Taran, and answer truthfully." Impatience laces his voice.

I shove an annoyed hand against his chest. He doesn't move so I'm forced to stand with my hand curved over his rock-hard pectoral muscle, the bare skin of his chest heating me. "I don't know how to answer and keep my integrity," I try to explain.

He gives me a light shake and forces my face up. "You belong to house Fuentes, your loyalty belongs to me."

"Loyalty is earned, Diogo!" I snap. "And to be honest, you've been destroying my initial impressions of you and replacing them with a man far more reasonable than I thought. I haven't had enough time to decide what this means to my life, if I believe we have a future. I won't give you rebel secrets any more than you're going to give me military plans."

His hands curve around my waist, squeezing until I'm uncomfortable, until I think there might be fingerprint bruises left behind in my flesh. His eyes burn on my face. "You do not get to decide your future, Taran, I do. It's your duty as my wife and the future mother of my children to tell me what I need to know."

I'm reminded of my place in the world in a few short sentences. I feel despair at his words, but they're passionately spoken. I know he cares about me, loves me and wants my happiness. Maybe the core of who I am will never reconcile with his intentions for me, but I need to remember that there is still hope for us as long as he cares.

I close my eyes against the heat of his gaze. He's too much right now. I can't think when I'm faced with all this emotion. Finally, I take a breath and look up at him. "We think differently, Diogo. And until our values align I won't do anything that might harm the people I consider family." He opens his mouth to argue, but I cut him off. "I will tell you this, because I can and because you've made compromises for me. There is no large rebel plot, as far as I'm aware of."

As the words come out of my mouth, it occurs to me that Diogo knows something I don't know. He has insider knowledge on the rebellion that he shouldn't have. Does he have someone on the inside, like we have in his police force? The more I think about it, the more it makes sense. He fed my forger false information on refugees that don't exist. He must've had a person close to the rebels in order to pull that off. Not close enough to know my real identity though.

Diogo lets me go and paces away, clearly trying to decide what he should do. He turns and points at me, pinning me to the spot with his intensity. "I'd better not find out you've lied to me, Taran."

Anger ignites quickly. "You insist I trust your word at every turn, Diogo. Yet you question mine. Every time you speak to me in anger you hammer another nail in the coffin of our marriage. We won't have a relationship without trust."

"You're wrong. Regardless of your feelings, you belong to me, Taran. End of discussion."

And he does end the discussion, by leaving. I'm left gaping after him on the rooftop terrace. I think about following him, but what's the point? He's angry and when he's angry he's unpredictable. I suppose I can understand. He's been carefully maneuvering every aspect of this city for decades. Now, suddenly, he has a wife to contend with. But not just any wife, a rebel leader. A woman with values and opinions and who will argue with him at every turn, try to change his world view.

I sink down on the cot and curl on my side, closing my eyes. I should be more patient with my husband. Life could be so much worse. He could've been the terrible tyrant I'd originally thought, instead of a thoughtful man with strong leadership qualities. I could've been kept as his concubine, forced to see to his needs while he continued on with his life with no thoughts to my comfort. I could've been tortured and executed.

With that chilling thought haunting my mind I allow myself to drift into a fitful sleep. My dreams are dark and nightmarish. I know I'm asleep but I can't seem to escape the binds of my dream world and force myself to wake up.

I'm running through Sanctuary, looking for a safe place to hide while a massive dust storm chases me. It has ripped through the wall, taking it down piece by piece. The city is empty of citizens. Somehow, they've all disappeared while I'm left in a desperate fight to save my own life. I'm running through buildings, climbing and jumping as fast as I can, faster than humanly possible. Then I'm standing on the rooftop ledge of One Church, my arms spread wide, the storm coming straight at me. I know it'll kill me, so I choose freedom instead. I leap off the roof, soaring through the air into nothingness. As I fall, I turn and look up. Diogo is standing on the roof watching me fall, his face completely void of expression. I reach out for him but the storm swallows him, taking him from my sight. I tense, preparing to hit the ground.

"Taran."

A voice reaches out to me, yanking me from the gripping nightmare. I reach for it, desperate to escape the fall that will surely kill me. Hands shake me and finally I open my eyes. I look up into the face of the last man I expected.

My ex-husband, Xavier Gunther.

I sit up with a gasp, covering my mouth and staring in shock. I reach out for the blanket to make sure it's covering my bare chest.

"How did you get in here?" I'm appalled. If Diogo finds him here, he's as good as dead.

"Told you, I have a man on the inside." His words come out laboured and he reaches for the edge of the cot, pulling himself down, his face twisting in a grimace. I pull my feet back to give him room.

"Did Garrett let you in?" I ask softly.

He looks confused for a moment and then nods his head vaguely, wrapping an arm around his middle.

I put a tentative hand on his shoulder. "What happened to you? Are you hurt?"

"Your husband attacked me," he growls. "Tried to kill me, but I got away with the help of some of my people."

"Oh no! He didn't tell me he saw you," I gasp, and run my hands over his chest. "Where are you hurt?"

"My ribs, in the back," he snaps. I tug his shirt up and my mouth drops open at the damage. Big purple and blue splotches cover the skin of his back over his ribs. I gently run my fingers over the area, probing. He shifts sharply in the seat.

"They're definitely cracked. The muscle between the ribs is swollen," I say and smooth his shirt back down. "Why did he do this?"

"Wanted to look me in the eye, see who your first husband was, I guess. The guy isn't exactly stable when it comes to you, Taran."

That sounds like Diogo. I suppose I should be grateful he didn't outright kill Xavier as he'd threatened to do. I clutch the blanket against my throat as anxiety presses in on me. I expect Diogo to walk in and find us here together. I've done nothing wrong, I wasn't expecting Xavier and I certainly didn't invite him, but I can't help feeling like that wouldn't stop Diogo's anger. Or the retribution that would follow.

"Why are you here, Xavier? This isn't smart. Diogo will definitely kill you on the spot if he finds you. Probably throw you off the roof. You won't get away with a few busted ribs."

"I'm not afraid of your husband," he sneers, but his eyes dart quickly to the door before settling back on me. "I need to talk to you, let you know what's happening in the rebellion."

"What is it?" I ask, worry for my friends overriding my need to rush him out of the apartment.

He shifts painfully in the chair. "We've lost some people. Fuentes," he spits the name out like it's poison, "and his men are tearing through the slums, arresting illegals and anyone suspected of being a rebel."

"But why would he do that?" I ask, frowning. "He hasn't seriously moved on the rebels since I've been in Sanctuary, and the rebellion has existed for a long time. And from what I've seen he has the intelligence and the firepower to take out our entire rebellion with ease."

"Sounds like you've switched sides," Xavier says accusingly.

I cross my arms and stare at him. "What it sounds like is I'm getting to know the other side and negotiating with him. It's much smarter to climb the mountain than to throw a rock at it and try to topple it. Now you tell me, what are these rumours I'm hearing about some kind of sabotage plot. Is that you?"

A flash of something suspiciously close to guilt crosses his features before he smothers it. His gaze is cool and detached when it finds mine. "We're always working on different plans, trying to gain power for the rebellion, bring in more supplies and refugees. The cause is all that matters. You need to remember that, remember who your friends are."

"I'm doing some good here," I defend myself. "I got Diogo to raise the age of marriage consent to 17."

Xavier waves his hand dismissively. I'm not surprised. He's never been one to concern himself overly much with women's issues. That was always my thing. It was one of the reasons I elevated to a leadership role, besides my ability to climb and hide from the authority. I've always been an outspoken advocate for women's rights, especially the women without a voice. Refugees, illegals, young women forced into marriage.

"There's something else you need to know."

His statement draws my attention back. "What?"

"There've been reports from our hunters of a small settlement of people in the mountains. Apparently, they've been around for a while... refugees that didn't make it into the city."

It takes a moment for the implication to hit but once it does my body is flooded with endorphins. The need to leave immediately is strong. I shake my head, reminding myself of the near impossibility that my grandparents could be alive after all these years of fending for themselves outside of a sanctuary. But if there's even a chance.

"I have to go," I murmur.

Xavier knows all of my history, he knows what this information means to me. He places a hand at my back. He isn't an emotive man but he has his moments. I lean into him a bit and take in the comfort he's offering. There can never be more than friendship between us, but that friendship is strong. Even when we don't agree.

"Your husband won't let you leave," he says seriously. "He's possessive and suspicious. I'm guessing you're the catalyst he needed to finally take control of the rebellion. He's been allowing us to rise to a certain level, have our little riots and rallies. But now that he has you, he can turn the tide of the people."

I tug on the end of my hair. This isn't good. This confirms what I've come to suspect. Diogo always had the ability to access the rebellion, to bring it down if he really wanted to. But something held him back. Now it would seem he's making advances to weaken the movement. "But why?" I ask out loud. "Why would he do this now if he always could? It doesn't make sense."

"It does." Xavier stands, pulling himself up with the edge of the cot. He turns so that he's hovering over me, though hunched in pain. "He has what he wants now. He has a major player in the rebellion, the Desert Wren, and having her here with him, capitulating to him, standing at his side willingly, will sway her loyal followers. All he needs is to get rid of the few that care most, the ones that'll try to bring her back into the fold."

"You and Emery," I murmur, a sick feeling rising up inside me. I continue to pace and think, his pitying gaze following me. "No, you can't be right. He can't have planned this entire thing."

"You don't want to believe it, Taran," he says softly, stepping in front of me and taking my shoulders in his hands. "But it makes sense. And I think you'll see that when you've had time to think about it."

Tears prick my eyes and I nod, not saying anything. My throat aches with the need to cry. I swipe a finger under my eye stopping the first tear from falling.

"Taran, you can't stay with him. The longer you stay, the more danger you're in." He brushes the hair off my face. It's a strangely intimate gesture considering we haven't been together as man and wife in more than five years.

I nod and say with a sigh, "I need to go to the mountains anyway, find out if the rumours of a settlement are real." Then reality kicks in. "Diogo won't let me leave though. Even if I do manage to escape my guard or scale down the side of this building, he'll have the city on lockdown faster than I can move sectors. He knows I climb the wall so he'll double-down on his people at the wall."

"Don't worry about that, Taran. We'll get you out when you're ready."

"What are you planning?" I ask, feeling numb. The thought of leaving Diogo makes me feel awful, dizzy and sick. Yet the thought of staying with the man who has planned every detail of my downfall from before we even met is worse.

"We'll cause a distraction, get you out of the city. I'll go with you, help you find what you're looking for."

I frown and shake my head. "The rebellion needs you here, Xavier, they can't lose both of us. Besides, if Diogo knows you've left with me, he'll tear this city apart and then come after us with everything he has."

"Don't worry about Fuentes, we'll keep him distracted." He squeezes my shoulders, a bit harder than I think is necessary, as though he's frustrated with my reticence. "No sweetheart, what we need to do is lay low for a while. We are the rebellion, you and me. If we're both caught, then the rebellion will collapse completely. But if we leave the city and hide out in the mountains, we'll be able to re-enter Sanctuary stronger and more equipped than ever."

I glance at him sharply. "What do you mean, more equipped?"

He gives me a shake before wincing in pain and letting me go. "We don't have time for that right now, Taran. Just be ready to go when I come for you."

"Why aren't you asking me to come with you now?" I ask suspiciously. "This seems like the perfect time for me to disappear. Diogo is out and busy with whatever rumour you've started." I hold my hand up when it looks like he's about to protest. "Don't bother to deny it, I'm not stupid, Xavier. You may believe in the cause, but you'll do what it takes to achieve your own ends."

"You aren't ready to leave that bastard yet," he snaps, backing away from me. "I wish you would come now, but we both know you're not ready. Not until you've talked to him, discovered the truth. But once you do, I'll be waiting."

I want to argue with him, tell him he's wrong. That he's wrong about Diogo and wrong about my reason for being here. My husband loves me, he wouldn't betray that love.

"Besides, as you pointed out, the Commander will tear this city apart looking for you. We need a clean break, get you out of the city and into the mountains where we can lose ourselves."

This whole thing feels wrong, like I'm betraying Diogo for even entertaining this idea. I'm about to tell Xavier that I won't go with him when he comes for me, but before I can say anything else, he turns and leaves the roof without another word. I run to the door, flinging it open. I run down the stairs and into the apartment. When I peek out the front door I'm surprised to find that no one is guarding the other side. I take two steps out into the hallway and look around.

No one. I could leave if I wanted.

But Xavier is right. If I'm going to leave Sanctuary to search for my grandparents, I need to have one last conversation with my husband. I need to know the truth about his intentions for capturing me.

THIRTY-FOUR

DIOGO

"Where's Stryker?" I ask coldly, dropping into my seat at the head of the war room table. I look around; everyone's there except my surveillance guy.

"He said he was coming in from outside the wall, desert side. Was doing a quick perimeter check," Jorje tells me.

I nod absently. Stryker is vigilant when he's running guard duty. The men on the wall hate him, but nothing ever gets past. I wonder if Taran ever attempted the wall with Stryker on duty. Or if she knew better than to attempt it. She seems to have our rotations figured out like clockwork, even when we switch them up. Perhaps I need to have a house cleaning among the police, find out if someone is working the rebel side. It would make perfect sense, I have people infiltrating the rebellion, not deep enough though. The rebels are not exactly a trusting.

"What've you heard?" I ask Jorje, the man that called this meeting.

He straightens in his chair, his serious gaze sweeping the room. "A rumour from our guy in the slums. According to him, there's a plot to bring down a section of the wall in retaliation for our crackdown on the illegals in their sector. Not sure if it's a single saboteur or the entire rebel faction."

Though murmurs erupt around the table, I don't react. I turn his statement over in my mind. Bringing down the wall is extreme, but then, the rebels are due for a little extreme. It's been three years since they rioted, creating havoc all over the city. I frown as the thought teases me. It'd turned out that they used the food shortage riots as a distraction to get their people smuggler through the gates and back in with dozens of illegals. People to shore up the cause.

Could it be? Could this rumour be another distraction? If so, who's being distracted and why? And is the rumour just a rumour or a full-fledged plot?

"I need everything you have from our man. If possible, I want you to bring him in. I'll talk to him myself. We need details if we're going to fight this kind of act."

I look around the room and start splitting up my men, giving them tasks. The majority will double shift their men on security duty. They'll organize the police, make sure everyone is on alert. Toward the end of the meeting, Stryker takes his place at the table.

He nods toward me and says, "All's quiet on the wall."

"Good," I acknowledge. "You'll stay on point there. Make sure our people detain anyone suspicious approaching the base."

I leave the meeting shortly after, arranging to meet with Jorje at the police station in a few hours. We'll meet with the captain and his top men, apprise them of the situation and a possible influx of detainees headed their way for processing. But before we do that I need to find Taran, make sure she's still at home and safe.

I enter our apartment, nodding toward Garrett on my

way in. He nods back, "She's been quiet tonight, not saying much."

Taran is sitting at the table when I close the door behind me, a lantern lighting her lovely features. A tomato sandwich sits half eaten in front of her. The look on her face is serious, wary. Her eyes flick over me and then raise back up to my face, a hint of relief in her eyes.

"No blood this time," she says dismally.

"Wasn't fighting anyone," I say on a grunt. I walk toward her, stopping a few feet away. Her expression, her posture, none of it is welcoming. I wonder if this has to do with our conversation before I left or if her agile brain has been working on a new problem.

"How many have you killed?" she asks, almost absently, picking up the sandwich to take a bite. Juice drips down her chin from the tomato slice and she catches it with the edge of her hand.

It takes me a moment to understand her question, then I ask coolly, "Primitive or human?"

She flinches visibly at the reminder that I'm a killer. That I've killed more than the monsters that hunt us. I wonder why she's dwelling on such a macabre subject. She knows what kind of world we live in and she's aware of the sacrifices involved in my job.

"Either," she says, eyes big and haunted.

I answer truthfully, "Five humans by my own hand, dozens of execution orders, and countless Primitives."

She swallows and then whispers, "Countless... as in you don't know how many?"

"No, I don't," I tell her. The more truthful answer would be hundreds. But I don't think she wants to hear that any more than she wants to know I've killed so many I can't keep count. "How many have you killed?" I ask, turning the question on her.

She looks up at me, appalled. "None! I've never killed anyone. Most people haven't, Diogo."

I crouch in front of her and place my hands on her knees, squeezing a little. "Exactly," I tell her gently. "You don't have to kill because there's people like me to do it for you."

"Th-that's horrible." Her eyes are wide and upset. She puts her hands over mine and runs her fingers soothingly over the skin. "I'm sorry you have to kill, Diogo. That you feel it's become your duty."

I shrug. "It's the price of protecting the things you love."

"But you didn't love anything before... before..."

I wait, but she lets the sentence sit unfinished between us. Finally, I finish for her. "Before you."

She nods, her eyes wide on my face.

I close my own eyes for a moment, trying to find the right words, then I look up at her, into her cloudy grey eyes, made sharper by the flickering light of the lantern. "You've given me the reason I need to keep doing this, Taran. To keep protecting Sanctuary. Before you I was losing myself in this city."

"But you couldn't have known I'd come along, or that you'd fall in love with me," she argues. I get the sense that she's searching for a way to say something or ask for something.

"I knew," I assure her.

She takes her hands from mine, her body stiff beneath my grip. "Did you know it would be me, or just some faceless woman? Did you plan on grabbing the Desert Wren and bringing her here? Marrying her?"

Frustration rises up as I search for a way to give her

what she's looking for while still telling her the truth. "Yes, I admired the Desert Wren before I met you. Her ethics, drive and passion have fascinated me for a long time. We live in a bleak and uncertain world, hunting a woman that does what she does for the simple love of people has long been something that drives me. I work for the people too, Taran, but I have no love for them. They are my burden. I became Warlord because it's what I'm trained to do. I run this city because I'm good at it, but at some point I lost my motivation. Did I know that I'd fall in love with the Desert Wren? No, I didn't. But I had some vague idea that I would meet you and a future path would unfold."

"Diogo," she whispers and touches my cheek tentatively then leans forward to press her forehead against mine. "I... I thought you were using me to sway the rebellion to your side."

I nod and lean into her hand. "I won't lie, Taran, the thought has crossed my mind. Even before I met you. But my feelings for you are genuine. Perhaps they began developing from your reputation alone, but the fire ignited once we met. Once I realized the real woman is as beautiful and noble as the Desert Wren."

She sighs heavily and shakes her head against mine, still holding onto my face. "How do you always manage to say what I need to hear? How are you this different from the Warlord I've grown up knowing was a bad man?"

"You make me a better person." I slide my hands up her thighs and wrap my arms around her waist, sliding her forward on the chair, tugging her closer to me.

She presses her lips to my face, right next to my eyebrow. I close my eyes and enjoy her feather light touch as she trails tiny kisses down my face, next to my eye, my nose, my cheek and my chin. She worships me with her caresses and I suck up every ray of sunshine she's willing to give. Taran is a saint and I'm a deeply lucky man to have her in my life.

Finally, she presses her lips to mine and though the heat rises within me, I sense that she's hesitating.

"What is it?" I ask, my voice husky with restrained passion.

She opens her eyes and looks straight into mine. Hers are anguished. My hands tighten on her in response. I don't like that she's looking at me this way or that her eyes appear haunted at all. But I know my girl, she's a deeply thoughtful woman who worries constantly over the state of our city and its citizens.

"If I told you I need to leave the city for a while, would you let me?" she asks. Her voice is tentative, soft and testing.

I frown and pull my face back from hers so I can read her expression. "You already know the answer to that," I tell her, hardening my voice. "Going outside the wall isn't an option anymore."

Her gaze takes on a faraway look and she nods absently. "I get it, Diogo. It's dangerous." Then she looks at me. "But I had to ask."

"Why do you want to go?" I ask her.

She drops her gaze before saying, "I heard a rumour that there are refugees in the mountains."

She's not telling me something, I can sense a reticence in her. She's accepting that I won't let her leave, but there's more to her reason for wanting to go. "There will always be more refugees, Taran. We can't save them all, much as I know you'd like to. But for your safety and the sake of my sanity, you need to remain within these walls."

Again, she nods. "I understand, Diogo."

I believe that she does understand, but I also think she'll

do as she thinks she must. If she believes there's another person to be saved and it's her job to do it, then she'll try to find a way to go. I'll have to tighten security on her. "You won't be leaving, Taran."

She smiles sadly and kisses me. "I know."

Why do I feel like I've lost a piece of her in just a few sentences? What am I missing?

THIRTY-FIVE
TARAN

The days following my conversation with Diogo are agony. He wants to talk about everything, discover every facet of my life. With each discussion, I can see his brain turning over and over, thinking about my upbringing and my time within his city walls. I feel that I'm on the verge of bringing our Warlord around to a new way of thinking. Knowing that I must betray him burns a hole right through me, eats me alive with every conversation. With every kiss and every touch.

I'm as in love with my husband as he is with me. But I'm going to leave him. If there's even the glimmer of a chance that one or both of my grandparents are alive and living in the mountains then I have to go. See for myself if the rumours are true, and if they are, I need to search the face of every person in the mountain settlement until I either find the ones I'm looking for or finally bury them in my heart.

Every time I think of them out there, living in the mountains, waiting for me to come rescue them I get the gnawing feeling of desperately needing to leave but not being able to. It obsesses my mind to the point that if I could walk out the door right now and scale the wall, I would. Diogo has added another man to my guard, posting him on the roof. I can't even sit up in the greenhouse without a silent companion shadowing every move. I know that I shouldn't hope, that the odds of finding my grandparents alive are astronomically slim. But odds don't matter to a grieving heart and I've been grieving them from the last glimpse I had as I was dragged through the city doors while they were pushed out.

The stack of plates I'm holding clatters as I drop them on the table. I sigh and try to focus on my task. Diogo has decided that we'll have guests for dinner. He's invited a few of his top lieutenants and their spouses. A total of six people including us. He told me I didn't have to do anything, but I need to keep my hands busy or I start to plot my escape. I can't escape yet, not until Xavier says its time, though I don't understand the hold up. Then I feel guilty because I plan on leaving a man who needs me in his life. A man that I've fallen in love with.

The food was delivered earlier. I'd stood staring in awe, hovering around the kitchen as loads of cooked meat, vegetables, gravy, bread and butter were brought in. I decide it's best for me to set the table, keep my hands busy, so I don't sneak into the kitchen and steal food. After I finish setting the table and lighting a couple of candles, I decide to change. I wasn't going to, even though Diogo provided me with a few nicer outfits when he replaced my wardrobe. I'll be eating with elites. Why should I try to look good for them? But now I want to wear a dress, look as good as I can. Show them that the poor people from the slums can look good, eat with manners and act like a human. I'll take this chance to show them that the people they push below them are just like them. Foster some discomfort at the way they treat others, even if indirectly.

Diogo enters the bedroom just as I'm tugging my new dress into place. I frown over my shoulder at him. "Does it look right?" I ask. "It's been years since I've worn one."

His eyes travel down my body, taking in the white fabric with its pretty blue flower print where it hugs my breasts, waist and hips before flaring out to land just above my knees. Then he walks up behind me and drops a kiss on my shoulder. "You look better than that meal out there. Bet you taste better too."

I grin and drop into the seat in front of my vanity. Brushing my hair in long even strokes I watch as he changes from his every day work clothes into his formal uniform. My mouth waters as he pulls on the jacket with its crest and insignia. I've come to have a better understanding and even an appreciation for what that uniform means. He's the man who watches over an entire region, protecting us from harm. I despise his practice of sacrificing some for the good of the many, but I understand why he does it.

His broad shoulders and tall, muscular body fill out the uniform, giving him a larger than life appearance. He comes up behind me, takes the brush from my hand and sets it on the table. Taking my hand, he pulls me around on the seat and helps me stand.

"Beautiful," he says, his grim mouth curving into a rare smile. "Are you ready to greet our guests?"

I give him a mischievous look. "I'll try not to scare them."

His own expression is serious when he says, "I want you to scare them, baby. I want you to be yourself and show them why they can't live in the bubble they've created up here."

I sigh and run my hand down his sleeve. "Diogo, if it were possible to change the minds of the elites, we wouldn't be living in this situation. Did you see any of them out in the streets defending us during the food riots? No. Because their bellies are full and it would endanger their way of living to lower themselves to help us. If caring about a group of people they don't know means changing their comfortable lives then they'll continue to bury their heads in the sand and deny the existence of a problem."

He takes my head in his hands and drops a kiss on my lips. "That's why I need them to meet you, Taran. It's harder to ignore a problem when the cause has a face. You'll speak for the people living in the slums, the rebels and the illegals. You'll become their conscience, the way you've become mine."

I laugh humourlessly. "That's a lot to ask of one person."

He shakes his head. "I'm not asking anything. Just be yourself and the rest will fall into place."

The guests include Jorje Cruz and his wife Milla, a man called Stryker, and a young widow named Dee. I'm immediately uncomfortable. The women are much fancier than I am, wearing long dresses made of a shiny material, shoes with heels and finely cut jackets. Dee is wearing a fur, which doesn't surprise me as fur blankets and coats have become more popular with the shortage of machine-made clothes. I have a blanket made of deer hide in my bedroom at home with Emery. But Dee's fur is made of something much rarer than deer, it looks soft and it's all white.

Everyone is polite to me, but I can feel curiosity with an edge of reserve to their gazes. I ignore them and leave Diogo to host while I stand silently at his side. Even though I'm his wife, I haven't had enough time to consider this my home.

Nor are these my friends. And I don't have the capacity to pretend I belong here.

Diogo either doesn't notice the tension in the room or it doesn't bother him. He simply places a hand at my back, endorsing my position as his wife as he introduces me. The greetings are polite but strained. It isn't until we sit down for the meal that things become interesting. A heavy silence lingers over the table as everyone eats quietly. Finally, Milla puts her fork down, side-eyes her husband and then lifts her eyes to me. Instead of hostility, as I was mostly expecting from this group, I just see eager curiosity.

"Are the rumours true?" she asks, her voice hushed, though it carries clear across the table. "Are you actually the Desert Wren, and did you actually climb the wall? Hundreds of times I've heard!"

Dee drops her fork and stares at me in expectation while Milla's husband sighs heavily and looks down at his food disapprovingly. I suspect it's not the food that's bothering him, as it's a fabulous mouth-watering meal, but his wife's fascination with the Desert Wren. The others around the table stop eating and listen with curiosity.

I shrug and set my fork down carefully too. I glance at Diogo, but he's only watching us with a neutral expression. I've come to know him well enough that if he didn't want me telling these women who I am, I wouldn't be allowed to speak, and they wouldn't be here at all, meeting me. He wants us to get to know each other.

"Yes, I suppose I am the Desert Wren. I lived in sector six before Diogo..." I glance at him, hesitating over the word 'arrested' and then say, "took me into his care. And yes, I've climbed the wall many times, but definitely not hundreds."

Dee grins suddenly and says excitedly, "I always wondered how you do it? It's such an immense wall and there are guards everywhere, with guns and orders to shoot anyone found on the wall. You must be very brave."

I laugh at her exaggeration. "Well, it's not an easy task, but it's not impossible. And I was always more likely to get arrested than shot at."

"Not true," Stryker mutters, his eyes flashing to mine, a grim set to his mouth. "Though we don't usually shoot at climbers, we will if we have to. At a guess I'd say you were able to keep yourself hidden from us."

I shrug and look down at my plate, then pick up a bun and tear the edge of it, placing it delicately on my tongue. I really don't want to tell these people, especially the military men, that I had a fair idea of their security rotations, passed on to me by Xavier who got them from whoever is working the inside for us. When I lift my eyes from my plate, Stryker's knowing gaze is on me. He doesn't look angry. I'm saved from having to explain myself when Milla pipes up.

"I heard you were doing it to rescue the refugees trying to come into the city, like a modern-day Robin Hood. So romantic," she sighs, her face dreamy in the candlelight.

I nearly laugh out loud, especially when Diogo catches my eye and I see the humour lighting his features. He's amused by the conversation. His lieutenants are uncomfortable and I have the strangest feeling I've become some kind of legend to these women.

"Umm, the story of Robin Hood has him stealing from the rich and giving to the poor," I explain. Both Milla and Dee nod eagerly leaning forward. Again, I have to suppress the urge to laugh. "Neither of which I ever did. I just escorted illegals safely into the city and found them housing, food and jobs."

"It sounds exciting and romantic," Milla says while Dee nods from beside her. They look at each other and then she continues, "We hardly ever leave Sector One. This is where we live and socialize. Where we get our supplies."

"Climbing the wall and bringing in illegals isn't romantic, it's hot and dirty." I try to explain the reality of the job but they're still looking at me like I'm Robin Hood. I shake my head at them. "I got the job because the guy before me was killed."

"Ferrier Dex," Stryker grunts the name, his eyes flashing to mine again, his expression unreadable. "Killed on the wall."

Dee gasps in horror. "Was he shot?"

"Fell." Stryker's eyes never leave mine, like he's trying to tell me something. Or warn me. I glance toward Diogo who's frowning at him, no longer amused.

Oblivious of any tension, Milla says, "You should come to our group and speak to the volunteers about your experiences. I'm sure they'd love to hear all about it."

"Yes, definitely," Dee chimes in, taking a gulp from her wine glass. "We'd love it."

"Volunteer group?" I ask curiously.

"A group of us wives who want to do more for our city." Milla's voice is shining with pride as she explains. "We create food and basic supply packages and organize welcome tours for refugees. We're involved in a few other things too, like creating food hampers to the poorer communities, planning holiday parties and organizing events for city workers."

"Milla created the group shortly after she arrived in Sanctuary and married Jorje," Dee chimes in excitedly. "The group has really taken off, we have twenty-seven members."

Life in the slums is so geared toward survival that the very idea of organizing 'groups' feels utterly foreign to me.

But I realize that I've heard of the hampers, even partaken myself when food rations ran low and I was in danger of not eating for a third day in a row. Though I truly believe their efforts can be much better utilized than for party planning, I am impressed by their drive to help. I'd always pictured the elites as a group of shadowy food-hoarding assholes. It didn't occur to me that they might also be working toward the common goal of aiding refugees and feeding the poor.

"You've done well," I murmur, gifting Milla with a smile.

Her answering smile lights up her face and out of the corner of my eye I see Jorje watching at her, his annoyance at her questions completely forgotten. To my eyes, he's a man in love. I watch them curiously, seeing in Milla a young, sheltered and passionate woman.

"You were brought into the city as a refugee?" There's only two ways into Sanctuary. Birth, and showing up at the gates. Many children don't survive the first few years, so refugee status is the most likely. Everyone needs Sanctuary, most can't survive without it.

She nods and lowers her eyes, the happy expression melting from her face. "I was turned out of the New Las Vegas Sanctuary. My parents had died of that horrific flu that took out so many people, and I was married off. The city officials found out... found out..." her voice trails off and she glances sideways at her husband.

He reaches over toward her lap. I assume he's taken her hand though I can't see it below the table. "It's okay, mi alma. You are perfect the way you are. There is no shame."

Milla straightens her shoulders and looks at me. "They found out I can't have babies and they banned me from the city. Luckily, I was able to join a band of other refugees who didn't make it into that Sanctuary. We headed South together and I ended up here."

I glance at Diogo, who is watching the scene with quiet contemplation. I wonder if he knew Milla was barren before she was invited into the city. I suspect not, otherwise she'd have been turned away, her sole purpose as a human woman having eliminated her as a candidate.

Jorje lifts her hand to his face and presses their linked fingers to his lips, oblivious to their audience. She seems to relax under his care and I feel something dangerously close to envy at their easy affection. I've been fighting my feelings for Diogo, and I realize that once I leave him, I will never have what these two have.

I'm surprised by the depth of affection Jorje has for his wife. The few times I've seen him in public and in Diogo's presence, he gives off a serious and disapproving air. I now see why he's become Diogo's right hand. He can do his job with cool precision, but under the uniform is a man capable of feeling deeply.

"You didn't miss anything," I tell her. "New Las Vegas fell in '60. If you'd stayed you likely would've gone down with it."

She gasps. "But that's the same year I left! What happened?"

"Flu weakened them to the point that they couldn't provide enough defence on their walls and they were overrun by Primitives." I study her carefully, hoping my words won't affect her too much. After all, she had a husband back there. Maybe she was attached to the man, maybe he wasn't party to her ejection from the city.

She nods, her eyes faraway. I wonder if she's imagining her ex-husband, or maybe her friends. Though naïve, I sense a depth of intelligence that I'd assumed was missing.

"When did you arrive here?" I ask curiously. She wouldn't have necessarily come here right away after being banned from her Sanctuary. Many people wander for long periods of time in groups, trying to survive, while searching for a new Sanctuary.

"I arrived here in '61."

I frown at Diogo. The same year I arrived. Back to Milla, I ask, "How old were you?"

"Seventeen," she says.

"And were you married right away upon entering this Sanctuary?"

"Of course," she says as though it should be obvious. And I suppose it is. All young women are immediately married on entering Sanctuary. The need for babies outweighs the need to provide women with proper care and choice. I grit my teeth at the realization that Milla would've been married twice by the time she was seventeen. Normally I would consider her lucky for living in Sector One and marrying an elite, thus becoming one herself. Now I'm not so sure. As happy as she seems, she never had a choice.

"And you?" I turn my gaze to Dee. "Did you come to Sanctuary as a refugee?"

"No," she says softly. "I was born here."

I'm not surprised. Many among the elites were born in their Sanctuary. It's the refugees that get punted into the lower classes. I wonder what happened to Dee's husband. He must've been important to land her a place at Diogo's table.

It seems odd to give this much thought to the lives of the elites. I never have before. But I'm coming to realize over the course of this meal that even elites have problems. Women are treated like cattle across the classes. I frown into my food and pick at it, which is unusual for me. I've known too much hunger to not eat with gusto. But, this time, I'd rather think than eat. I glance toward Diogo. His eyes are on me, his look thoughtful and almost pleased. As though this dinner has gone exactly according to plan. Which doesn't make sense. If he thinks I won't organize a rebellion among the female elites, he's dead wrong. I was born to cause dissent where I see injustice flourishing.

He flashes me a quick smile, as though he's reading my mind and he approves. I flush in response. How has he come to know me so well in such a short time? And more importantly, how has he come to love me? I'm a pain in the ass.

I realize that Stryker is watching us, a slight frown between his brows. Does he approve? I suspect of everyone sitting at the table, Stryker's opinion means the most to my husband. I can't read him though, Stryker is good at hiding his feelings. Not one to let an uncomfortable silence pass, I open my mouth to ask Stryker about his job within the military.

But before I can speak, a deafening banging sound echoes through the room followed by rumbling that shakes the walls and the table. One of the women shrieks as we all leap to our feet. For a few seconds silence reigns as we stare at each other. I look to Diogo, whose gaze is hard. His relaxed façade is melting away and in its place is the Warlord, standing tall and serious.

Radios go off all around the table. I jolt in confusion before I realize all the men are receiving the same message. "The wall has been attacked. Repeat, the wall has been attacked. All hands to HQ."

Milla gasps and turns to clutch her husband's arm. The door flies open and Garrett hurdles in from his guard position in the hall, his radio waving in his hand. Diogo nods sharply at him and Garrett falls back, the alarmed look on his face quickly changing into something more professional.

Diogo lifts his radio and barks, "Fuentes here. Report."

The room falls completely silent as we all stand tensely waiting for the response. Finally, the radio crackles and the man on the other end shouts, "Rebels have attacked the West wall, bringing down a section of it in an explosion."

Diogo's hard gaze finds mine. I'm lost for a moment as to why he's staring at me with such a cold look, then I realize he thinks I knew. I shake my head feeling sick to my stomach. Even before I met him I would never have been on board with such a plan. Bringing down the wall is one of the stupidest things a Sanctuary can do. Though not impenetrable, the walls have proven effective at keeping out Primitives. They can't seem to sense the humans on the other side and don't bother going to the effort to find out if anyone resides within the walls.

Without the protection of that wall every part of the city is left vulnerable.

"The roof," I whisper.

Diogo nods, giving his permission and I bolt from the table, heading for the roof. The others follow close behind me, pounding up the stairs to our rooftop terrace.

"Oh, this is lovely," Dee says as she steps out and looks around.

Everyone ignores her as all eyes turn to the West. A huge cloud of dust and smoke billows out from the wall. My heart leaps into my throat and I hold myself tight as the full impact of what the rebels have done sends a chill down my body. Diogo comes to stand beside me, his hard gaze fixed on the destruction. Hushed murmurs rise and fall around us from the dinner guests.

Diogo lifts his radio and barks orders at whoever is on the other side. The military men group around him, awaiting his command. Trepidation and awe war inside me as I watch my husband in action, the man born to lead with an iron will. When Diogo puts his radio back on his belt, he sweeps everyone with a glance. His eyes settle on Garrett, "I'll need you to escort Milla and Dee home." His gaze flicks to me, but he doesn't actually look at me. My heart sinks. Does he still think I was part of this rebel plot? "Take Taran with you," he tells Garrett. "It's your life if she leaves your sight."

"Of course," Garrett says and makes a move to usher the women back down the stairs while the men prepare to leave with Diogo. We all file back into the apartment and I look to my husband, hoping for just a glimmer of the warmth I've come to know from him.

"Diogo," I say, pulling his attention back to me.

He locks eyes with me for a moment, then says, "Go with Garrett, don't give him any trouble."

I'm hurt by his tone of voice and I have to swallow past a lump as I nod. I remind myself that this city is his responsibility. This isn't about me. He needs to take care of everyone else. We'll sort ourselves out. But as I watch him leave, I can't help feeling that I'm watching my future walk away.

As if sensing my despair, Milla moves to my side and tentatively touches my arm. "This isn't his first emergency. He'll be fine."

I smile up at the taller woman and nod absently, my eyes on the door as the men leave.

TARAN

I'm shocked by the dust and smoke filling the air as we step out the front doors of the Tower. The cloud from the explosion seems to have moved quickly, swathing the city. All four of us, Garrett, Dee, Milla, and I, stare to the west where great billows of smoke are rising up into the air and being pushed outward by the wind. It's difficult to see the extent of the damage past the other buildings, but the sheer amount of dust flying toward us indicates that the rebels meant business when they decided to take down a section of the wall.

"Explosives," Garrett mutters as he opens the door to a vehicle. Milla and Dee climb in without a second thought. I pause for a second, torn. The destruction of the wall is a huge step in the rebellion. I don't know why they've done it, but I do know they would have to have a good reason. Even if I don't agree with the method. Someone could've been killed.

"Taran," Garrett snaps impatiently from next to his vehicle indicating that I should get in.

I slide in beside Dee as he slams the door shut. We

hurtle through what used to be downtown Tucson. The streets are filled with people checking out the source of the explosion. Garrett is forced to dodge them and when the crowd becomes too thick for him to pass, he presses something on his steering wheel that makes an awful blaring sound. All of us jump and he musters, "It's a horn, ladies. Most vehicles have them, but only a few still work."

A few blocks later we arrive on the outskirts of Sector One, where houses line the streets in what used to be an upscale urban neighborhood. The homes are still lovely, but the same disrepair that marks everything is here as well. Garrett stops in front of a large house with pretty, freshly painted trim and actual grass in the yard.

"I think I'll stay with Milla, if you don't mind," Dee announces, sliding out the door with her friend. "I'd rather not be alone until this fuss is sorted out."

Garrett grunts his acknowledgment and tells them, "Stay inside, lock the doors. Go to the cellar if there's any trouble. Keep your radio on you in case you need to be moved."

They murmur their agreement and then hurry inside, slamming the door shut behind them. I'm still staring in bewilderment at what looks like a lawn ornament in the shape of a tall pink bird standing on one leg. "So this is how the elites live."

Garrett grunts a laugh, though the sound doesn't hold much humour. "Some of them. But most of us live like the Warlord. Even on this side of the checkpoints, there aren't a lot of resources to go around. Some of the people around here have decided that extravagances, like paint and lawn care will bring back the normalcy and comfort of the 20th century. Others of us are more practical."

I think about it for a few minutes and then I say, "I

suppose we do the same sort of thing in the slums. We want to preserve the parts of our dying world that bring us a sense of nostalgia, even if it doesn't serve a purpose."

"Part of being human," Garrett agrees, and I nod.

As we attempt to make our way back to the Tower, the streets become even more crowded with concerned citizens. Some are holding children, some are shouting and pointing, while others are just frowning and watching the action. Finally, Garrett is forced to stop the car as we're surrounded by people. They recognize him as Authority and start banging on the windows, wanting information.

"What's happened?" Someone shouts.

"Are we under attack?" Another asks hysterically.

"It is the Primitives?"

I flinch back as someone bangs hard on the window next to my face. Garrett reaches out and squeezes my arm. "We'll be okay," he tells me. "But we can't stay here. I need to get you to the Tower, where it's safe."

"I don't think we'll be able to drive through this crowd," I say worriedly.

"We'll have to walk," he agrees, failing to keep the concern from his voice.

I take a breath and reach for my door. "We'll be fine, Garrett. I trust you."

He nods. "Let's go."

We open our doors and get out. Garrett slams his door shut and fights his way around to my side where I stand clinging to the frame. He takes my arm in a firm grip and starts manoeuvring me through the crowd, away from the worst of it. Once we reach a clearer section he speeds up, forcing me to run behind him.

"We're going to take a shortcut," he growls over his shoulder. "I don't like having you on the street like this. If anyone decides the rebels are to blame and recognizes you, you could get hurt."

Before I can respond he drags me into the nearest side street. As soon as we're clear of the street he starts running. I'm forced to sprint to keep up with his longer strides. There are still people everywhere, but some of them definitely don't belong in the elite sector. I recognize one person, a rebel. A troublemaker, not just a critic of the city officials. The man stops when he sees us and starts following our hurried footsteps. I twist around as I run, watching him, beginning to suspect this rebel plot might involve me in some way.

As if sensing trouble brewing, Garrett stops and turns to me. "Sorry about this, Mrs. Fuentes," he mutters. I wonder why he's suddenly calling me Mrs. Fuentes instead of just Taran, when he hauls me toward him and swings me up into his arms. I cling to him as he runs full tilt back toward the Tower. Footsteps dog our progress, hitting the pavement all around us. I try to see what's happening but I'm being jostled, my view cut off by Garrett's hulking form.

He zigzags through the streets, but he doesn't know them like I do, like the other rebels who've memorized every building and every street, until we learned how to move through them like shadows. Dark figures jump out of buildings, blocking our path and forcing us to turn abruptly and run in another direction. I realize quickly that we're being herded. Soon after, Garrett realizes the same thing.

He stops abruptly before we can hit the dead end of a street. He drops me to my feet and swings me behind his back faster than I know what's happening. He covers me with his body while pulling his sidearm and a knife. I reach for his arm and then stop myself. I don't want to hinder his movements if he needs to defend us.

"Be careful," I say to him desperately as shadows begin to converge, stepping through the dust filling the air around us.

My heart pounds in fear as we're completely surrounded. I peek around Garrett's shoulder. 6 men, all wearing heavy clothes with either scarves covering the lower half of their faces, or ghoulish Day of the Dead face paint.

One man steps forward. He's wearing a scarf over his face and a felt cowboy hat pulled low over his eyes. I've seen that hat before. "Drop your weapon, Authority, and we won't kill you. We just want the Desert Wren."

Garrett steps back, crowding me into the wall behind us. "Not a fucking chance," he says, doing his best to shield me from view. My heart sinks. I know who he's talking to and he won't hesitate in killing Garrett to get to me.

"Suit yourself." Xavier lifts his rifle. "Taran, duck."

I squeeze out from behind Garrett and fling myself in front of him. He grabs my arm and tries to drag me back, but I dig my heels in and elbow him in the stomach, forcing him to drop his hand while he catches his breath. I might be small but I'm tough when it counts. Climbing around the city has given me a hidden strength most people under-estimate.

"Taran." Xavier sounds satisfied to see me.

He can't have been the one who created the explosion on the wall. He wouldn't have been able to get into this sector so quickly. But he was certainly involved in the plan-ning. My heart sinks as I realize this is the distraction he was talking about.

"Did you do this?" I ask, disgust clear in my voice. "Did you fuck with the wall just to get to me?"

He shakes his head. "Don't flatter yourself, Taran. I'm

using the bomb as a distraction, but we've been planning this for a while. We need to get the Authority's attention, show them we can't be pushed aside or squashed like the pests Fuentes thinks we are."

"Well you did an excellent job there!" I snap. "All you've proved is that you're just as stupid as the Authority thinks, but even more dangerous than they thought. That you're willing to draw the attention of Primitives and bring them inside the walls, just for a little attention. And not good attention. I guarantee the cause will suffer from this idiotic move. If the Primitives don't kill us all, then Fuentes and his military certainly will. You've sunk the rebellion, Xavier."

Xavier paces forward a few steps. "Yes, the wall creates a vulnerability, and it will keep those assholes busy defending Sanctuary. It gives us an opportunity to make our move, overrun the city."

I've known he was getting more and more extreme over the past several years. Maybe it's why I drifted away from having a real relationship with him. Even though, in many ways, we'd be the ideal couple, passionate and driven by the same cause. But I'm turned off by his methods. He's too focused on his own goals to cultivate any kind of real friendship, let alone a romantic relationship.

He takes a step closer to me, pointing his finger as he says, "Your idealistic world doesn't exist, Taran. It never has. Passive resistance doesn't work."

Garret grips my shoulders and drags me back into his body. He's about to yank me back behind him, but Xavier lifts his gun and points it at me. Both Garrett and I freeze.

"She's coming with me, or you both die," Xavier snarls. "I'm losing patience."

"Promise you won't hurt him if I go with you?" I

demand, tugging my arm from Garrett's grip. He lets me go. Maybe he knows that there's no way we can stand and fight all six of them together. That the best we can do is negotiate for his life.

I can't see his mouth, but I can see his eyes, and the look Xavier is giving me tells me everything I need to know. Without turning, I yell, "Run, Garrett!"

He doesn't run. Instead he shoves me so hard, I stumble and fall to the pavement, landing hard on my hands and knees. A shot cracks through the space, echoing off of the surrounding buildings. I shriek as blood hits me from behind and Garrett's body falls next to me, his gun clattering to the pavement.

"No, no, no!" Tears fill my eyes as I twist around, reaching for him.

It's too late. As I grip the material of his military jacket, I watch the life leave his eyes. His face goes slack under my shocked gaze. Tears splash down my face and hit my hands as I reach for his wound, intent on staunching the blood pouring from his neck. He was just doing his job, protecting me when Diogo isn't around. Now he's lost his life.

A hand grips my arm and I'm hauled to my feet. I swing around, flailing my fists toward Xavier as he drags me down the road, away from Garrett. He grabs hold of my fist, swinging me around to his front. He pauses for a minute, his cold blue eyes drilling into me. Then he lifts his gun and presses it to my temple.

"You want to stay behind with your man back there?"

"You motherfucker!" I snarl. "Do your worst."

It's foolhardy and stupid, but in this moment I don't care. I've always underestimated Xavier and his approach to the rebellion. Now a man I respect is dead and I'm being dragged away from my husband. Fire flashes in Xavier's eyes, then he reaches up with his free hand and drags the bandana down, revealing the harsh lines of his handsome face. A few days growth of blond whiskers covers the chin I once considered beloved.

"I don't want to kill you, Taran, but I don't have time to fight with you. This city needs the Desert Wren." He's trying to moderate his voice, but I can hear the frustration. "The Warlord will be hot on our heels as soon as he realizes that explosion was a distraction. We need to leave the city now."

"Go to hell!" I shout at him, jumping back. "You don't know what the fuck you're doing."

He stalks toward me and grips the front of my dress, lifting me up onto my toes. "And you don't have the balls to follow through on our mandate; equality at all costs. Or have you forgotten, everyone has an equal right to survival? Your words, not mine."

"Don't you dare," I hiss angrily, shoving at his chest, breaking his hold on my dress. I straighten and rub my chest where his knuckles dug in. "Yes, my words, twisted by a man bloodthirsty for vengeance on the elites. You spout equal survival at me while you kill my friend in cold blood."

"Your friend," he spits venomously. "What did he do for you, Taran? Did he give you a home, give you clothes and food? Teach you how to survive in a toxic world? Did he give you Sanctuary?"

I brush impatiently at the tears that begin to flow once more. Xavier is describing everything he did for me when I was brought into Sanctuary and given to him as a child bride.

"No," I say to him, lifting my chin. "He gave me the things you never could, friendship and protection."

Xavier takes a threatening step toward me. "Will you

leave the city with me, or will you stay with your *friend* back there?"

"Are you going to kill me if I don't?" I demand.

"No, I never intended to kill you, Taran. But you have to see how important this is. The rebellion needs its Desert Wren. It needs its leaders, intact and united." Though his words are cajoling, the manic heat in his gaze is unsettling. He wants to use me to his advantage.

I stand silently for a moment, torn, knowing that my heart lies with the man commanding his troops. A man, that while cold and often cruel, would never compromise an entire city to achieve his own ends.

"Don't forget about the settlement, Taran," Xavier says, softening his voice. "There are people in those mountains, and we might be their only chance at survival."

Fuck. In the wake of the explosion I'd forgotten about the settlement. The possibility that my grandparents might be among them. Though my heart lies with Diogo, my loyalty, my life, lies with the desperate and destitute that fight for their basic human right to live.

"I'll go with you," I tell him. Then give him a grim look. "I'm going for the refugees though, Xavier." I step toward him, pointing at his chest. "But what you've done today is utterly unforgivable. You and I are finished."

THIRTY-SEVEN
DIOGO

"Commander!"

I turn my gaze from the chaos surrounding the fallen section of wall toward an officer striding quickly toward me. I've been supervising the wall cleanup and rebuild. We have to work quickly since a hole in the wall will attract predators into the city. The noise of the explosion itself has already drawn several curious Primitives, pulling them from wherever they were hiding out. I have men on the other side of the wall, taking them out as they approach.

"What is it?" I ask impatiently, flicking my eyes back to the mess in front of us. Cars, concrete slabs and twisted metal beams from buildings have been flung in every direction from where they were hurled away from the wall. It'll take months to rebuild to the height and strength that it was. But work must begin immediately. We don't have a minute to spare in the protection of our Sanctuary.

"Garrett has been found dead."

I freeze the officer with my gaze. "Where?" I demand in a sharp voice, hesitating before I ask, "And was my wife with him?"

The man shifts uncomfortably but meets my gaze head on. "He was found in sector one, several blocks away from the Tower, at Hastings and Veranda. Your wife is missing."

"I want her found," I bark without hesitation. "Close all checkpoints and grab anyone that even looks remotely like the Desert Wren. Have someone on my place in case she shows up."

"Already done," he says. "Anything else, Commander?" he asks.

"Get Jorje Cruz to supervise the rebuild and security," I snap, turning on my heel and striding away from the wall. Though I know the officer will do as I say, I still speak into my radio, "Jorje, you're needed on the wall. Now."

I leapt into my vehicle and tear away from the site of the wall destruction. As I drive, I bring the radio back up to my lips. "Stryker."

"Here." His reply is immediate.

"Taran is missing, I need you to have your men watching the wall. Orders are to detain, not shoot on sight." I'd given the brutal order after the wall attack, to discourage any citizens from using the weakness in the wall to their advantage. Now it occurs to me that Taran might be doing exactly that. Using the explosion to escort illegals into the city. It's exactly something she would do.

Ten minutes later, as I kneel next to the body of her security guard, I realize that no matter how passionate Taran is for the rebel cause, she would never do this. He was shot in the throat by someone trying to get to Taran. They might've even created the wall explosion as distraction in order to grab her during the chaos. I'm content in the knowledge that Garrett gave his life trying to protect her. I know my man. I know all my men. They'd follow my orders until the end.

I stand and leave the corpse of a good man; someone who gave his life to protect my wife.

Worry gnaws at my gut. I can't help but think that Taran's with Gunther. The one and only conversation I'd had with him doesn't give me confidence that he'd treat her well if she resists his efforts to reintegrate her into the rebellion. She's well-loved by the lower class, a symbol of hope and unity. He would've realized since her disappearance that he needs her. There's little doubt in my mind that he's the one who has her now.

I don't entertain the possibility that she might've gone willingly, because that would mean that she knew about the plot to bring down the wall and she kept it from me. I can't have that on my mind as I search for her. The need to ferret out any that have betrayed our city and kill them is strong. I don't know what I'll do if my wife is caught up in this rebel plot.

The thought of her delicate body standing bravely on a dais about to be hung or beheaded isn't something I can contemplate. Yet, if the Desert Wren is part of this sabotage, she'll have to be punished, along with her fellow rebels. The city residents will demand their heads, including hers.

"Commander," the radio crackles with Jorje's voice on my personal frequency.

"Speak," I growl into the radio.

"As per orders, we're sweeping up all known rebels and illegals."

"Good, start the interrogations immediately. I want to know what happened today." I pause, thinking, and then say, "I want an immediate curfew, get these fucking people off the streets. We can't move around properly while they're out here.

"Yes, Commander. Consider it done."

Seconds after we finish the call, sirens go off around the city emitting three sharp bursts, falling silent for a few beats and then sounding again. This goes on for a minute before silence reigns once more. Panicked voices sound as people rush home, fearful of being caught after curfew and arrested. Everyone knows the sound of the curfew siren. We trained them well.

Jorje always does his job to the best of his ability, following my orders to the letter. He's the best for a reason. As much as he's able to love and show compassion for his wife, he's one evil son-of-a-bitch in the interrogation room. If any of his detainees have information on Taran, or the explosion, we'll know by the end of the day.

After giving instructions to the police on what to do with Garrett's body, I head back toward my jeep. Just as I'm climbing in my radio goes off again, this time with Stryker's voice. "Commander, I need you on the wall. Eastern guard tower."

"On my way."

With the streets clear of people, I'm able to make it to the Eastern checkpoint in minutes. I park my jeep at the base of the wall and jump out. One of the regular guards strides toward me, meeting me halfway to the lift.

"He's at the top, waiting for you."

I nod sharply and get into the lift without a word. He pushes the buzzer, which tells the top guard the elevator is on its way. I wait impatiently, gripping the edge of the cage as I'm transported up at a painfully slow pace. Smoke from the explosion is beginning to settle across the city, only the Western wall still holds dust in the air surrounding the demolition site. From this height I'm able to see the extent of the damage.

Rage rushes through me once more and I grit my teeth

to keep my cool. Anger won't bring my city back into order. It won't bring my wife home safely. And it won't allow me to dispense well deserved justice. The way I'm feeling, if I get my hands on the people responsible for this mess, I will murder them with my bare hands. And I don't want to - they deserve a much more prolonged drawn out death.

"Commander." Stryker greets me as I reach the top, holding the cage door open.

I don't speak, just follow him to the stairs taking us the rest of the way up to the guard tower. I swing up through the trap door and into the hut, stepping to the side to give Stryker room to follow. We stand on each side of the built-in machine gun, staring out across the desert. We're so high up, I have a clear view right to the base of the Tucson and Catalina mountain ranges. Without speaking he turns to me and hands me a set of binoculars then points into the distance toward the closer Tucson range.

I hold them up to my face, focusing them. It takes me a minute to see what he's pointing out, but I finally catch the movement. A few miles from the base of the wall a couple are running at top speed toward the foothills. Once more I adjust the binoculars, taking a closer look at the people. I can't make out much more than a tallish person wearing a hat and a much smaller person by his side, her bright auburn hair streaming in the sunlight like a beacon. Hair the exact same shade as Taran's.

"Check the base of the Tucson range," Stryker directs me.

I lift the binoculars and point them straight at the foothills. It takes some scanning before I see what his eagle eyes have already picked out. A dust cloud left behind from a vehicle, or likely more than one given the size of the cloud, disappearing into an outcrop of rocks at the base of the foothills.

"Not sure if they climbed the wall, but the people running toward those rocks definitely came from the city. Too much chaos after the explosion for us to monitor everything and everyone."

"The explosion was a distraction," I growl. "To get Taran safely out of the city."

"She ain't safe out there," he says.

He's right. I sweep the binoculars across the landscape. Primitives are everywhere, running toward the site of the explosion, their faces twisted in manic glee as they head toward the sound of humans. They're skin and clothes hang off them in tatters. For the moment, there are no massive hordes, no groups larger than ten. My people have done a good job of culling any that get too near the city, but that explosion will have echoed through the mountains surrounding our Sanctuary, bringing all the Primitives out in the open, making it incredibly dangerous for any humans outside the city.

"Motherfucker," I snarl tightening my grip, watching helplessly as several Primitives change direction and head straight for Taran and her companion. The Primitives are several miles off, but closing in, moving much faster than her.

"You won't have time to get to 'er before they do. I doubt whoever's in the car will even make it out of the foothills before the zombies take them out. Better hope those men know how to take on a horde attack, because she's a sitting duck out there."

I throw the binoculars toward Stryker and hurl myself down the ladder, yelling up at him, "Get me a clear path through the city gates. I want them open and ready. I want you on my tail with backup. Get someone else up here."

"Commander," he snaps and reaches for his radio as I descend out of sight.

As I take the agonizingly slow lift back down to the ground I'm forced to contemplate the idea that there was one thing I didn't see in the binoculars. Taran wasn't resisting. She was running full-tilt across the desert, the willing companion of a man I have no doubt is her ex-husband. I'm forced to consider the idea that she may be complicit in the bombing of the Western wall and the death of her guard.

Unable to hold in my frustration any longer, I slam my fist against the cage wall, rocking the lift as it lowers back into a city on the brink of destruction.

"I can't... keep... running!" I gasp clutching at a stitch in my side.

Xavier turns to grab my arm, dragging me closer to him, but he doesn't slow his pace. My breath is coming out in fast, sharp gasps and I feel as though I'll collapse. We climbed the wall in record time, using the chaos within the city to cover our escape. Xavier forced me to keep pace with him, though his legs and arms are longer. I have more climbing experience though and was able to make it over with only a few cuts and bruises. A dress isn't the ideal outfit for climbing so my arms and legs have taken the brunt of the scrapes. Xavier has it worse off, he slipped a few times and fell once, landing several feet below on a ledge jutting out from the wall. He groaned in pain and cradled his aching ribs, taking a minute to recover before forcing us to get moving again.

"We're almost there," he grunts and points to the Tucson foothills.

"This is stupid!" I snap. "The explosion would've attracted every Primitive in the area, we should be hiding inside the city until the guard take them all out. We're as good as dead out here in the open."

He laughs bitterly, the sound caught in the wind as we run. "Your *husband* has locked down every sector in the city by now and stationed extra guards on the wall. I'd be surprised if he hasn't already spotted us. We wouldn't have been able to escape the city without the explosion taking everyone's attention."

I gasp and almost stumble as I twist to look over my shoulder. Xavier is right. The wall looms large in the distance, the watchtower a speck against the landscape. We'd be easily spotted with a pair of binoculars. If Diogo is looking for me, I'm positive he'll think to look outside the wall. Then my gaze drifts, the cloud of dust still marring the area from the explosion grabbing my attention.

"Oh god," I moan breathlessly. "Please tell me you didn't do this because of me."

"Don't flatter yourself," he snaps. "I already told you, it's time for the rebellion to show what we're capable of. Take our cause to the next level. Collecting the Desert Wren at the same time only recently became part of the plan."

"And what exactly do you intend to do with me?" I ask scathingly.

He stops running so abruptly that I slam into his back and bounce away. I hunch over, grabbing my knees and gasping for air. He bends with me, getting right in my face.

"You're going to rally the rebels, show them you're safe and that we're a united force." His voice is hard, his eyes glittering with the manic energy that has become more and more prevalent lately. "You're going to do your job."

"How exactly am I supposed to do that out here?" I

argue with him. "The rebellion is inside Sanctuary, not out here in the desert."

"You're going to do your job," he says again, his voice harsh and commanding. "You're going to lead a group of refugees into the city."

"What refugees?" I demand.

Instead of answering, he straightens, grabs my arm and starts running again. I cling to him in order to keep up, my feet flying over the hard-packed earth, dust flying with every step. I'm covered in it by now, the grit infiltrating every part of me, my legs, my eyes, nose, mouth. I've made this trip many times, but I've never done it with such recklessness. I've always covered my face, worn heavy clothes to protect against the sun, and jogged at a reasonable pace.

I'm on the verge of collapse, stumbling helplessly behind Xavier when he finally slows. "We're here," he says, pointing toward a rocky outcrop.

"Where?" I ask, looking around with bleary eyes.

He doesn't answer, just drags me toward the rocks. I'm too winded to argue or resist. I clutch at the agonizing pain in my side and blink back tears caused by dust. As we round the outcropping I'm surprised to see a grouping of vehicles with men surrounding the area. They all have weapons and stand alert to possible danger. I jerk back, yanking my hand from Xavier's hold. He takes hold of me again and drags me forward, leading me to the biggest, meanest looking man in the group. The guy is wearing dark, heavy clothes, a bandana over his mouth and nose and a hat. Scars cover every inch of his face and hands. I suspect scars cover the rest of his body too, though I've no desire to see.

"Gunther," he snaps, stepping forward. Though he addresses Xavier his strange light green eyes take me in with mild curiosity, flicking over my dusty dress and hair. "You were supposed to meet us an hour ago, lead us into the city before the zombies catch wind that we're out here." He stabs a finger out past my shoulder. "They're on your fucking tail and closing in fast."

I twist around to see, squinting into the brightly lit desert, but I don't see anything. He must've used binoculars. My stomach sinks and I feel queasy at the thought of Primitive's being so close.

"You worry too much, Talon. Your cars'll move faster than them," Xavier says, tugging me toward the nearest one. "We'll hide out in the Catalina mountains until they pass."

The man steps threateningly toward Xavier, grabbing him by the throat. I'm shoved backward as Xavier jerks in his hold. "There's no fucking time, you idiot. We'll have to set up a perimeter here and hope there's enough of us to take them out."

He throws Xavier away from him and strides back to the vehicle. Over his shoulder he says, "The woman can hide inside my car, you'll take point with me."

I turn scathing eyes on Xavier as he rubs his throat and glares after the man. "Are these the 'refugees' you want me to escort into the city? These are mercenaries, Xavier! Outsiders! They're in it for the resources. They don't want Sanctuary!"

"We need them," Xavier mutters. "We don't have a chance at taking the city without them."

"Is that your plan?" I ask incredulously. Then I realize it goes even further than that. "You want to take down Diogo and replace him, don't you?"

"Diogo, the military, the Authority, the elites." He fixes his eyes on the city in the distance. "All of them."

"Replacing one dictatorship with another isn't what the rebellion stands for!" I shout at him. "At least his is a stable government, you don't know what you're doing. All we wanted was change, not this," I sweep my hand around indicating the armed men preparing for a Primitive attack. "You're going to bring the whole city down."

Xavier turns on me, his eyes vicious, his mouth twisting bitterly. "Your precious idealism means nothing in the real world, Taran. Sanctuary doesn't work the way you want it to. We won't be able to negotiate with the Authority. Fuentes won't allow it. In order to instill democracy again we need to topple and replace the Commander. I wish to God you weren't the one the rebels decided to flock around. You weren't meant to make the tough decisions, I was. I've been the rebellion since day one. I've sacrificed everything for the cause, given up every comfort. Given up any chance at reconciliation with my wife..."

"Xavier..." I reach for him, forgetting where we are and what he's done for a moment. "I didn't know you wanted anything with me. It never worked out for us."

He shakes my hand off and paces away from me. "We could've worked, Taran, if we tried."

"Relationships require more than presence, Xavier."

He flicks his eyes to mine. "Like love? I've always had that. Always."

I stare at him open-mouthed, no idea what to say. I'd been married to him for twelve years, until Diogo dissolved our union. He'd never once declared his feelings. And now, it's too late. Too much has happened to separate us.

"I'm sorry, Taran," he says, his shoulders slumping in defeat. "Sorry I dragged you into this, used your reputation to gather the rebels. Brought you out here. I'm so focused on the cause I didn't consider what I was doing to you."

I watch him for a moment, trying to reconcile everything that's happened with the husband I knew; an impatient and driven man, but he was never deliberately cruel. "You killed an innocent man today, Xavier. You're too involved. There's no going back now."

His eyes light with passionate fire once more, replacing the momentary defeat. "There is no innocence in the Authority." His voice is hard. "And you're right, there's no going back. Only forward, with the weapons I've bought and the mercenaries we'll pay for once the city is taken."

I straighten in an instant, all sympathy for him fleeing. I'm about to tear a strip off him, when someone shouts from behind us, "Heads up!"

I turn just in time to see Talon and his men start shooting. I assume they're shooting at the approaching Primitives, though I don't see any yet.

"Fall back!" Talon shouts. "They're right on top of us. To the vehicles!"

Xavier grabs my arm and hauls me toward the nearest vehicle. He opens the door and flings me inside, slamming the door shut. I turn onto my back just in time to see a Primitive slam against the door I'd just crawled through. I scream and scramble back against the opposite door. It crawls up the door, bleeding hands pressed against the window and stares in at me through dark bruised eyes. I've never seen a Primitive so close before. I think it's a woman from the long, wild hair and delicate bone structure. But it's hard to tell from the strips of flesh hanging off her face, the pieces of wood and metal jabbed through her skin and into her skull.

Time slows as we stare at each other, only the glass of the door separating us. Her eyes travel over me, watching me as I'm watching her. I thank God that this vehicle still has its glass, that it's still intact compared to most others. She slowly starts banging her fist against the window, gaining speed and force with each hit until she's slamming her hands against the window so hard it rattles in the frame. I stare in fear and awe as she mangles her hands, breaking the bones in her fingers as she tries to get to me.

Explosive pops fill the air around us as the men battle against the horde. I can hear screams of agony as, one by one, the mercenaries are taken out. I straighten up and twist around in every direction, desperately trying to catch a glimpse of Xavier. But I can't tell friend from foe in the melee. A gun goes off right in front of my car and I whip around to look. Talon has shot the head off a Primitive.

He turns to look at me, giving me a grim smile before leaping back into action, yanking a Primitive off one of his men and turning his knife on the creature, severing its neck in one stroke. Bile rises up and I look away before I see the body collapse.

A cracking sound reminds me of my own predicament.

"No!" I yell just as she shoves her fist right through the window, scrambling to reach me as the window shatters all around her arm. She drags it back through the opening and claws at the window until she manages to pull it right out of the frame.

I twist around reaching for the handle at my back. Just as she launches through the open window, shoving herself inside I manage to open the door and scramble out. I don't look over my shoulder, I start running on all fours as soon as I touch the ground, pushing myself up as soon as I'm clear of the car. Her shrieks follow me.

Tears stream down my face as I run faster than I've ever run in my life. The sound of her uneven gait follows me, picking up speed as I do. Hysterical sobs bubble up my throat and join the cacophony of noise all around us. I don't make it far when she launches herself at me, slamming into my back, digging her fingers into my shoulders.

As I'm driven to the ground, instinct kicks in and I roll, taking her with me and disorienting her. I'm able to shove her off, despite her superior strength. I crawl away from her, kicking out at her face. A crunching sound tells me I've broken something. But it doesn't slow her down. In seconds she's on my back again, shoving me face down into the dirt. This time as she grabs hold of me, she sinks her teeth deep into my neck. I scream in agony as she starts to tear.

But before she can finish the job, tearing the flesh from my bones and killing me, she goes slack. I twist around as she falls away. I shove myself backwards, staring down at her lifeless corpse, the head lolling on the ground next to her body. My gaze goes up and I find myself crouched under the shadow of my husband, standing motionless over me with a rifle in one hand and a knife dripping blood in the other.

I gasp, my hand flying to the bite on my neck. My shaky fingers come away bloody. She broke the skin. With tears dripping down my face, I look up at him, into his hard, pitiless gaze.

"Diogo – "

TO BE CONTINUED...

CONTINUE READING...

ALL THREE BOOKS IN TARAN AND DIOGO'S STORY ARE NOW AVAILABLE!

SANCTUARY ON FIRE
BOOK 2 OF THE SANCTUARY SERIES

ALSO BY NIKITA SLATER

If you enjoyed this book, check out some other works by #1 International Bestselling Author, Nikita Slater. More titles are always in progress, so check back often to see what's new!

Sinner's Empire

Book 1 - Sin of Silence - Preorder

Book 2 - A Silent Reckoning - Coming Soon!

Book 3 - Goodnight, Sinners - Coming Soon!

The Queens Series

Book One – Scarred Queen

Book Two - Queen's Move

Book Three - Born a Queen

Book Four - The Red Queen (Coming 2021)

Alejandro's Prey (a novella)

The Queens 4 Book Box Set

Fire & Vice Series

Book One – Prisoner of Fortune

Book Two – Fight or Flight

Book Three – King's Command

Book Four – Savage Vendetta

Savage Boss (a novella)

Book Five – Fear in Her Eyes

Book Six – Bound by Blood

Book Seven – In His Sights

Book Eight - Burning Beauty

Book Nine - Chasing Ecstasy (Coming soon!)

Fire & Vice 6 Book Box Set

The Driven Hearts Series

Book One - Driven by Desire

Book Two - Thieving Hearts

Book Three - Capturing Victory

Novella - The Princess and Her Mercenary

Driven Hearts 4 Book Box Set

The Sanctuary Series

Book One - Sanctuary's Warlord

Book Two - Sanctuary on Fire

Book Three - The Last Sanctuary

Book Four - The Road to Wolfe

Book Five - Skye's Sanctuary (Coming soon!)

The Sanctuary Series 3 Book Box Set

Loving The Bad Boy Series

Loving Vincent

Loving Jared

Loving Rico (Coming Soon!)

Standalone books

The Assassin's Wife

Because You're Mine

Mine to Keep (a novella)

Luna & Andres

Kiss of the Cartel

Stalked

After Dark

In collaboration with Jasmin Quinn

Collared: A Dark Captive Romance

Safeword: A Dark Romance

Chained: A Mafia Marriage Romance

Good Girl: A Captive BDSM Romance

Hostile Takeover: An Enemies to Lovers Romance

The After Dark Box Set

Visit **nikitaslater.com** for more information
and the latest updates!

ABOUT THE AUTHOR

Nikita Slater is the International Bestselling dark romance author of the Fire & Vice series, Angels & Assassins series, The Queens series and several standalone novels. Her favourite genre is mafia romance, the bloodier the better, though she loves to write about every subject under the sun. She lives on the beautiful Canadian prairies with her son and crazy awesome dog. She has an unholy affinity for books (especially erotic romance), wine, pets and anything chocolate. Despite some of the darker themes in her books (which are pure fun and fantasy), Nikita is a staunch feminist and advocate of equal rights for all races, genders and non-gender specific persons. When she isn't writing, dreaming about writing or talking about writing, she helps others discover a love of reading and writing through literacy and social work.

9 781775 278269